S0-AGP-948

Snow White and Rose Red:
A Modern Fairy Tale

Snow White & Rose Red

A MODERN FAIRY TALE

by

Regina Doman

Regina Doman
for Emily
God bless you!

BETHLEHEM BOOKS · IGNATIUS PRESS
WARSAW, N.D.   SAN FRANCISCO

© 1997 Regina Doman
Artwork © 1997 Joan Coppa Drennen

ISBN 1-883937-23-X
Library of Congress number: 96-80078

Cover art by Joan Drennen
Cover design by Davin Carlson

"Only to Rise" © 1996 Nathan Schmiedicke, used with permission.

It's Only a Paper Moon, by Billy Rose, E.Y. Harburg, Harold Arlen © 1933 (Renewed) Warner Bros. Inc. Rights for Extended Renewal Term in USA controlled by Glocca Morra Music, Chappell & Co., & SA Music All Rights Reserved. Used by Permission. Warner Bros. Publications U.S. Inc. Miami FL, 33014

Bethlehem Books • Ignatius Press
15605 County Road 15, Minto, ND 58261

Printed in the United States of America

For Billy, Joan, and Raquel
who started it all—
and Ben
who helped in a small but significant way

Acknowledgments

My thanks to Amber and Katie, who wanted me to write the story down so that they could read it; and to my sister Maria, who was among the first to read it; along with my brother John; thanks to my mother and father for their terrific encouragement; also for my friends of the Steubenville writer's group—Helen, Ronda, Judy, and Rebecca—for their enthusiasm and constructive criticism; grateful thanks to the Bethlehem Community for liking this odd story enough to want to publish it, especially for Jean Ann, Lydia, and Peter; thanks to my brother-in-law Mike S. for his plausibility and grammatical editing during the final stretch.

From start to finish, the one person who has given me the most encouragement, who seemed to see what I saw and feel what I felt about this story was the man who was to become my husband, Andrew. He knows this story wouldn't have been finished if it hadn't been for his inspiration, his support, and his love.

SNOW WHITE AND ROSE RED:
A MODERN FAIRY TALE

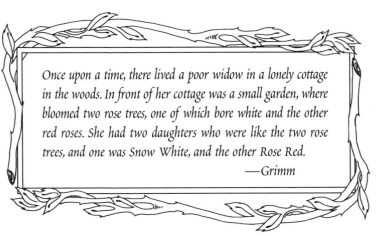

Once upon a time, there lived a poor widow in a lonely cottage in the woods. In front of her cottage was a small garden, where bloomed two rose trees, one of which bore white and the other red roses. She had two daughters who were like the two rose trees, and one was Snow White, and the other Rose Red.
—Grimm

One winter night, while they were sitting together, someone came to the door.

—*Grimm*

Chapter 1

THE TWO GIRLS were alone in their house that night.

Inside was safe enough—the living room where they were sitting was crammed full of familiar furniture from their old country home. There were bookshelves and knick-knacks, lamps with cheery fringed shades, and homemade afghans. Golden ovals of lamplight on the floor and ceiling sufficiently dimmed any shadows that might have crept into the little room.

But outside, it was a different story. Outside was New York City, vast and dirty and dangerous. And a howling January snowstorm was wreaking its fury upon it.

Blanche, the oldest at eighteen and therefore somewhat responsible, was nervous. It was almost an hour past the time when their mother should have been home. She had once or twice considered calling the hospital where Mother worked as an emergency room nurse, but had stopped herself. It was very likely that traffic accidents and other weather-related incidents were keeping her and the rest of the hospital staff busy right now. But it didn't make Blanche feel any more at ease.

She could tell her sister Rose wasn't worried—if she had even noticed that Mother was late. Rose was two years younger than Blanche. Right now, she was curled up in the armchair, in theory studying trigonometry, but in reality, reciting poetry to herself and drawing lines around the border of her notebook. Blanche could see her lips moving as she chanted some favorite line. Rose had long shining red hair, which contrasted sharply with her outfit: a paisley skirt in a jewel box of colors and a bright green sweater. Her sister always wore bright colors—blue, purple, gold, and green; she was like a bright new color herself, vibrant and alive.

Blanche, prosaic in a pale yellow sweater and blue jeans, was wondering again if anything mattered—life, faith— specifically, finishing homework assignments. Twisting her fingers in a long strand of her hair, which was black and straight as a poker, she tried to read Camus and keep out the disturbing thoughts that continually circled inside her head. She was struggling again in that murky pool of lassitude that had tormented her ever since their father had died last year. Moving to a chaotic, threatening city hadn't helped assuage the pain. Life was like that storm outside, "ignorant armies clashing by night," as Matthew Arnold had said.

A car door slammed right beneath their window, and Blanche jumped as a woman cried out. Pushing aside the quilt she had wrapped around her legs, she got up and ran to the window. You never knew what might happen in New York City. Blanche lifted one of the heavy slats of the blinds and peered out the window. The only thing she could see in the swirling darkness were the window boxes outside, snow-covered humps where their rosebushes from home had been. Frustrated, she shoved aside the floral print curtains and the blinds and pressed her face to the pane, trying to decipher the darkness.

Out on the street, she could just make out their family car. Mother *was* home! But there was someone else, too. Two shapes were moving around the vehicle. The one that appeared to be Mother was waving her arms, while the other larger shape loomed alarmingly over her.

Rose, hearing Blanche gasp, finally looked up from her book. "What's happening?"

"Someone's outside with Mother," Blanche said tensely.

Rose got to her feet in one flashing movement and ran to the door. She jerked it open and dove into the little entrance way, where she began to undo the bolts on the house's outer door. In two seconds, she was creaking it open. Blanche stood, half-paralyzed, wondering if she should make for the door or the phone.

Rose yanked the door wider, letting the full-blast of the storm inside. "Mom!" she cried out.

Her mother turned away from the towering dark form she had been facing. Rose could see her calm features in the light from the outdoor lamp. "I'm all right, Rose," her mother's voice came reassuringly through the wind and snow.

Blanche had crept up beside her sister, and the two of them now stood looking out the front door of their brownstone. Mother came towards them, limping slightly, her arms full of soggy brown paper bags, her long grey-brown braid trailing out the side of her damp parka hood.

"I slipped on the ice, and this man came to my rescue," she explained as she mounted the steps and moved out of the storm into the entrance way. "I didn't want to go shopping in this weather, but I know we have practically no food left in the house." She smiled sheepishly at her two daughters and handed the paper bags to Blanche. Then she turned to the looming shape which hung back in the dark, out of reach of the house light. "Come on in for a minute, sir."

"That's all right," said a rough, muffled voice. The shape approached the steps and started to set down the three bags it was carrying on their stoop. All Rose could see of him was a dirty brown winter coat with a furry hood, the sort she'd seen homeless people wear.

"Just bring those bags inside," Mother called from the doorway, and the shape reluctantly straightened and shuffled up the steps. Mother put a hand on Rose's shoulder and drew her inside the apartment with her. The bulky hooded form filled the little entrance way. Rose could see that there was a face beneath the fur-trimmed hood—a red face, surprisingly young looking, with large brown eyes, a straight nose, and a scrub beard.

"Here's your groceries," said the face, sounding embarrassed.

"I really appreciate this," Mother said, pushing the door shut, squelching the noise of the storm. Turning to Blanche and Rose, she explained, "I took one step out of the car and fell flat on my face. The groceries went all over the street. Then this young man came out of nowhere and helped me up."

"It's nothing," the hooded form murmured, ducking his head as Rose took the bags from his arms and set them inside their apartment. He stood there, looking more and more uncomfortable. Rose, stealing another look at him through the concealing drape of her hair, decided he would have a nice face if it were a little cleaner and less uncultivated.

"Could I give you some money?" Mother was fumbling in her pockets for her wallet. She never carried a purse.

"No, please don't. I just wanted to help. I couldn't leave you on the ground there, could I?" the stranger hastily assured her. "I'm all right."

"Do you have some place to go?" Mother asked, looking at him critically for the first time. "You look as though you've been outside for a while."

"I guess I have," he admitted, reluctantly.

"Why don't you come in and warm up?" Mother invited. Blanche, who had been carrying the groceries to the kitchen in order to be closer to the phone, heard this and groaned inwardly. *My mother, the Good Samaritan.*

"Nah, that's all right. I'd better get going." He turned and fumbled for the door knob.

"Sir—what's your name?" Mother queried, obviously trying to keep him there for another minute. Blanche hoped he would brush the question aside, but instead, he paused.

"Bear," he said.

Rose mentally raised an eyebrow. What kind of name was that?

"Thank you, Bear, for your help. Do you have some place to stay tonight?"

"Oh yeah. Don't worry about me. Like I said, I'm all right. I'd better be getting home." Again, he tried to leave.

"How far is it from here? Do you have to walk?"

"It's a little ways, but I'll make it," Bear said.

"How about if I give you a subway token? It's very cold out there."

"No, really, I'll be all right."

Mother turned to Rose, who was hanging on the door jamb. "Go get me a token from the can, please."

Rose hurried to comply, but by the time she reached the kitchen, Blanche had already dug one out of the tin by the phone and handed it to her.

Good grief, Blanche thought, *can't Mother see the poor guy just wants to get out of here? Next time he'll think twice before helping strange ladies with their groceries.* Besides, the sooner he left, the sooner Blanche could breathe normally again.

Bear stared awkwardly at his feet. Noticing that his shoes were melting all over the entrance way, he apologetically scuffed the snow from his feet on the side of the door. Mother gasped just as Rose swirled dramatically to her side with the token.

"Bear, you're only wearing canvas sneakers!"

"Um, yeah."

"They hardly give your feet any protection at all!" Mother was horrified.

Blanche slumped against the kitchen doorway, foreseeing what was coming. Her mother was determined to be a ministering angel, and Rose was entering into the drama whole-heartedly.

"Can you feel your feet?" Rose demanded, unconsciously imitating her mother's anxious tone.

Bear turned red but sounded nonchalant. "Well, sort of."

"How long have your feet been numb?" asked Mother.

"Well, maybe a couple of hours."

"That's very dangerous! Bear, come inside this house at once," Mother said imperiously, her blue eyes snapping with authority.

Bear hesitated, then meekly complied. Mother shut the

apartment door and waved him towards the couch. She brushed past Blanche into the kitchen and began filling up a basin with water. Rose urged their reluctant guest to sit down, and while he gingerly sat down on the very edge of the sofa, she perched on the arm of the stuffed chair next to it. He pushed off his hood, revealing a head of long, dark, matted hair in twisted dreadlocks. Rose heard Blanche draw in her breath sharply and looked up in time to see her sister put a hand to her mouth in a gesture of fear, her white face paler than usual. Wondering, Rose looked back at Bear, but the guy wasn't doing anything unusual, just looking a bit overwhelmed by the situation. *What's she upset about? His long hair?* She shrugged off her sister's reaction as typical.

Bear bent down, and tried to take off his sneakers, but had to stop to pull off his grease-spotted gloves first. He had trouble getting enough of a grip to pull off the first glove, and Rose almost wanted to lean down and offer some help.

"Are your hands frostbitten, too?" Rose asked, poised attentively on her chair arm.

"I don't know. They hurt a bit, so that's a good sign, I guess," he said, starting to work on his laces.

"How long have you been outside?" Mother asked as she came into the living room with the basin full of water.

"Since sometime this morning."

Mother's brow was furrowed. "It's been terribly cold out. Several homeless people with severe frostbite were brought to the hospital today." She knelt on the floor and began to help him with his sneakers.

There was silence while she eased off his shoes and peeled off his grubby sports socks in her best emergency room manner. The large feet were red, and the tips of the toes were slightly blue.

"My goodness, I'm glad I made you come inside. If you'd walked home, you'd have had some permanent damage." She sunk his feet into the basin of cold water and began to rub them gently. "I've got to warm your feet slowly or I'll damage the tissue."

The young man said nothing, but his face was as red as his feet. "I'm sorry you're having to be bothering about me—"

"Nothing to be sorry about. This water isn't cold enough. Rose, get me some ice cubes from the freezer."

When Rose went into the kitchen, Blanche slipped in next to her. "Rose, do you recognize that guy?" she asked in a low voice.

Rose glanced back and shrugged. "Looks like a lot of homeless men I've seen around the City. Kind of young, though."

"I'm pretty sure I've seen him hanging around the school parking lot in the mornings." Blanche's blue eyes were round and worried in the contrasting frame of her white skin and black hair. "He could be a drug dealer."

Rose pursed her lips, then shrugged, scooping ice cubes into their pottery salad bowl. "Well, I don't think he'd have any luck trying to sell drugs to us." She whisked back out of the room.

Blanche slouched against the counter, muttering, "My family is hopeless."

Rose handed the ice cubes to Mother and surveyed the stranger inquisitively. "Why do you call yourself Bear? Is it because of your hair?"

Bear gave a faint smile. "That's part of it."

"What's the other part?"

Bear stared at the floor for a second. "Well, actually, I spent some time in juvenile detention. I sort of picked up the name there." He looked at her with a half-jesting expression, but his remarkably dark eyes were serious. Rose decided she liked his eyes, even if his face was rough.

"Sounds like you've had a pretty tough life," Mother said.

Again, Blanche groaned inwardly. Her mother was giving the guy a wonderful opening to tell them his whole tragic life story. Blanche had no doubt he'd probably tell them one, only it wouldn't be the real story. Rose, now leaning forward with an avid expression, was practically begging to be led down the path of fabricated misery. *Why are Mother and Rose so intent on dragging themselves into these situations? Why am I the only one with any sense left? If only Dad were here. . . .*

But to Blanche's surprise, the strange figure didn't seem any more anxious to give out information about himself than Blanche was to hear it. He cracked his knuckles apprehensively. "Yeah, in a way. Look, I don't want to make you nervous. I could just go to the emergency room. You don't have to be doing this for me." His eyes seemed to be searching for a way out of the room, out of this predicament.

Mother laughed. "Bear, believe it or not that's where I work, though I did think I was done for the night. But really, it's better for you not to go outside yet."

Rose was grateful for her mom's cool handling of the situation. She felt proud, watching Mother as she knelt there, still wearing her coat, rubbing this stranger's feet with practiced efficiency.

"What were you in juvenile detention for?" Mother asked. Blanche was grateful that Mother hadn't completely lost her store of caution, after all.

"Drug possession."

A long breath escaped Blanche, unnoticed by the others.

Mother squinted up at him. "You don't look like someone who uses drugs."

"I don't," he said.

"I'm glad to hear that," Mother said. "Blanche, fill up the spaghetti pot with cold water and bring it out here. And put some water on low heat on the stove. Rose, I'll need you to get me another basin and a coffee mug. I'm going to start taking these ice cubes out and put in some less cold water."

As Blanche jumped to follow orders, she wondered if Mother really believed that Bear didn't use drugs. Mother was experienced in recognizing the physical signs of drug use, that was true. But was it possible that even she could be fooled?

Rose returned with the items requested and hung on the edge of the sofa. She studied Bear's profile, a bit miffed that Bear didn't seem willing to talk about himself.

"How was it, being in juvenile detention?" she asked. "I can't imagine what that must be like."

"It was pretty bad," Bear admitted. "I was glad to get out. I'm making sure I stay clear of that scene altogether."

That could mean two things, Blanche recognized. *Either he had stopped breaking the law, or he was hoping to not get caught breaking the law.*

"So why did they start calling you Bear?" Rose persisted, still hoping to learn something.

Bear rubbed his chin. "Well, one day these guys were

beating up my brother. When I found them, they had his head in a sink full of water. It looked like they were trying to drown him, just for kicks, though they denied it later. I never used to fight anybody. I don't like it. But I just saw red and threw the three of them against the wall." He winced, whether from the memory or from the pain in his feet, Rose couldn't tell. "I knocked the one guy out and the other two were scared pretty bad. I got sent to the disciplinary unit for two weeks, but nobody ever picked on my brother again. That's when they started calling me the Bear."

"Wow," Rose breathed. "So, what's your brother called? Did he get a nickname out of that too?"

A closed look appeared over Bear's face. He shrugged.

"Was he in juvenile detention for the same reason?" Rose asked.

"Yeah. Same as me. Drug possession with intent to deliver." Bear paused. "I'd rather not talk about my brother."

Blanche came out with the pot of water, her dark hair falling around the sides of it. She knelt by her mother as she set it down, but she wasn't looking Bear in the face. Rose knew she was still wary, and probably irritated that they had let this disreputable character into the house at all.

"What does that mean—'possession with intent to deliver'?" Rose wanted to know.

"Possession with intent to sell." Mother explained, sitting back on her heels for a moment. "It means they were caught with a large amount of drugs on their person."

"Gee, Mom, you know all about this stuff!" Rose said.

"She probably sees a lot where she works," Bear said.

Mother tested the water with her hand and put Bear's feet into some slightly warmer water. "Yes, I do. Too much, unfortunately."

"Have you lived here in the City all your life?" Bear asked.

"I was born here, but I moved out when I got married. My husband died last year, and my old supervisor offered me a staff management position in the hospital. So we moved back."

"I'm sorry," Bear said quietly. "What did he die of?"

"Cancer." Mother added some warm water to the basin from the pot Blanche had brought.

"That's what my mother died of," Bear said, after a pause.

Blanche, still kneeling, looked up at Bear when he said that, but lowered her eyes again quickly.

"I'm sorry," said Mother. "It's hard, isn't it?"

"Yeah, it is." Bear was silent for a few minutes. Then he winced.

"Does that hurt?" Mother looked up at him. "Good! Good! I was thinking that I was going to have to go back to the hospital with you after all." She continued rubbing. "How sharp is the pain? Faint or does it really hurt?"

"Um—it really hurts."

"Good! Well, I'm sorry to tell you it will probably get worse before it gets better."

As if to distract himself, Bear looked at Blanche and met her eyes. "So, what's your name?"

Those black eyes seemed to see too much of her. She almost flinched, but stopped herself. "Blanche," she said stiffly. She wished she could at least pretend to be friendly, but these out-of-control situations unnerved her. The storm continued to roar in the blackness outside, and this person still seemed part of that blackness—and her mother had brought it right inside their house.

"We go to St. Catherine's high school," Rose informed their guest. "Blanche is a senior and I'm a junior."

There was Rose, spilling out information. Wasn't it somewhat dangerous to be telling this unknown person where they went to school? And there sat Mother, not saying anything to her chatty daughter. Pretty soon this Bear person would know every last thing about them. Wretchedly, yet defiantly too, Blanche got up and walked over to the rocking chair. She picked up her quilt and sat down, folding and smoothing it over her knees.

"How do you like school?" Bear asked, leaning over to gently touch his feet. His jawline was taut and he shut his eyes just a bit. *He's really in pain,* Blanche thought. *He's trying hard not to show it, but he can't help it.*

It was odd to see him like this. Here, on their living room couch, surrounded by their quaint little tables and books and lamps, he looked huge and out of place. The room itself seemed smaller with him in it. He seemed far more in his place in St. Catherine's parking lot, where she usually saw him.

St. Catherine's was an ugly rectangular block building, four unremarkable stories high. The hallways were long and narrow, and the three stairwells were always crowded between classes. But in the morning, the top of the south stairwell—the one leading into the library—was usually empty, and that was where Blanche went to hide when she felt besieged by her classmates. It had a window, and it was from there she had seen the boy who called himself Bear.

Sometimes on those mornings, she leaned her books on the sill and studied. Usually, she just looked out on the grey cracked square of the parking lot and the surrounding dirty streets and felt trapped and lost. Before homeroom started, different groups of students hung out in the parking lot by the chain-link fence and smoked. There was a lot of rough-housing. Every once in a while, Blanche saw some money change hands, and she would get a hard, cold feeling inside. She knew there were a few kids who did drugs at St. Catherine's. Everyone knew that type of stuff went on, even if not everyone knew which ones were involved.

At the beginning of the school year, she'd also noticed the tall, burly figure at the corner of the school grounds, solitary and defiant in dark glasses, a kerchief over his lengthy dreadlocks. He'd pace up and down the periphery with cool indifference, someone you wouldn't want to meet in a dark alley. Sometimes he'd stop and talk to a student, or to another suspicious-looking character. Once she'd seen a police car crawl slowly through the traffic near the school, and the boy with the dreadlocks had sauntered casually off.

And this was the same guy who was now sitting in their living room, having his feet washed by her mother. At the moment, he looked more shabby and bewildered than ferocious, but Blanche couldn't forget his usual appearance of disguised danger. She felt wooden inside.

Her blithe younger sister was apparently quite taken with this boy of conflicting faces and sat babbling away on the arm of the sofa.

"This is our first year of regular school. Our parents taught us at home ever since we were babies. Mom always said it was a more natural way to learn. She must be right, because Blanche and I are way ahead of the other kids at school in everything except science and health studies. I hate science, but Blanche is good at it. Blanche almost didn't have to go to high school at all—but she needed one more year of English and her math scores were a little low, so Mom thought it would be best for us to go to school for at least one year. I don't mind the work, but I don't like the kids, generally. Some of them are okay, but the popular girls like to pick on my sister, and almost all the guys are so gross. I don't know why guys are like that. Do you?"

"Simple immaturity, usually," Bear said. He seemed to be enjoying Rose's chatter. At least it was keeping his mind off his feet, thought Blanche gloomily.

"So you think they'll grow out of it?" Rose asked.

"Oh, it's not impossible," Bear said.

"Well, there's a sign of hope. The boys at school are so degenerate that it makes one feel pessimistic about the future of the male gender in general. Some of the senior boys are nice enough, although I've had to yell at them when they tease my sister."

Bear looked at Blanche. "What do they tease you for?"

Blanche shrugged her shoulders. *How should I know?* "Something to do, I guess," she said.

Bear seemed to be irritated by that. "Yeah, I used to get picked on myself in school. It's not fun."

This was a new dimension. Blanche wondered if he had ever felt as overwhelmed by the teasing as she did.

Mother had gotten the warm water from the kitchen stove and was pouring it into Bear's basin. He leaned over. "Are you getting tired of rubbing my feet? I can rub them myself. Come on, let me. I feel strange sitting up here just watching."

"Well, if you want to. Rub slowly and gently. You won't gain anything by doing it faster. Yes, that's the way."

Mother sat back on her heels. Slowly she began to take off her coat. "You must be roasting in that parka," she said to Bear. "Let me take it for you."

"No thanks, thanks. I'd better be going soon," Bear said.

"What were you doing outside for so long?" Rose wasn't done with questions.

"Personal business," Bear said briefly, without looking up from his rubbing.

"Too private to explain?" Rose asked, interested.

"Yes," Bear said in a forbidding voice that made Blanche feel justified for her continuing doubts. Even Rose got the hint and changed the subject.

"How are your feet?"

"They hurt, but it's bearable now. How soon can I go, Mrs.—? I'm sorry, I don't know your name."

"Brier," Mother said. "Jean Brier. You should probably stay inside until you've recovered total feeling. I'm going to have some dinner. Would you like anything?"

"No thanks, you've been very kind to me."

"What about a sandwich? There's one already made up in the refrigerator."

Bear's resolution seemed to waver. "Well, okay." He straightened up, lifted up a foot from the basin, and hesitantly began to dry it with his dirty sock.

"Here, I'll get you a towel," Rose said as she hopped up and headed toward the bathroom. She returned with one of their company towels, a blue paisley terry-cloth. As she handed it to Bear, she caught her sister's disapproving eye and grinned, as if to say, *well, what other company do we have?*

"Thanks," Bear said gratefully.

"Keep your feet wrapped up for a bit," Mother said from the kitchen. "Blanche, let him use your quilt."

Reluctantly, Blanche handed him the quilt that Mother had made her when she was seven years old.

Bear wrapped his feet in it carefully enough, and began to look around him. His eyes gravitated towards the wall-to-wall bookshelf at one end of the room. "You folks like books, I see."

"That's only half of our books," Rose informed him. "When we moved here, we had more books than anything else. The rest are upstairs in the hallway and our bedrooms. One of our favorite things to do is go to used bookstores and library sales. We're book addicts!"

"That's great," Bear said. "What authors do you like?"

Mother brought him a sandwich on a plate and a glass of milk. He took them with thanks and began to eat with relish.

"Oh, Carroll and C. S. Lewis and George MacDonald. Blanche has read more of the classics than I have. She likes the Brontës best."

"Second best to Jane Austen," Blanche murmured.

"Do you like to read?" Rose asked Bear, who was already halfway through the sandwich.

Bear scratched his neck, shaking his dreadlocks. "There's this guy G.K. Chesterton I've read a lot of," he said at last. "I like him."

"What, you too?" Rose yelped. "Nobody reads G. K. Chesterton these days, except theology buffs like my Dad. I love him! Have you read his romances, like *Manalive* and *The Napoleon of Notting Hill?*"

"Yeah, I have, though it's been quite a while," Bear said

slowly. "You're right, not too many people read him these days."

Rose intoned,

> *"The men of the East may spell the stars,*
> *And times and triumphs mark,*
> *But the men signed of the cross of Christ*
> *Go gaily in the dark."*

"That's the *Ballad of the White Horse*, isn't it?" A smile crossed Bear's face. "I like his poetry. I like poetry in general."

"Do you know any? I mean, to recite?" Rose wanted to know, tossing her red head from side to side excitedly.

" 'When in disgrace with fortune and men's eyes, I all alone bewail my outcast state . . .' " Bear paused. "That's Shakespeare. I used to know more of it, but I'm afraid I've forgotten." He took another bite of the sandwich.

"Blanche, you say something next. It would only be fitting," Rose urged. Poetry went to Rose's head like wine. Her cheeks were flushed with eagerness.

Blanche searched her mind, and at last said quickly, without emotion, " 'Dust I am, to dust am bending, from the final doom impending, help me, Lord, for death is near.' "

"That sounds like Tennyson," Rose said.

"T. S. Eliot," said Bear, setting down his glass, empty. "*Murder in the Cathedral.*"

"You're right," Blanche said, surprised.

"It's a favorite of mine," Bear admitted.

Rose clapped her hands. "Oh, Bear, you must come visit us again. We haven't found anybody interesting in the City to be friends with and it would be such fun to talk poetry with someone again!"

"Well, maybe I will, if you like." Bear's face reddened.

"Do, please. I beg you," Rose clasped her hands.

Bear grinned suddenly. "All right, but only if it's okay with your mother." He swallowed the last of the sandwich and bent down to put on his socks and shoes.

Mother had been sitting on the chair with her dinner tray on her lap, listening to their conversation. "You're welcome to come any time, Bear." She stopped him. "Wait, you really shouldn't put on those wet socks again. Rose, go look under the stairs for that box of your father's I've been saving for the Goodwill collection. I think you'll find some men's wool socks in there. And see if there's that old pair of overshoes, too. They might fit him."

Bear started to protest. "Look, I couldn't take—"

"You don't really have a choice when Mother makes up her mind," Blanche said, so grimly that Bear was silenced and Mother glanced quickly at her daughter.

"Well, uh—thanks a lot for saving my feet," Bear said awkwardly, accepting the socks and overshoes Rose had speedily found for him. "I'm really grateful."

"Glad to help. And make sure you come back," Mother said, setting her tray aside and rising. Bear hastily finished pulling on the boots and stuffed his wet socks and sneakers into the pockets of his jacket. He rose to shake her proffered hand.

"Goodnight, then," Bear looked at all of them. He smiled, and his face seemed to come alive. He looked far happier than when he had first come in. Blanche thought that he could almost pass for a nice person. Feeling a bit sorry for her callous attitude, she waved a tiny good-bye at him as he passed.

"Goodnight!" Rose said, escorting him to the door.

"Make sure you lock your door," Bear said to her, putting on his hood as he went out the apartment door. He shot her a half-mischievous glance. "There's lots of strange people on the streets these days."

"Ah yes, we know," Rose laughed. He shut the house door carefully behind him and tested it to make sure it was locked. Blanche, who had gotten up to peer through the blinds, saw him bound down the snowy steps and disappear into the night, vanishing almost as suddenly as he had appeared.

She shivered again as she turned from the window. Rose and Mother were talking about what a pleasant person he seemed to be and how they hoped he would come back. She retrieved her beloved quilt from the floor and folded it into her arms. It made a warm, comforting bulk against her chest.

"So, you've seen that guy around school?" Rose queried as Blanche started for the staircase.

Blanche tossed her heavy curtain of black hair behind her shoulders. "Yes." For Mother's benefit, she added, "I always thought he was a drug dealer."

"Well!" Mother sipped her glass of milk meditatively. "He certainly doesn't seem quite like what I'd have expected, then."

"You never know," Rose said. "Maybe he's just a lonely guy."

"You never know," her sister repeated ominously. "He could be lying to us about not using drugs. He could be planning to—rob us, or worse. And those awful dreadlocks! Why on earth would anyone do that to themselves?"

"You're just being a stick-in-the-mud," Rose said airily.

Mother silently listened to both of them. "Well," she said at last. "We'll see if he comes back. Don't worry, Blanche. I know you're trying to be sensible, and that's very wise of you to be cautious. But I must admit he doesn't seem like a dishonest person. We can't judge a person by his looks. Not even by his hair."

Blanche did not feel that Mother's judgment was always entirely accurate. A bit annoyed that she was apparently the most sensible person in the family, she countered, "Maybe something so bad will happen that we'll be sorry that we ever let him in."

"Nonsense!" Rose stuck out her chin. "I'm glad we let him in. Who cares what happens next?"

"Don't worry, Blanche," Mother said unexpectedly. "After all, we were sheltering the stranger and tending the sick, weren't we? That wasn't wrong, no matter what may happen from hereafter. And I may be foolhardy, but I believe that God gives a special protection to those who step out in faith to care for their brothers."

As Blanche took this in, Mother set down her cup with a sigh. "Now, I think it's about time we went to bed."

The two girls went upstairs, Blanche first and Rose afterwards. A few minutes later, Blanche sat on the bed, brushing out her hair, a time-consuming chore with hair as long as hers. She could hear her sister in the bathroom doing her nightly facial scrub and humming a sixties song about taking time to make friends with a stranger. The song irked Blanche. She couldn't help her fears, could she? Rose was one of those people who found it easy to be daring. Try as she might, Blanche couldn't, or at least didn't, want to be. The world needed sane, prudent people too, didn't it? Not everyone had to be fighters, did they?

The world was a fantastic, marvelous, awesome place, Rose decided again as she threw herself down on her rumpled bed and dug herself comfortably under the covers. She breathed one last breath of the cold bedroom air before snuggling beneath her comforter to think of the swirling world of the storm outside, which tonight had deposited such a puzzling enigma of a person as Bear on their doorstep. She meditated upon this happening, and felt that this was the nature of God's world. You were constantly coming across the unexpected, the unexplainable, the tremendous mystery of creation. It was lovely and romantic to ponder in the dark, while lying in bed, listening to the further mystery of snow and wind, waiting for sleep to come. Her deep thoughts were disturbed by Blanche's getting up to fumble around the room. "What is it now?" she asked, mildly exasperated.

"Just looking for matches," Blanche explained in a whisper.

"Setting us on fire, are you?" Rose turned over in a hump and watched her sister's shadow huddle over the vigil light on the dresser, trying to light it.

"Are you scared?" Rose asked softly. Blanche usually lit the candle when she was disturbed or couldn't sleep.

Blanche didn't answer. She watched the little flame of the votive candle lick away at the darkness before her picture of the Virgin Mary. Then, before returning to bed, she stole over to the window and peered out into the night of the City encased in storm. There was no dark figure, sinister and solitary, lounging in the corner of an alleyway, watching their house, waiting for them to come out into his territory. But in her fearful thoughts as she dropped off to sleep at last, he was there.

The two girls were quite close and always held each other's hand when they went out into the world together.
—Grimm

Chapter 2

LUNCH TIME was not Blanche's favorite part of the school day.

She really didn't mind the classes very much. Some of the teachers were interesting, especially Sister Geraldine, who taught literature. Occasionally Blanche was teased by her classmates for being too smart. Which was stupid, because her grades weren't always that good.

But lunch time and homeroom—those times when there was little structure and kids were free to mill around, socializing—were hard for Blanche. Her first problem was having no one to talk to. She hadn't made friends with any of the girls in her class, who had been together since their freshman year. So she usually spent her lunch hour reading a library book.

This would have been a good arrangement, except for a certain group of seniors in the popular set.

The day after Bear had come to their house, Blanche sat in the storm of shouting and talking in the crowded cafeteria, trying to read *Jane Eyre* over peanut butter and jelly.

"Hey, Blanche!" a guy shouted at her from the other end of the table.

She half looked up. It was Carl, the pimpled, loud-mouthed boy from science class who thought himself a great comedian. This was a set-up.

"Can you give me the answers to our homework for Biology?"

Whatever she said, he'd play off it, somehow. "I'd rather not," she said at last, brushing the crumbs off of her plaid uniform skirt. Carl's companions laughed.

"Pleeeasse?" He slid down the bench towards her. "Come on, Blanche, be my friend."

Nervously, she glanced at him, and his friends burst into laughter.

Confident of his audience, he said, "You got a date for this Friday?"

She bit her lip. With Carl, it always ended up this way. She wished for the umpteenth time that she had some of Rose's nerve, or at least that she could think of some decent reply to shut him up.

"Aw, playing hard to get, are you? Wanna go out with me Friday night? I could show you a real good time."

Grimly, she stared at her book, trying not to look frightened. He went on.

"Come on, Blanche. You gotta start sometime. You and I would be good together, I know." Her face went red as the other boys hooted. She got up as he pleaded, mockingly, "Aw, now don't run out on me!"

She gathered up her things as quickly as she could while he continued to hassle her, and walked as fast as she dared from the cafeteria, her face scarlet.

It was a relief to find the girl's bathroom empty. Feeling cold and clammy, she leaned against the nearest bathroom stall and tried to fight off the faintness. The last thing she needed was to keel over on the bathroom floor. "Oh, stop it, please, not now," she said beseechingly to her body, which always seemed to cave in on her when things became stressful. She undid the top button on her blue oxford uniform shirt. The tiny black specks that had been dancing before her eyes receded, and she breathed deeply. *Thank God for that, at least.*

When she felt more normal, she took some bathroom tissue from the stalls and blew her nose. There was one kid in the school who had seizures, and everyone made fun of him. God forbid they should ever find out about her fainting spells. She had enough strikes against her already.

Still shaky, she stared at her face in the mirror—a round white face with pale blue eyes (red-rimmed) and long straight black hair that (the fashion magazines said) only made her face look rounder. It was a child's face, and Blanche wished that it was still possible to be a child. But here she was, stuck in an adolescent body in an adolescent world, and apparently failing miserably.

And her skin was *very* white, the heritage of an Irish ancestry. She rubbed her cheeks irritably and fumbled in her book bag for the necessary blush. *I look like a china doll without the pink cheeks. Goodness, I could be dead, staring in the mirror, and not know it.* She found her tiny compact and brushed on some of the pink powder. Better, but her eyes and nose were still red. She wet a paper towel and pressed it to her eyes, feeling very fragile.

The bathroom door banged open, and Eileen Raskin, one of the top girls in the food chain, walked in with her entourage. The blond girl's green eyes alighted on Blanche and her mascara-heavy lashes lowered. "Hey, it's the Immaculate Complexion!" she laughed.

Blanche had no idea why her one blessing—a lack of acne—should have become the target for her classmates' ridicule. She put away her compact and turned from the mirror, hoping that it wouldn't look like she had been crying.

Eileen's sidekick, Lisa, a tall redhead who wore her uniform skirts as short as possible, sneered. "What's up, I.C.? How's the book reading?"

They think I'm their personal chew toy, Blanche thought irritably. "Woof, woof," she muttered below her breath, making her way to the door.

"Have you found a date for the prom yet? Better start early!" Lisa called after her, and Eileen said, "Carl Rogers is willing!" Blanche heard their laughter as the door slammed shut behind her.

Now there was no place to go. Blanche didn't think she could handle the lunchroom again. Slowly she started up the nearest staircase. Maybe she would just hang out in the halls until her next class started. But if she did that, she would risk being questioned by teachers, who seemed to have an inherent distrust of solitary students. As she walked onto the second floor, her eyes fell on the door to the chapel. Without another thought she slipped inside.

In the dark room, a converted classroom with stained-glass windows installed, a red electric light flickered by the round plain tabernacle in the corner. Blanche genuflected and gave the unadorned box a grim smile.

The room was sparsely furnished, although it had apparently once been nicer. Blanche guessed the pillars in the corners had once held statues, but there were now only artificial ivy plants. The altar was a bare wooden table, the crucifix above it, unremarkable. On the wall beside the altar hung a liturgical banner celebrating Peace and Justice Month. In the back of the room was a lone statue of Mary that Blanche touched lightly with one finger as she passed.

She leaned against the wall by the windows—there were no pews, just floor mats—and tried to formulate a prayer. Instead, pictures of her dead father began to flash through her mind—Dad coming home from work, looking tired and relieved; Dad slicing potatoes to make his famous home-fries; Dad reading out loud to them after dinner, his wire-rimmed reading glasses making him look distinguished. *Dang it, this was not the way to stop crying.*

To steady herself, she began to look at the only concession to beauty in the room, the stained-glass windows, a triumphant medley in blue, gold, red, and purple. Today, the winter skies made the colors murky, but the hues still glowed with an unearthly light that comforted her, some-how.

She rested her hot forehead against the cold glass and tried to find a transparent panel. Through a chink of white glass, she could make out the parking lot below. Was Bear there today?

She could not see him through her tiny peephole. He might be there, or he might not. If he was not there, where was he?

Turning back to the room, she stared at a dedication plaque, stating that the windows had been donated by friends and faculty to honor the memory of Fr. Michael Raymond, chaplain of St. Catherine's. There was a picture of Fr. Raymond in the hallway downstairs. He was a formidably hand-some priest whom the girls said looked like James Dean in his fifties. There wasn't a chaplain at St. Catherine's any more. Instead, a Sister Melanie was the school's spiritual counselor. Blanche had spent a few hours in her office at different times, being forced to talk about her feelings. Sister Melanie was very sweet, but she seemed to think that Blanche's problems would be solved if she made more friends and joined the Yearbook Staff. Blanche liked Sister Melanie, but felt that for all the nun's sympathy, she sort of missed the point.

The bell rang, shocking Blanche into the present crisis. *If I don't get to class on time, I'll end up doing personality tests in Sister Melanie's office again,* she thought. That was enough to drive all metaphysical and social terrors from her mind, at least for the moment. She knelt down before the tabernacle to say a quick formal prayer, then carefully opened the door and stepped out into the hallway.

Blanche straightened her posture in her desk as Sister Geraldine came into the room. The English teacher in her long white Dominican habit and black veil was about eighty years old, shriveled and walking with a cane. She had continued teaching English because she liked to, and had reached the stage where she was no longer offended that many of her students were not interested in literature. She simply taught the course as if they were all college literature majors, and never graded on a curve. That meant that even the laziest students had to work hard to keep up the pretense of passing, and Blanche enjoyed being pushed academically. If only the other nuns would stop trying to push her socially!

Today, Sister Geraldine returned their poems. In general, Sister Geraldine frowned upon "creative writing" as a diversion from studying the classics, but when they had reached the section on poetry, she had reluctantly directed the students to write an original poem in one of three classical styles, just for practice: sonnet, villanelle, or terzanelle. It hadn't been an easy assignment.

Blanche had spent long hours laboring over her sonnet, and was dismayed to find it returned covered in blistering red slashes and writing. Sister Geraldine, who seemed to like Blanche in an odd, roundabout way, had criticized the poem harshly. The poem was "technically well done, but suffers from a poor handling of the subject."

Blanche had written about flowers at sunset, because she could find the most descriptive words to use on this subject. She had some thought about trying to work in her grief over Dad's death, but the rigid form of the sonnet wouldn't allow it. Every line she came up with about death that rhymed just sounded stupid. So she got rid of death and just talked about flowers. Sister Geraldine's caustic remarks hurt, because she had intended the poem to be so much better than it was.

Apparently, she wasn't the only one who was upset by her grade. Lauren Berger, who had written what Blanche thought was a pretty funny villanelle about studying for an algebra test, raised her hand and complained. Lauren was the top student in the senior class, and was used to getting "A's". Sister Geraldine had never given her more than an average grade, which Lauren resented bitterly. Sister Geraldine listened to Lauren's hurt remarks for a few seconds, and launched into a lecture which Blanche thought didn't really answer the question. Sometimes she was sure that Sister was a little deaf.

Well, maybe not. Leaning on her cane and staring at Lauren with beady blue eyes, Sister expostulated, "The problem is not in your technique, which was fairly good, but in the handling of your subject matter. Two qualities of great poetry are that it deals with a universal subject matter in an original manner. Now, while everyone might be able to relate to the frustrations of studying for a test, your poem didn't adequately convey what we might call the 'human realities' of that sensation. It was clever and even humorous, but was too exclusively 'yours.' You provided your audience with too few avenues through which they might become immersed in the experience and so sympathize, identify, and participate in the poem's sentiments. Now, Miss Brier—" here she indicated Blanche with a wave of a shaking hand, "spoke with a familiar voice that the reader could emotionally respond to on a universally significant topic—death—but her thoughts on the matter were poorly formulated and unoriginal, although she handled the sonnet form nicely."

How did she know that I was writing about death? Blanche was silently amazed. Sister Geraldine went on, and Lauren continued to look glum and irritated. At last, Lauren said, raising her hand again, "So I think you're saying that it's impossible to get an 'A' in this class unless we're Shakespeare or something."

The class chuckled, and Sister Geraldine permitted herself a rare smile. "Oh, it's not impossible, just very, very difficult."

She paused. "Actually, if it will make you feel better, I did give out one 'A' to a student poem, once."

Really? Blanche and the rest of the class were interested in the poem immediately.

Sister sensed that, and opened her briefcase. "We had just studied Robert Frost, one of the moderns, and I gave the poetry assignment then. One remarkable student turned in this poem. It is meant as a response to Frost's famous poem, 'Nothing Gold Can Stay.'" She pulled out a folder and paused. "Perhaps it might not make sense to you if you're not familiar with the poem, but I think that it stands on its own."

With her white, veined hand, she took out a piece of paper and read aloud, her thin voice rounding out the words:

> "*The first tree-flowers float,*
>   *wisp on water, though it's air.*
> *Each prism parallel—*
>   *Suspended there.*
>
> *Suspended there as sap is rising.*
>   *Growing as it stays.*
> *Bending under sap's height*
>   *Giving praise.*
>
> *Giving praise but oh, they have been bent,*
>   *growing green for which they fade.*
> *Singing only to be silent.*
>   *To rest laid.*
>
> *To rest, laid low in the earth's brown dust,*
>   *the Autumn grey dust they had been.*
> *Again themselves to dust—but born*
>   *again to all things then.*
>
> *Again to all things then they're flying—*
>   *tallest mountains, highest skies.*
> *All things green and good are falling,*
>   *Only to rise.*"

She cleared her throat at the end. "Perhaps I was a bit hasty in giving it an 'A,' but I did, so I let it stand. For a student composition, I thought it was excellent." She laid the paper on the desk. "Please open your literature books to page 103."

Lauren turned to a girl across the aisle and whispered. "*That* didn't sound like a villanelle or a sonnet. Huh! I bet the one who wrote that poem was her special pet."

"Must have been, to crack Sister Geraldine," was her friend's remark.

Blanche wasn't sure. She expected Sister Geraldine to be far more objective than that.

As she found page 103, Blanche thought about the images in the poem. The apple blossoms on the farm that was no longer theirs were dead now, though the promise of next year's buds slumbered in the black frozen branches. Would she ever see them again? *There's such a thing as hope,* she thought resentfully. *Mom has it. Rose has it. Just not me.*

After class was over, she hesitantly went up to the old nun who sat at her desk, checking off items in her schedule.

"Sister, I wondered . . . may I have a copy of that poem you read us?"

Sister Geraldine looked at her over her bifocals with sharp blue eyes. "Certainly. Take it to the School Office and ask Sister Maureen to make a photocopy of it for you, then bring it right back here."

She handed Blanche the poem. Blanche did not dare disobey, though it would probably make her late for her next class. As she hurried down the hall, she scanned the poem again. It was signed "A. Denniston." Blanche wondered if A. Denniston was a boy or a girl.

When she opened the office door, Mr. Edward Freet was talking to the nun who was the office manager, a formidable woman with a stylish haircut. Mr. Freet was a commonplace sight at the school, although Blanche had never been able to figure out if he held an official post there. A short, older man in his sixties with iron-grey hair and a red, wrinkled face, he seemed to be friends with all the teachers and secretaries, although he was more brusque to the students, at least to the girls. In his patterned vests and collared shirts, he was a peculiar and distinctive figure. Blanche had heard he was the principal's brother and owned an art gallery in Greenwich Village.

"What do you want?" the nun said to Blanche as she approached them.

"A photocopy—for Sister Geraldine," Blanche faltered.

Mr. Freet looked annoyed at the interruption, but the nun took the poem from her and went to the copier. He continued to talk in petulant tones about art and music.

"You can't pretend that this trash that they're putting out today is really music," he was saying. "It's abysmally inferior to just about anything from the eighteenth century. Take Mozart, for instance. None of these contemporary composers can hold a candle to him!"

"Truth can be found in all times, in many forms, even ugly ones," the nun intoned mildly. "I disagree. I think that the light comes through even a distorted mirror."

"Art isn't about truth, it's about form," Mr. Freet said indignantly, rapping on the Formica desktop with his fingernails. "That's why the absence of a beautiful, structured form destroys music. Yes, and art, too. That's why I don't hold with your modern churches and their formless abstractions. Garbage and tripe, all of it."

He shot a look over at Blanche, who couldn't help following the conversation with interest, and glared at her.

Blanche swiftly dropped her eyes and pretended to read the fire drill procedure taped to the top of the counter.

"So you'd have us remain frozen in admiration of Michelangelo's nudes?" the nun said over the noise of the copier.

"Why not? Stay with the perfect. I agree with the Greeks."

"There were a lot of flaws in the philosophies of the ancient Greeks."

"Oh, I suppose you mean because they revered the male body over the female body as exemplifying perfection," he said. "So what's wrong with that? Here again, Michelangelo is a perfect example. Take his *David* for instance, over his grotesque female nudes."

The nun crossed to Blanche and handed her the poem and its copy with a reassuring smile, then turned back to her conversation. "You see, that's your view of the truth, Mr. Freet. It's perhaps different from other people's point of view."

"Which is why I say art is about form and not truth!"

Blanche closed the door, thoughts whirling around her head. She would have to repeat the strange conversation to the family at home and try to make some sense of it, if there was any sense in it at all. It sounded terribly refined and reasonable, but somehow she found herself lost in the middle of it.

When she came back into the classroom, the elderly nun was standing at her desk, rearranging papers in her briefcase with delicate precision. Her cane was on her elbow.

Blanche gave the original poem back to her teacher and

asked hesitantly, "How did you know my sonnet was about dying?"

"I read between the lines," Sister said cryptically. "It's a difficult subject for a young person to handle."

Blanche stared at the nun's gnarled hands, and thought, *That may be true, but young people still have to deal with it.* But, of course, she couldn't say that to Sister, who might not know about her father's death. So, she thanked her teacher hurriedly and went out to her next class.

"Hey there!" Rose hurried towards her sister as Blanche left Sister Geraldine's room. "How are you doing?"

"The usual." Blanche gave a bleak smile.

"You don't look too good." Rose studied her sister's white face anxiously.

"I was feeling a little dizzy after lunch. That's all."

"Was someone teasing you again?"

"Do they ever stop?"

Rose felt an angry flush pass over her face. "Who? The boys or the girls?"

"Oh, both," Blanche admitted, pushing back her hair from her face. "Don't worry about me, Rose."

"You know I do, though." Rose bit her lip. There really hadn't been a need to ask her sister who had been tormenting her. It was inevitably the same cast of characters. "You know, some of the kids in this school must have awfully low self-esteem to get such a charge out of being bullies."

"You'd think they'd have grown out of it by now," Blanche agreed. "It's probably just the competition coming out that you find all over the City—raise yourself up by putting someone else down." Blanche already seemed less tense, being able to talk about it, just as Rose had hoped. Rose was heartened. She and Blanche had always been very different people, but since they had come to this new school together, Rose felt a closer kinship between them. She was Blanche's sole ally in an environment neither of them felt a part of.

"Keep your chin up," Rose urged. "I'll find those boys and pound them." Rose was not afraid of any kind of male creature. She'd already made a reputation among the boys at school by bawling them out for harassing her sister. Some of them looked the other way when they saw her coming, but she couldn't care less.

"Sister Geraldine gave me this neat poem," Blanche said, changing the subject. "I'll show it to you at home. It was written by one of her old students. Just our luck—the one student here who seems to have any grasp of the higher things graduated a long time ago. But it's a cool poem."

"We'll read it together tonight," Rose said, smiling at her sister. "Two more hours!" Blanche grinned back, some of her old fire showing again. She turned into the doorway of her next class.

Rose had the last lunch period of the school day, which was sarcastically nicknamed "the supper lunch" since it came so late in the day. As she walked down the stairs to the basement where the cafeteria was, she saw Rob Tirsch at his locker. She couldn't help slowing down a bit. Rob was tall, black-haired, and terribly good looking. Unfortunately, he seemed to know it. He was part of the popular crowd in the senior class, but he had been pretty friendly to Rose.

"Hey, Red," he said to her as she passed him.

"Hi, Rob," she said, smiling, and he turned around.

"What you been up to?" He flashed a smile at her, indicating that he'd like to talk.

"Oh, nothing much." Despite herself, Rose leaned against the wall to talk to him, hoping that the three zits on her face weren't too obvious.

"Break's over. Can you believe it? It went by so fast," Rob ran his hands through his curly hair.

Rose, whose Christmas vacation had been lonely, if leisurely, simply nodded. "What did you do over break?"

"Went skiing a couple of times. You ever gone?"

Rose shook her head. "I've done cross-country a few times, but not downhill."

"It's the best. Man, this year is dragging by. I can't wait till I'm out of here." Rob glanced behind him and winked at her. "Hey, bet you didn't know this. See that iron door over there?" He indicated a much painted-over door beside the furnace room.

Rose nodded.

"D'you know there's a tunnel there?" Rob asked.

"Really?" Rose was intrigued.

"Yeah," Rob lowered his voice mysteriously. "It goes over to that abandoned church next door. A long time ago, the two buildings were connected."

"Why was the church abandoned, anyway?"

"Ah, the roof was going to fall in or something. So they closed it down. They say there's all sorts of treasure buried in the basement."

"You're kidding," Rose said, not sure whether to believe him.

"No, no, I'm not." Rob was earnest. "The old priest over there—Fr. Raymond—he used to collect hundreds of chalices and gold stuff for the altar—all the stuff churches were throwing away when they stopped having Latin in the Mass. He collected it all, and hid it in the church. Then one night, when he was polishing his collection, he was murdered."

"Murdered?!"

"Yeah. Some crazy guy came and shot him in the back, right behind the altar. They say they've never gotten the bloodstains off the floor." He grinned at Rose, who was shuddering. "You're pretty gullible, you know that?"

"Did he really shoot him?" Rose flushed. She *was* gullible.

"Honest, he did. The guy who shot him stole everything. All the gold and stuff. My old man says most of it was junk. They've never found the guy who did it."

"That's horrible!" Rose was indignant.

"Yeah. It happens. They had to close down the church because they said they couldn't raise money to fix the roof, but it was really because they couldn't find a priest who would work in that church again. You see, it's haunted now."

He looked at Rose to gauge her reaction. She half-believed him.

"It's the truth," he said, cocking his head. "Just be careful when you pass the church after dark. The ax murderer who lives there will get you!"

"I thought you said the priest was shot," Rose accused him. The bell rang.

"Yeah, by an ax murderer who had mislaid his ax. Next best thing. Oh, and he strangled the priest, too." Rob grinned, slapping his books out of his locker. "Must have been a real sicko."

He punched Rose playfully on the shoulder. "That should put you to sleep at night. Did you know they took the word gullible out of the dictionary?"

Rose made a face at him as he bounced off down the hallway to class.

He was about the only boy at St. Catherine's that Rose felt a more than passing interest in. It was a pity he acted like a jerk sometimes, usually when he was with his buddies. Blanche disliked him, but Rose found him appealing. He was almost always nice to her, and that was flattering. Just about every junior girl she knew had a crush on him. He had this fascinating charm that melted the hearts of even the most sensible teenaged girls. His singling Rose out hadn't made her terrifically popular among her classmates.

But unlike Blanche, who seemed to be picked on or ignored by everyone in her class, Rose got along pretty well with just about everyone—except those senior jerks who kept tormenting her sister. Blanche had resigned herself to occupying the lowest social strata in the school; Rose preferred to stand defiantly outside the structure.

Going into the cafeteria, Rose found a place at a table with some girls from her biology class. They were all good students, and Rose found herself welcomed in their circle. She wasn't close with any of them, but at least she had someone to sit with at lunch who could hold intelligent conversations.

Something cold touched the back of her neck right over her collar and she jumped. There was a burst of male laughter behind her, and she turned to see Manny sitting at the next table.

"Hi, Rose," he grinned, tossing and catching the cold pack he was carrying around for his leg in one hand. He played on the basketball team with Rob and always seemed to be recovering from some kind of injury.

Rose allowed a deliberate look of disgust to come over her face, and cued her eyes. She had chameleon eyes—hazel eyes—and she believed that she could make them change color on command. So now she mentally cued herself. Show temper. Let him know he's in trouble if he keeps this up. Eye color: stone grey.

With a toss of her red hair, she turned back to her sandwich, took a bite, and began to chew slowly. She rolled her eyes at the girl across from her, who grimaced back.

"Hey, Rose," Manny leaned over beside her. "You going to the senior prom?"

"Of course not," she said, not looking at him. "I'm a junior."

"Would you go with Rob Tirsch if he asked you?"

Rose's heart almost stopped beating for a minute. *Rob?* She gave a faint gesture. "Probably," she said at last, with feigned lightness.

"Ooh," Manny said, and moved back to say something to his friends, who all laughed.

Probably? She had meant to say "maybe!" She moaned inwardly and crumpled her napkin. Nothing like looking desperate. She glanced around at the other girls, most of whom hadn't overheard Manny's remarks, and shrugged.

Inwardly she debated about asking Manny what he meant. He was probably just teasing her. Guys thought it was terribly funny when girls had a crush on one of them (Rose, apart from her own situation, found it pretty funny too, considering). Manny was no doubt looking for ammunition to tease Rob with.

Her heart sank inside her. If Rob knew she liked him . . . how embarrassing! *But he probably has some inkling already,* Rose thought mournfully.

She sighed and tried to join the conversation going on around her. *I won't say anything to Blanche about this unless something real happens,* she decided.

When two-thirty came, Rose bounded the steps to the south door to meet her sister. Blanche was already there, looking out, her petite figure almost overwhelmed by her black hair. Her books were held in front of her defensively as she gazed at the chain link fence at the other end of the parking lot. She looked upset again.

"What's wrong?" Rose asked worriedly.

Blanche nodded with her head towards the fence. "That's where I usually see him standing."

"Who?"

"Bear. He wasn't there today," Blanche said.

"Are you sure it was him the other times?" Rose glanced skeptically towards the fence, where Rob and a group of other guys were standing in clumps, talking.

"I'm almost positive." Blanche turned towards her sister, tossing her heavy curtain of hair back over her shoulders. "Rose, he really might be a drug dealer, for all his talk about poetry and whatnot."

"Can you picture Bear hanging out with people like those?" Rose asked derisively, mentally excluding Rob from that group.

"I don't know. There's a lot of contradictions in him," Blanche admitted as they started to walk home.

"Well, we'll see if we ever see him again," Rose said amiably.

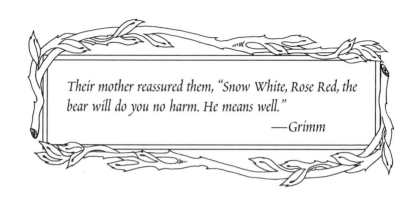

Their mother reassured them, "Snow White, Rose Red, the bear will do you no harm. He means well."

—Grimm

Chapter 3

IT WAS ROSE'S turn to do the dishes that night, so while she and Mother chatted in the kitchen, Blanche slipped out to the living room to play the upright piano that stood in one corner against the wall. She used to practice all the time, but now only played occasionally as a way of consoling herself when she'd had a bad day. Dad had bought the piano for her and its worn walnut surfaces reminded her of him in a way that was distant enough to be comfortable. She pulled out her sheet music, spread it out in front of her, placed her hands on the keys and began.

First, some scales. Then, Mozart's "Rondo," because it gave her fingers a good workout. Then the "Arabian Dance" from *The Nutcracker Suite*, a Chopin interlude she was learning, and Beethoven's "Für Elise." She tried her hand at a new duet for piano and violin that Rose had gotten from her violin teacher. Back in the country, she and Rose had often played together for their family and friends. Rose still took violin lessons—now from a teacher at school—but Blanche had laid aside her study of piano, maybe for good.

She ran quickly through the piano part of the new duet once, then put it aside and took out the "Moonlight Sonata" by Beethoven.

From far off in the city came a car alarm, and the wailing warning of a police siren. Blanche shivered to herself and moved the bench closer to the piano. Fingers adjusted, she began to play the first bars of the "Moonlight Sonata" and let the notes murmur from her fingers in a ceaseless repetition that carried her away down a broad river in her imagination. When she felt she had the current going sufficiently, she moved her right fingers into the melody, let the notes drop haphazardly from her fingertips, like rain on the surface of a pond with a deep undercurrent. She let the melody slide away until she felt like playing it again, barely glancing at the music. This definitely wasn't the conventional way to play the "Moonlight Sonata," but it was very relaxing.

Eventually she began the rising melody of the piece, the uncertain question that drove her eyes back to the notes and made her left hand unsteady. Striving to keep the continual motion of the lower notes, she pounded out the hard, short, anxious notes of the climax, then let her right hand fall. Beethoven never answered the question in this piece. The left hand just kept doing what it had been doing all along, until it eventually sank to the lower end of the keyboard, and then into silence.

Blanche was still, contemplating the vibration of that last low note when the doorbell sounded. The delicate tranquillity she had experienced was shattered.

"I'll get it," Rose sang out, drying her hands on a dish towel as she went to the door. Blanche remained on the piano bench, wary.

"Oh, it's Bear again," Rose sounded surprised. Blanche

heard the house door open, and Rose say, "Come on in, Sir Bear!"

"I just wanted to drop off a thank-you gift and bring back the boots and stuff," Bear was saying.

"Well, come on in!" Rose replied merrily.

Mother came in from the kitchen and stood smiling at Bear. Tonight she was wearing an old denim dress and had her long hair braided and pinned up like a Swedish housewife. "Welcome again, Bear," she said.

Bear came into the living room uncertainly, a small package in one hand and a lumpy grocery bag in the other. "I just thought I'd get you a little gift to thank you for saving my toes last night," he said, a bit sheepishly.

"Take off your coat and stay a while," Mother said. "We were just finishing in the kitchen."

"I was going to make hot chocolate—would you like some?" Rose took Bear's coat, hung it on the old-fashioned coat stand, and skipped to the kitchen to get out the mugs.

"Well, okay, if you don't mind," he said awkwardly. With his coat off, he looked a little smaller in a khaki flannel shirt and old jeans. He sat down carefully on the sofa and crooked his fingers through his matted dreadlocks. His eyes met Blanche's as she sat guardedly in her corner.

"You play piano?" he asked.

"Not in front of other people," she said defensively, getting up from the bench and sitting down on the chair.

"You know, I've seen you before," he said finally, when Mother moved into the kitchen to help Rose.

Blanche said nothing.

"At St. Catherine's," he said. "On the school grounds."

"I've seen you there, too," she said flatly.

A faint red came into his cheeks. "I keep pretty lousy company, don't I?" he observed, quietly.

Blanche still said nothing. Rose came into the room with mugs of hot chocolate.

"I feel like talking poetry," she said cheerfully. "Blanche, where's that poem you got today?"

Blanche felt irritated at being forced to share something that moved her with a stranger. But what could she say in front of Bear without being rude? So she went to fetch the paper.

Mother opened Bear's package. "Italian cookies!" she exclaimed. "Bear, how did you know to get our favorite kind?"

"I didn't know, but I've always liked them, too," Bear admitted, clearly pleased.

"The perfect thing with hot chocolate!" Rose said approvingly, and went to fetch a plate. She arranged them artistically in a spiral on the plate and set them on the coffee table for nibbling. Mother and Rose both ate them with relish, but Blanche didn't take any until after Bear had helped himself a few times.

Rose read the poem by A. Denniston with interest and passed it to Bear, who perused it with a frown on his face. "I like the rhyme scheme," Rose said. "Really good for someone our age. What do you think?"

Bear coughed. "Well, I think it's a bit overdone myself," he admitted. "But I can be super-critical."

"The images are good," Mother said, looking it over as she rocked on her rocker.

"Well, what don't you like about it?" Rose wanted to know, sipping her hot chocolate.

"It's an okay rhyme scheme, but I get the feeling the guy

who wrote it didn't know much about death, or suffering," Bear said. "He just seems to answer the question too easily. It's sort of trite, really."

Blanche cupped her warm mug in her hands and felt her cheeks flame. *Of course he wouldn't like it, or understand it.*

"I think it's a remarkable attempt," Mother said, taking another cookie. "It makes me think of our apple orchard back home."

Mother handed the poem back to Blanche as Bear asked casually, "Where'd you find a piece like that?"

"Sister Geraldine read it to us in class," Blanche said quietly, still hot. "She said it was the best poem she'd ever seen written by one of her students."

Bear shrugged. "Well, that may be her opinion. But I still like Robert Frost's poem—the one it's copying off of—better." He paused, and quoted, " 'So Eden sunk to grief. So dawn goes down to day. Nothing gold can stay.' "

There was a stillness in the room, and Bear looked so pensive that Blanche almost forgave him for not appreciating A. Denniston's poem.

"Sister Geraldine is one of those rare specimens of people," Rose announced, after some musing. "I don't have her for a teacher, but I like her. Do you know, I don't think she's really who she says she is. Well, I suppose that she really is a nun, but she's more than just an old schoolmarm." She eyed Bear carefully. "Do you know what I mean?"

"I'm not sure," said Bear, looking interested.

"Have you ever felt that there was something going on in life that not everyone was aware of?" Rose asked, turning her mug around in her hands.

Bear relaxed a bit more deeply into the couch, and put on a mock-solemn look. "Explain thyself."

"As though there's a story going on that everyone is a part of, but not everybody knows about? Maybe 'story' isn't the right word—a sort of drama, a battle between what's peripheral and what's *really* important. As though the people you meet aren't just their plain, prosaic selves, but are actually princes and princesses, gods and goddesses, fairies, shepherds, all sorts of fantastic creatures who've chosen to hide their real shape for some reason or another. Have you ever thought that?"

"Tell us more about this view of reality you have, Miss Brier," Bear said straight-faced.

Rose shook her head, sending her red hair flying from side to side. "No, silly, I'm not psychotic. I'm not even sure if I'm serious. Well, I am, but I'm not, if you know what I mean. It makes life so much more interesting that way. I mean, for instance, our real estate agent—the one who helped us find this place—looks like any other lady who sells real estate—suits and hairspray and all that. But she always wore these incredibly wild earrings. Didn't she, Blanche? Just perfectly exotic ones, with all sorts of tortoiseshell and beads—so I decided that who she really is—" Rose leaned closer to Bear for dramatic effect, "—is a gypsy woman of a lost tribe, a pure descendant of the oldest line of Pharaohs. But see, she's lost contact with her tribe when she was a little girl—"

"Stolen away in the night by non-gypsies?" Bear suggested.

"In a terrible act of reverse discrimination," Blanche added.

"Shut up! I'm serious! She *is* a gypsy. She has these large, soulful eyes, but she's incredibly shrewd—anyhow, she was separated from her tribe, and, being a gypsy in her heart, body and soul, she is completely unhappy in modern life. She has searched for her own people in vain. So, she's come to New York City and is selling real estate to make ends meet, hoping that in this way, she'll be able to keep track of people coming into the City and just maybe, someday, she'll find her lost family," Rose sighed. "It made it so much easier to go around with her looking at houses once I realized that she was a gypsy."

Mother smiled at her daughter fondly. "I know what you mean, Rose. I thought there was something unique about Lois Cohen. I must say she did have excellent taste in houses."

"The sad thing is that I don't think that Mrs. Cohen realizes that she's actually a gypsy. Or maybe she once knew, but forgot. I wish she would remember. It would probably make her much happier in her sorrows." Rose gazed sadly at the half-eaten cookie in her hand.

"You know, you're right, Rose. I think there's a lot of people who have that problem—forgetting who they are in the larger scheme of things," Bear said thoughtfully.

"Can you imagine anything more tragic?" Rose asked. "To be born a princess—native and to the manor born—and then to forget who you are and settle for being something horrible like an—an accountant!"

"Or a stock broker," Bear said.

"But, you know, there's something not so bad about a princess becoming a house-cleaner," Blanche said, feeling compelled to stand up for the underprivileged. "Or even a hairdresser, or a waitress." She had forgotten about her irritation with Bear.

"Yes, princesses are still princesses even if they're poor. You can't help being poor, especially if you're a displaced princess," Rose agreed. "Can you imagine a princess who works as a counter girl in a fast-food restaurant? I'm sure there's one somewhere. Imagine if all the people who come in to place orders were to realize that their meal was served by a princess! I don't think most people could handle it."

"I think it would be hard for a real princess to have to do menial work like that," Blanche reflected. "She might think it was beneath her."

"Oh, but a *real* princess would know that hard work ennobles the soul," Rose objected. "That would be one of the signs."

"I think that if a real princess was lost in this modern world, and she could be whatever she wanted, she would be a musician," Blanche said slowly. "A violinist, or a harpist. That would be the only place where she could find solace for her lost kingdom."

Rose turned to Bear, a terrible thought having struck her. "By the way, what do you do for a living? You're not an accountant, are you?"

Breaking into open laughter and subsequently choking on his cookie, Bear asked, "Why? Do I look like one?"

"I didn't want to hurt your feelings," Rose explained.

"Well, I just pump gas part time, so you don't have to worry about me," Bear chuckled.

"Oh, good. That makes sense," Rose nodded. "You seem like that type."

"I'm grungy enough," Bear agreed.

"No—I mean the type who knows about hard work ennobling the soul," Rose objected, finding herself accused of yet another injustice. "You could be a handsome prince in disguise."

Bear was seized by another fit of coughing and wiped his eyes. "So your theory, as I understand it, is that everyone in the world just might be something extraordinary, but very few of them know it?"

"Oh, a few know it. Or at least, they have an inkling. I think Mrs. Cohen knew it, somehow, because after all, she did buy the right kind of earrings for a gypsy, and the radio in her car was always on the folk music station." Rose took a generous sip of her hot chocolate and sighed.

"So, what does this have to do with Sister Geraldine?" Bear asked, draining his mug.

"I think that Rose suspects that Sister Geraldine is a queen of some sort—a dispossessed queen." Blanche raised an eyebrow at her sister.

"You're right. I think she was a queen who became a nun. Or better yet, a battle-maiden who forsook her shield and sword for holy vows," Rose said. "But she still fights battles."

"Yes, you can tell," Blanche reflected. "Everything *means* something to her. You just look into her eyes and know that she sees things as they really are, not as they seem. She sees the purpose and the implications of everything."

"Even improper grammar," said Bear, smiling. "No doubt."

"Well, of course," responded Blanche. "You can't find truth so easily in disorder. Grammar—and biology—and chemistry—and math, too—they keep things in order. We wouldn't know much without order. Good grammar *does* matter."

"It's as though what we call reality is a huge chess game," Rose said aloud, still sketching her marvelous vision on the conversation, "but today, most people don't realize what's going on. They don't know anything about chess. So they don't understand most things that take place. Only a few people know what's really happening any more. And even if you do know, it's hard to keep that inner vision."

"True. But when you catch a glimpse of the real meaning of life, it's easier to find others who also have that insight," Mother said.

"That's why you found us, Bear. You're one of those kinds of people. You *know*," Rose told him solemnly.

Bear said nothing for a moment, looking up at the ceiling. When he looked back down, he said teasingly, "And are you two girls princesses in disguise?"

Blanche and Rose exchanged glances. "I don't think so," Blanche mused. "I feel too ordinary."

"But maybe real princesses feel ordinary," Bear said.

"Oh, I don't think so. How could a princess feel ordinary? I think we're too rough and plain. We're probably just peasant maidens," Blanche said.

"Of course, either one of us could have a marvelous destiny in store for us," Rose added, twisting a strand of hair around her finger. "Just look at all the peasant girls in fairy tales!" She grinned at her sister mischievously.

Bear accepted Mother's offer of the last cookie and asked, "So what other extraordinary people have you found in the world, aside from nuns, real estate agents and grease monkeys?"

"What about Mr. Freet—the principal's brother?" Blanche asked Rose, turning her mug in her hands to the last of its warmth.

Rose made a face. "Him? Oh, he's such a grouch! I hear he hates women, except intellectual ones. I don't know why he's always hanging out at our school. But he does wear cool clothes for a man."

"That's what made me think," Blanche admitted. "Those silk waistcoats and walking sticks. He doesn't look funny in them. It's as though he's dropped out of another era into ours. He doesn't fit, if you know what I mean." Blanche glanced at Bear and caught a look of interest in his eyes.

"Yeesss," Rose meditated upon the empty cookie plate as she scooped up the crumbs with her finger. "That's exactly it. He doesn't fit. And yet, he does."

"What do you know about this guy?" Bear asked casually, scratching his head.

"Mr. Edward Freet? Dr. Robert Freet is our principal—Mr. Edward Freet is his brother. I think he owns an art gallery, and he comes by our school every once in a while to argue with the nuns and scowl at people. He's quite an enigma." Rose continued to scrape crumbs from the plate and eat them, unconcerned over her breach of etiquette.

"He says art is about form, not truth," Blanche said, adding as an explanation, "I overheard him say that to the office manager."

"Art's about truth," said Bear. "Even I know that."

"But it seemed to make sense when he said it," Blanche argued, feeling that Bear was right. "Art's almost always beautiful—"

"Because beauty is truth," Bear said.

"But not always," Blanche thought she had at last found a point to contest. "The devil was beautiful once—"

"That's because he reflected the beauty of God," Bear answered.

"But what about beautiful witches and siren songs?" Blanche dug in. "And the beautiful girls in bad advertising and things like that? Evil things often look beautiful."

"But that's because they've stolen the beauty from the good." Bear was looking uncomfortable. "Evil isn't beautiful on its own. You know?"

"Well, good people are sometimes ugly—" Blanche said at last.

"I don't know about that. Not really," Bear shook his head. "If the good's there, and you look for it, you'll see it in some way."

"I think Bear is right," Rose said decidedly. "Fairy tales teach you that. No one who's *really* good ever stays ugly. It's always a disguise."

"So do you think Mr. Freet is good or evil?" Blanche asked Rose, feeling besieged.

"Good," Rose said promptly. "I always assume that until I know otherwise."

"I don't like his eyes—" Blanche said. "They're too cold. He's got a very—very small soul, I think."

Rose giggled at the thought, but Bear looked thoughtful. "You might be right. I think I know the guy you mean, Blanche."

"But there's something *large* about him at the same time—as though he sees what Rose calls 'the big picture,' but doesn't quite agree with it. But I think he knows, somehow, about the inner meaning." Blanche felt she was talking too much and fell silent.

"We should get to know him," Rose said suddenly. "I think that might be fun."

"Rose! Now that would be dangerous," Blanche protested.

"Why? Why shouldn't we? He might just be lonely and need someone to cheer him up."

Bear looked as if he didn't like Rose's idea. "I agree with Blanche. I'd stay away from him."

"Oh, come on. You're both giving into fear and suspicion," Rose shook her head. "Mom, aren't we supposed to overcome evil with good?"

Mother sighed, "Yes, that's true, but I tend to agree with Bear and Blanche."

"Well, there, then!" Rose drank the last of her hot chocolate with finality. "Let's invite him over for supper!"

With a laugh, Mother shook her head. "You're far too impulsive. Just like your father."

Blanche wondered how Mother seemed so at ease with the loss of her husband. It was as though he was still present to her, somehow. Feeling as though she were the only one who still missed him, she got up and began to stack the mugs on the empty cookie plate.

"Hey! There's still some crumbs left!" Rose complained.

"I should be going," Bear got to his feet.

Rose was doubly grieved, but stood up as well. "I'm glad you came over, Bear. I really enjoyed talking with you."

"Thanks, I did, too." He looked around at all of them. Blanche met his eyes briefly and went to the kitchen with the mugs.

"You're welcome to come by again," Mother smiled at him. "Any time."

"And don't just vanish on us," Rose begged. "We're starved for company. Come by tomorrow if you like."

Bear chuckled at her. "Don't worry. I'll take you up on your offer."

"Oh, good! So, we'll see you again." Rose went to get his coat.

Blanche came back into the room and saw that he was looking at her, a bit uncertainly. *He knows that he makes me uncomfortable,* she realized, and felt guilty for her ungracious attitude earlier.

"Yes, please come again," she said.

To her surprise, he smiled back at her. "I will. Thank you." He took his coat from Rose and said good night. Blanche followed after her mother who had walked him to the door. As before, he bounded down the steps and vanished into the shadows of the City.

Once again, he seemed part of the wildness outside and Blanche couldn't help but be glad when her mother closed the door and locked it firmly.

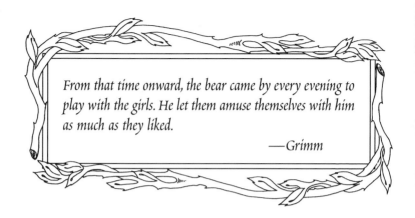

From that time onward, the bear came by every evening to play with the girls. He let them amuse themselves with him as much as they liked.

—Grimm

Chapter 4

DESPITE BLANCHE'S misgivings, she began to look forward to what became Bear's frequent evening visits to their home. She never saw him on the school grounds any more, and she began to wonder if he might have re-formed. There was certainly an aura of trustworthiness—or just plain *worthiness* about him. And he appeared to enjoy all stripes of their talk—both their deep discussions and their girlish silliness. At least, he tolerated the latter.

As for Rose, she had felt an implicit kinship with Bear from the first moment she saw him—or so she claimed. She didn't discount her sister's occasional doubts about his character, but she found them much less threatening than Blanche did.

"Well, beggars can't be choosers," she would say when Blanche cautioned her. "You've got to admit that Bear is about the closest thing to the only friend we have in this city."

Which didn't make Blanche feel much better, even though it was true.

One Friday night a few weeks later when Bear came by, he looked a bit more mysterious than usual. "Tell me something," he said, slightly embarrassed. "How do you girls feel about buying illegal tickets?"

"You mean from scalpers?" Rose asked. "I don't know. I guess it's pretty wrong."

"Well, maybe these aren't so illegal as that. The guy wasn't a scalper. It's just that his friends had canceled on him and he was trying to get rid of them."

"Tickets to what?" Blanche wondered.

Bear flushed again. "Standing-room-only tickets at the Met. They're doing *The Marriage of Figaro* tonight and I was wondering if you all wanted to go."

"Oh!" Rose had jumped to her feet, eyes shining. "Oh, Mom, may we?"

"My, my," Mother said with a smile. "That's a pretty upscale show, Bear."

"It was an odd thing. I just happened to be passing by the theater on the way to the subway, and this frustrated guy pointed to me and said, 'Hey, do *you* want these tickets? I'm ready to give them away!' So of course I asked them what they were for, and he told me. He would have just thrown them at me, but I gave him some money for them. There's three tickets, so you all can go."

"Why don't you just take the girls, Bear? They'd love the show, and I'm a bit too tired tonight. It'll be a rare treat for them," Mother said. "They've never been to the Met."

"Would you want to?" Bear asked the girls.

"Sure thing! Oh boy, should we wear gowns?" Rose danced around, all in a tizzy.

"Not for standing-room seats. Just wear what you have on," Mother advised.

"Oh, but that would be too ordinary! Can't I just go change, Bear?" Rose begged. "One doesn't go to the opera every day!"

"Yeah, but hurry! The show starts in a half hour, and it'll take us twenty minutes to get there on the train," Bear urged.

Rose raced up the stairs and Blanche followed her.

Blanche put on her favorite royal blue sweater and brushed her hair back into a loose pony tail while her sister wildly threw clothes out of the closet onto the bed. "Oh, if only I had a black dress!" Rose lamented. "That would be *so* appropriate! How does this look?" She whipped out a purple dress and hung it in front of herself. "Too fancy? Okay, how about this one?"

"Rose, there's no time for going through your whole closet," Blanche insisted. "Here, just wear your black sweater."

"Yes! With a pink turtleneck and my grey silk skirt and black hose! Perfect! I knew I kept you around for some reason." Rose started changing at a lightning pace, then stopped and moaned. "Oh! Rob Tirsch said he'd call me tonight!"

"Well, too bad. You'll have to call him tomorrow night."

"But I promised . . ."

"Mom'll tell him. Hurry up and get dressed!"

It was amazing that they managed to get downstairs and into their coats within the next five minutes. They hurried out the door with Bear, Rose issuing a stream of orders all the time to Mother about what to tell Rob. Blanche was thankful when they at last got outside into the cold and dark. Heavy white flakes were sifting down from the sky, and even though Christmas was long over, there was holiday in the air.

They had to run to keep up with Bear's long stride. "There should be a train leaving in about a minute. It'll be close—do you have tokens?" he said over his shoulder.

Blanche held up two tokens in her mittened hand. "Yes. Do you?"

"Yes! We're set, then. Be ready to run when we get down the subway. Follow me!"

He pounded down the steps, avoiding all the people coming up, and took off running for the train.

"Augh! He didn't tell us he would run so fast!" Rose wailed, dodging after him through the Friday night crowds in line for tokens. Bear whipped through the turnstile with such velocity that Blanche had to hold it still a moment before she could go through it.

They flew after him down to the lower level where the train to Manhattan had paused, its lights flashing and the "close doors" signal sounding. Bear got onto the packed train and held the doors open for them with his hands as it started to pull away. Blanche and Rose dove beneath his arms and were safely on the train as it began to move in earnest. They stood beside him, gasping for breath and laughing as the train plunged into the tunnel.

"Do you know, I always imagine that the subway trains are dragons," Rose said to Bear as they clung to his coat for support in the swaying car. "Tearing back and forth across the city in their underground caves, devouring people and spitting them out at random destinations."

"Well, it *is* rather dangerous to ride the subway these

days," Bear said. He winced as another train passed them in a deafening roar. "They certainly are as loud as dragons."

"Hey, weirdo," someone said to Rose, poking her in the back. She went pale, her eyes flashing green. But when she turned, she gasped and the color came back into her cheeks. "Rob!"

It was the man himself, his blue eyes and black brows snapping at her beneath a ski cap. "What are you doing out here tonight?" he grinned at her. He and his buddies were sitting in a row on the other side of the train, an army in sports jackets and hooded sweatshirts.

"Going to the opera. What are you doing?" Rose wanted to know, turning to face them. She had forgotten all about Bear and Blanche.

"The oh-per-ah!" Rob mimicked. "Getting some culture shock, are you?"

"I thought you were going to call me tonight," Rose said.

"Well, I can't. You're not home, are you?" he said teasingly.

"Yes, but—So where are you going?"

"Ah, over to Lisa's house for a party. Want to come?"

"No, I've got to go—"

"To the oh-per-ah! Yeah, that's right. You said that."

Bear watched Rose talking animatedly with Rob and bent down his head to Blanche. He said in a very low voice, "So this is the famous 'Rob'?" One couldn't talk to Rose these days without hearing some allusion to Rob.

"It is," Blanche affirmed dryly.

"Tell me something. Why does Rose like this guy?"

Blanche shrugged, a bit irritated. "It beats me."

"He's just nothing like the type of guy I'd expect your sister to like, with all her talk about princes and gypsies."

"Rob—is a nice guy. And he's very popular," Blanche hedged. Bear's remark was odd in one respect. Rob definitely fit the image of Prince Charming, with his good looks and style. *He looks more like a prince than Bear does,* she thought. But of course, she couldn't say that to Bear.

"Well, we'll catch you later," Rob was saying to Rose. The train was stopping. His buddies shouldered him out.

"Call me tomorrow night!" Rose called after him. "If you want!"

To Blanche, she turned and whispered, "Oh, can you believe it? What a coincidence! I'm so glad I saw him—I would have felt so bad if he had called and I wasn't there!"

"He wasn't going to call you anyhow. He was going to a party."

"Oh, he would have called from the party. That's what he said he was going to do. Oh, gosh, I can't believe I saw him. He's just *so* good-looking. Doesn't he look like the man who played *Ivanhoe?*"

"Hush," Blanche said sharply. Bear was taking them on an outing. It was rude not to include him in the conversation. Besides, she couldn't help but feel put out with her younger sister, who always seemed to be the center of attention.

Standing in the back of the dark opera house and gazing at the huge stage before them, gay with gold-scrolled scenery and sumptuously costumed singers, the air vivid with bright music, was one of the most enthralling experiences of Blanche's life. For a time, she forgot her doubts about reality in the sheer delight of illusion. But, as Rose reminded her during the intermission, perhaps it wasn't illusion. Perhaps it was a glimpse of what reality was really like.

It was a puzzle. Which was more true? Their own dark existence or the grace and brilliance of Susanna, Figaro, and the Countess? Most people would say that daily life is more real, Blanche supposed, and that the opera was merely a frivolous and expensive diversion. Then why was the loveliness of Mozart's creation filling a hungry gap within her that no "reality" could fill?

Many people left after the second act, so Bear suggested that they should snag some seats. Blanche didn't want to, in case the people came back, but Rose thought it was a good idea. So they found three good seats much closer to the stage and huddled there to enjoy the rest of the show. Despite Blanche's nervous glances at the ushers, no one ordered them back to their posts at the rear.

"We should always get standing-room-only seats!" Rose gushed when they came out into the frosty night air. "It was wonderful!"

Bear chuckled. "Well, I'll only accept those kind of tickets from now on, if you say so," he said.

They all laughed, and Blanche felt the metaphysical heaviness she had been sensing lift. She felt lighthearted suddenly.

"Come on, there's another subway down this way a bit." Bear led them off in a different direction. "It's a little safer this time of night."

This time, they were in no hurry. The snow continued to come down in heavy showers, and there were fewer people around. The streets in this part of New York were broad and the sidewalks were wide. Huge glass windows looked into all sorts of upscale shops. Rose and Blanche dawdled, looking in the windows of the shops they passed, and Bear let them take their time.

"Oh, just look at that dress!" Rose breathed, coming to a stop and gazing at one of the mannequins in a fashionable boutique. "Now that's what I would buy if I had the money!"

"Yes, but it would be almost sinful to buy it—it probably costs so much," Blanche agreed, looking longingly at the dress in question. It was a long white linen dress with a lace collar and covered buttons. The slim mannequin wore white ballet shoes and a modest straw hat with white ribbons trailing down the back.

"Couldn't you just die? Imagine wearing that—on a windswept field—surrounded by wild flowers—ah, rapture!" Rose whispered.

"Couldn't you make a dress like that?" Bear asked, looking critically at the motionless figure in white. "I thought you girls sewed a lot."

"Oh, probably," Rose agreed. "But it would be so elegant to buy one—just once, you know."

"The material is nicer than what you can get in the fabric stores, and those dresses really are well made," Blanche added.

"Although I suppose we could scour the garment district for fabric like that, if we really wanted to . . ." Rose trailed off. "But it wouldn't be the same, somehow." She sunk into thought as they continued walking, the girls giving a wistful farewell to the white dress.

"It's more the idea of the dress than the actual dress that attracts me," Blanche admitted to Bear as they walked on.

"That's it! I mean, how often do you have a chance to

wear a white dress like that?" Rose pointed out. They passed another clothes store where a tall mannequin modeled a fluted silk gown with a long train. "Oh! How exquisite! I intend to have one some day, just to wear around the house for fun." Rose gave another sigh.

Bear whimpered softly and put his hands to his face in pretended despair. "I had no idea you girls thought so much about clothes."

"You should be grateful that we think about anything else," Blanche said with a straight face.

As they reached the opening of the subway tunnel, Bear halted. "Say, would you girls like to see a special place of mine? It won't take long. It's on the way home."

Rose and Blanche exchanged glances. Bear quickly said, "You don't have to come. Not if you'd rather just go straight home. It's just—well, I can't really go there during the day, and—I sort of wanted to show you this place. It means a lot to me."

An adventure unlooked for was staring them in the face. Rose tugged on her sister's hand. This was a chance to find out more about Bear and his mysterious life. Blanche's brow was creased, and she stood stiffly, unsure what to do.

"You're sure it won't take long?" Rose asked Bear.

"It won't, I promise. I just thought—it might be interesting for you."

Blanche started to shake her head, and Bear looked so crestfallen that Rose's heart ached. *Oh, come on, Blanche,* she thought. *Don't play the grown-up now.*

"All right," Blanche said at last. "But please, let's get home soon."

"All right, then!" Bear gave them a grateful smile and turned eagerly into the subway tunnel.

"I'm not so sure about this," Blanche whispered to her sister as they followed him.

"Cut it out, will you? We'll be fine," Rose whispered back. "Besides, if we can't trust someone like Bear, who can we trust?"

Blanche didn't respond, but Rose could hear her praying a "Hail Mary" under her breath.

The subways were much less crowded at this stop. The three of them stood waiting in the train's subterranean cavern, hearing the far off screams of other rail cars in the distance. Blanche stared into the round black tunnel in front of her, wondering whether the train would emerge from this hole or the other one.

A black man in a tattered orange hat and ancient overcoat approached them, holding out his hand and muttering something about food. Bear gave him a dollar. Rose whispered, "God bless you," but the man didn't seem to hear. Blanche continued to look at the blackness uneasily, her thoughts troubling her.

Who could you trust, really? Anyone you knew might suddenly turn on you and become someone else. People had free will. Even the holiest saint, however unlikely, could decide to become a devil. The people who seemed most stable might suddenly fall away, swallowed into the earth when you looked away, and not be there when you turned back. Anyone could die. The world was spinning with dire possibilities, and nothing, no one could be relied on.

She heard the roar of the dragon behind her and looked

to see the flashing malevolent lights and hissing nostrils of their train. It hurtled past them even as she looked, and halted, snorting, waiting for them to enter its belly.

Rose stepped excitedly inside, her eyes dancing (color: bright green). Already her heart had fallen into a steady drum beat. Where were they going? What perils awaited them at their destination? Who knows? Who knows? The very uncertainty was exhilarating. She sat down in the closest empty seat and Bear and Blanche sat on either side of her.

Blanche sat stiffly, wrapped in her typical iceberg. Rose decided to ignore her. Bear was hunched over, his arms folded on his knees, studying the floor. Rose stared at their reflections in the window opposite and watched Bear carefully as the train began to move. His mood had changed from enthusiasm to reticence. Was he regretting having asked them to come with him? He looked so lonely to Rose she felt a sudden urge to give him a hug.

Blanche gazed woodenly at her image in the opposite window, watching her sister watch Bear. Where were they going? Where might they end up? The dragonish train could be taking them anywhere. Stations flashed by them, red lights flared in the windows suddenly and vanished, noises tumbled over each other and passed by from dark to dark. The lights in their compartment went out for a minute. Her own image in the reflecting window disappeared. Light slashed across Bear's face like a dagger, and he vanished.

The lights came on again. The world was weaker, yellow. The car rushed on as before, but the squalid interior seemed strange. Blanche could not feel or hear her own body. She, Rose, and Bear had diminished. Only their reflections in the window remained. In the dim light of the grimy car, their images seemed stilted, absurd. They were automatons, substitutes for real people, puppets dangling over a convulsion of dissonance and confusion. She felt dizzy for a moment.

The lights flickered off again. Were they gone for good? Would the train ever stop, or would it hurtle on forever, now that it had reduced its passengers to ghosts and shadows? Were they to be prisoners forever in its tumultuous innards? She could not breathe.

The noise changed. The dragon gave in to friction and slowed sullenly, tearing and snapping at the ground. Ordinary light—ordinary city noise poured into the car as the doors opened with a hiss and a bang. The crowd propelled them out of the car onto the pavement. A guitarist was plucking away on the far side of the track, emitting a melancholy air.

They had escaped—for now. Blanche shivered in the wispy breath of the dragon and wished she were safely at home in her bed, familiar reality enshrined around her. The heady joy of the opera had vanished, and she felt even more unprepared than usual for an adventure.

And the bear cried out, "Snow White, Rose Red, would you beat your wooer dead?"

—*Grimm*

Chapter 5

L EAVING THE UPROAR of the subway tunnel, Rose felt a little overwhelmed by the silence outside. The snow was still falling thick and fast, smothering the City in a layer of downy white. It was almost as though the weather had drawn a muffling hood over the City's head. An occasional taxi flashed past, making furrows in the white roads, but otherwise, this section of the town was deserted.

"Where are we?" Rose asked Bear, looking around.

"You'll recognize it in a moment, I think," he said. He had started to walk faster now, so the girls had to hurry to keep up. There was a change in him. He now seemed much taller, casting off his habitual slouch in his eagerness. He was in his own element, following some other purpose, something familiar to him but foreign to the girls. It was as though he was transformed into a denizen of fairyland, about to enter his own haunted realm.

Blanche reached out and clung to her sister's hand. Rose felt her thin mittened fingers clutching her own. She knew her sister was beginning to be frightened. But

Rose was too caught up in the mystery to be afraid. She strained to hear the enchanted song Bear was listening to. Her heart was pounding, but to the rhythm of a marching drum, not fear. There was a sense of purpose here, and although she did not understand it, she rejoiced to be a part of it.

As the three of them moved down the snowy streets, Rose became aware of the three pointed towers of a Gothic church challenging the skyscrapers looming beyond it. A black rose window spread its wings across its facade, a whorled eye staring, entranced, beyond the world. She realized that Bear was heading for the church. And all at once, she recognized it. It was St. Lawrence, the abandoned church beside St. Catherine's.

"We're right by our school!" she blurted in excitement.

"Yeah, I thought you'd figure it out. We just came from a different direction, that's all," Bear said.

Blanche cast glances towards the school fearfully. Rose knew she was remembering the times she had seen Bear hanging out in the schoolyard with the druggies.

"Are we going to the school building?" Rose asked.

"No. We're going to the church," Bear said.

"Really? But I thought it's been locked up." Rose gave a skip of anticipation.

"I happen to have a set of the old keys. I used to be an altar boy there." Bear said the last sentence offhandedly.

Rose laughed at him. "I can't imagine you as an altar boy."

Bear gave a ghostly smile. "Believe it."

They crossed the snowy street slowly, as though wading through a river of slow water, with the traffic light heedlessly changing colors above them. Bear leapt up the steps to the church in three bounds. The girls scrambled after him, breathing hard. He pulled out a key from beneath his coat, looked around once, then said, "Follow me," and pushed it into the lock. The door opened and he slid inside, cracking it for the two girls to follow.

Rose squeezed her sister's hand tightly and plunged into the pitch-black cavern. Blanche followed, and Bear shut the door with a click behind them.

The chilly smell of must and grime assailed Rose's nostrils. She heard Bear and Blanche breathing hard, but she could not see anything, although she felt they were standing close by.

"This is so neat!" Rose exclaimed, and at once felt hollow, shallow. This place was sacred.

Blanche wrapped her arms around herself tightly. This was a strange experience, and she didn't like it at all. She desperately hoped Bear wasn't planning on doing anything—well, sacrilegious. Everything was becoming so bizarre that she could imagine anything happening next. It wasn't very comfortable to be alone in a locked, abandoned church with a guy—even a guy like Bear. She shouldn't have allowed herself to be talked into this.

"My violin teacher told me what a beautiful church this is—or was," Rose said. "Blanche, they used to have school masses here, instead of the assembly hall, before it was abandoned. The floor is unstable."

"Oh, just wonderful," Blanche said in a restrained voice. Not only were they in an eerie, forsaken church, but there was the sheerly material danger of falling through the floor as well.

"It's only unstable in certain places," Bear hastened to

assure her. "Don't worry—I know where the weak spots are."

Rose chided herself for babbling and making her sister even more tense. Her eyes were adjusting to the dark, and she could make out that they were standing in a narrow vestibule. In front of them were doors with dark glass windows. Through them, faint light showed.

There was the sound of scuffling as Bear's shape turned to one side and hunched over a low table. "I keep some vigil candles over here with matches. Hold on, and I'll get a light."

Then there was a scratch, and a faint glow. Blanche temporarily lost perspective as the flame of the candle made the shadows briefly impenetrable once more. Her eyes adjusted again, and she saw Bear's face with its mane of hair floating above the wax taper. He had become a cave man, his face gaunt with dark eyes alert and cunning like some strange beast. The light grew, illuminating his shape, and casting light on their faces. Blanche was disconcerted to see that Rose looked different—her green eyes were odd, almost fey, as though she had been snared in a spell. Between the two of them, Blanche felt as though she were a mouse about to be pounced on and eaten.

Bear looked up at the ceiling, listening to something the girls could not hear. But this time, it was something material.

"Hear that? I think it's a rat. I'll go first. Don't worry, I'll scare them away." He put a hand on the door behind him, illuminating a panel of dark colored glass and dropping a pool of light onto a tiled floor. The door opened, and he led them into the church.

Something scuttled away in the gloom before them. "I've got to set some traps," he murmured, holding up the candle like a torch.

They found themselves in a large, spacious place full of indistinct forms. Bear led them down the main aisle, boards creaking beneath his boots. Rose could make out pillars and an occasional jeweled glimmer of a stained-glass window catching the glow of a streetlight outside. Their footsteps echoed weirdly in the emptiness that was full of something.

"Can you see anything?" Bear asked them in a whisper.

"Pews," Rose whispered back.

They reached the end of the aisle and stood before the sanctuary. Bear pointed with the light to the roof. "The roof leaks, and it's been rotting the floorboards in the sanctuary. That's where the floor problems are. I wish the parish would have fixed the leaks when they first started. The problem will only get worse as time goes on." He set the vigil light down on the marble altar rail with a deep sigh. "But the diocese seems determined to let this place run down. It's a crying shame. You can't see much of it now, but it was a magnificent church."

"You really seem to care about this place," Rose commented.

Bear looked at both of them, a fleeting look of mischief on his face. "Well, this is my ruined palace. I'm an enchanted prince, aren't I?"

"Oh yes!" Rose said. "I had forgotten."

He turned to the sanctuary. "There's a marble facade with statues of saints and angels in the wall behind the altar." He stepped inside the sanctuary carefully. "This is the part of the floor that's weak. Wait here."

He passed the barren altar and went out through a small door into what must be the sacristy, and returned with a brass candle-lighter. He leaned over and lit it from the small candle he had been carrying. Then he began to light the candles of various heights which stood in dusty branched candelabra on the altar. Slowly, the altar was illuminated with halos of gold, as though it were the stage for a play. It was a high altar, layered like a palace, with niches where men and women with wings and robes stood frozen in adoration. Lastly, Bear, a hulking stagehand, lit the candles on either side of the carved tabernacle which was fixed to the wall behind the altar. The gold box was closed, but the red glass holder where the sanctuary lamp would have stood was empty.

Bear stood there a moment, silent, gazing at the floor. He seemed to have forgotten about them altogether. As he stood in the flickering glow of the candles, his long matted hair hallowed in amber, he had changed yet again. Blanche couldn't tell how, but she sensed, dimly, a quiet, enormous sorrow overwhelming him. She couldn't see his face, and there was no change in his silhouette, but a feeling emanated from him—it emanated from the very walls of the church—of a deep and potent loss.

Her eyes traveled upward to the empty tabernacle, to the pallid faces of saints and angels, to the darkness of the weakened roof, and she felt that sorrow beginning to slip in at the edges of her consciousness. And beyond that sorrow was a blackness, a terror, mixed in with the larger terror of the void and chaos of the City. Something had happened here—something terrible. She felt a coldness grip at her rib cage and she clutched the altar rail in sudden fear. There was something trying to get at them—no, trying to get at Bear. It was almost as though he was not resisting, but was allowing it to overwhelm him.

Rose stood behind Blanche, erect and composed. The heat of the candles radiated against the frosty air of the nave, and the candle in front of them warmed her face. Again, her heart was beating the hard cadence of a march— questions falling and rising in her mind. Who was Bear? Why had Bear taken them here? What was his connection to this place? She sensed a bit of the abandonment and fear that Blanche experienced, but she wasn't troubled by it. The sense of danger made her lift up her head higher. There were battles coming. But life was meant to be a battle, wasn't it? There was nothing to fear.

They could have dropped into the stillness of eternity for an hour or more. None of them moved or spoke for several minutes. Only the candles continued their ceaseless dance on the forsaken church walls. Blanche felt her dread recede a bit as she watched the tiny lights burning away at the darkness.

At last, Bear roused himself and set the candle-lighter to one side. He turned to face the girls, and his features were enigmatic in the candle light.

"I'm glad you came," he said simply.

"It's—lovely," Rose said at last. "I've never seen such an altar."

"If we could come here in the daytime, you'd see much more of the church's character," Bear said. "But you can feel it, even in the dark. Can't you?"

"Yes, I can," Rose affirmed. Blanche, uncertain, said nothing.

He walked towards them in a roundabout fashion. "Careful of the floor. Come around behind the altar. You can see the statue of Christ best from behind it."

Rose hadn't even noticed the marble statue of the Savior towering above the tabernacle, and felt somewhat guilty. But when they reached the spot Bear indicated they should stand, her mind was arrested by something else, completely different—there were stains on the carpet behind the altar.

Even in the shadows, she could make them out—faint, irregular marks on the light plush of the carpet. Suddenly, Rob's story about bloodstains behind the altar flooded her mind, and she felt nauseous. But that was silly. Rob had been joking with her. She drove it from her mind ruthlessly, a profane distraction in this holy place. But the thought still teased her.

Gazing at the statue of Jesus, Blanche found the courage to look at Bear's face once again and was shaken by the hardness in his expression. It was as though he were struggling to contain a silent fury inside him. Suddenly he noticed her gaze and all at once, averted his eyes, as though he hadn't meant to drop his guard.

"You ready to go?" he asked, and his voice sounded tired.

Blanche nodded, but Rose seemed to be distracted by something and didn't answer. As Bear went back and forth, extinguishing the candles, Blanche watched the barren church slowly succumb once more to its habitual gloom.

Outside, they all stood on the steps of the church in the snow. The spell had dissipated, but the girls still felt the remnants of its strangeness.

"What time is it?" Bear said at last.

Rose held her watch up to the street light. "Two o'clock."

"Let's go," he said, setting off. "I hope your mother won't be worried about us. We really should have given her a quick call."

"Why did you take us there?" Rose asked as they set off for home.

"I don't know," he confessed, "It's just my secret place. You let me in your house. I thought I'd show you my place."

"Do you live there?" Rose wanted to know.

"Oh, no. But I go there, now and then," Bear said, kicking at a clump of snow with his foot. "What did you think?"

"It was—breathtaking," Rose admitted. She felt terribly drawn to asking him about the stains in front of the tabernacle.

"Uh—you know, since it is my secret place, you wouldn't tell any of your friends that I took you there, would you?" Bear suddenly seemed a bit flustered.

"Oh, we don't have any friends to tell," Rose assured him. "Just Mom."

"Oh, I don't care if your Mother knows. She's as solid as a brick."

They lapsed into an unnatural silence on the walk home which Rose found stifling and unbearable.

So, as they came to their block, she scooped up a mittenful of snow, packed it, and tossed it at Bear's face.

"Hey!" he yelped in shock, and even Blanche had to laugh at his expression.

"Oh, so that's what you want!" he exclaimed, and thrust two big gloves into the snow. He let loose two snow balls at Rose while Blanche ducked to get out of the way of Rose's return fire.

She laughed at them and suddenly felt brave enough to

slip a mittenful of slush down Bear's neck when his back
was turned.

"This is betrayal!" he roared, and took off after her. She
squeaked and ran, while Rose heroically pounded him from
behind.

He chased them both to their doorstep, and they stood
on their stoop and rained snow missiles down on him,
keeping him from gaining the porch quite effectively. He
raged and protested and pleaded while Rose kept a stream
of well-aimed snow balls coming at him and Blanche managed a few lucky pot shots of her own. At last he fell on
his knees and begged to be let back into the house.

"No mercy," Rose grinned, and whomped one square in
his chest.

With a grunt, he flopped over on his back, rolling his
eyes and sticking out his tongue in feigned death. Blanche
muffled a scream of laughter with her mittened hand, and
Rose had to harden herself to stand firm. At last, finding
them pitiless, he rolled over on his stomach, shielded his
head and moaned, "Snow White, Rose Red, will you beat
your lover dead?"

"Oh, have some mercy, Rose," Blanche protested.

"Well—I suppose in charity we should relent," sighed
Rose. "You there! Sir Bear! We have decided thou shalt
receive our pardon and our favor, if thou so desirest."

"A thousand blessings upon you," panted Bear, crawling
up the steps on his hands and knees.

"Only—" Rose stopped him, "if thou will kiss our royal
feet."

"Fair maiden, I will," he returned, and actually kissed
Rose's proffered dirty boot. Blanche dissolved in giggles as
he then pretended to bite it.

Rose whipped her boot away indignantly. "I protest, foul wretch, thou must take no revenge, and must prove thyself a noble, valiant lord before we allow thee to re-enter our graces."

"Oh, I vow I will be ever most noble and ever most meek," Bear beat his breast, "in thanksgiving for your many favors to such a peon as I. I promise you riches and many blessings if you will only allow me to serve you and will bestow upon me the joy of your company again."

"Well, since it is cold out here, we shall relent," said Rose. "It's too late tonight, most noble Sir Bear, but return tomorrow and we shall wine and dine thee upon hot chocolate and cookies."

"For such a promise, fair ones, I shall return. I'd best say farewell, my lovely ones, before the neighbors call the police!" And with a smile, Sir Bear leapt from the porch and bounded off into the night.

The girls so accepted their strange friend that they never locked the door until he had arrived.

—Grimm

Chapter 6

THE NIGHT-TIME sojourn to St. Lawrence had an interesting aftermath. It should have made the girls more curious than ever about who Bear was. It had the opposite effect. Perhaps they felt that he had earned their trust, and they decided to allow him to keep his secrets.

Nothing much of note happened the rest of the winter, except that the friendship between Bear and their family deepened. Bear continued his regular visits, and the girls continued to enjoy his company and talk.

"I had a weird dream last night," Rose said to Bear a few weeks after the St. Lawrence visit. February was turning into March's thaw, but spring refused to come quickly. She, Blanche and Bear were talking one Friday night after Mother had gone to bed. "Do you know how to interpret dreams?"

"Do I look like I should?" Bear was lying on the floor, poring over a book of medieval art that Blanche had taken down for him to look at. She was also on the floor, with her back propped up against the couch.

"Sort of. Those dreadlocks make you look like a sha-man." Rose, curled up on the couch, prodded him with a toe teasingly. "You know, I've never seen a white guy with dreadlocks. How did you get them?"

"With great difficulty." Bear yanked at one matted lock thoughtfully. "I had a Jamaican roommate in J.D. He thought I should try dreading my hair. I've just sort of kept it that way. It looks rather hideous, but a great disguise for a prince, don't you think?"

"Ah, yes indeed, Sir Bear. Well, anyhow, I thought you might be able to interpret dreams. But not because of your dreadlocks. Some people have that gift, like Daniel in the Bible. I don't think *he* had dreadlocks." Rose picked at her nails meditatively. "I always think my dreams mean some-thing."

"Maybe they do, and maybe they don't," Bear ventured.

"Well, see if you can interpret this one. It was actually kind of funny. I dreamed that those mean girls from school had kidnapped my sister. I didn't see them, but I knew it was them. And I was running downstairs and through the rooms trying to find my mom. You know how you can never seem to do what you want to do in a dream? Well, at last I found her, and she was in the kitchen ironing, and I said, 'Mom, they kidnapped Blanche. What can we do?' and Mom just shrugged and said in a slow, careless way, 'Well, those things happen.' 'But Mom,' I said, 'we've got to do something! Call the police! Don't you care about your own daughter?' And she said, 'If you're going to be so sassy, why don't you do something about it?' Now, my Mom isn't like that at all, which is why it was so weird. And then the doorbell rang, and I ran to open the door, and it was the girls from school—the ones who kidnapped

Blanche, and I said to them, 'Where's Blanche?' and they said, 'We have her.' 'What are you going to do with her?' I asked, and they said, 'We're going to stick her head in a box of Styrofoam balls.' 'Is that painful?' I asked, and they said, 'Yes, very painful.' And that's all I remember. Isn't that weird?"

Bear, who had been trying to keep a straight face, burst out laughing.

"A box of Styrofoam balls?" Blanche giggled.

"Yes," said Rose perplexed, "It seemed normal in the dream, and I guess I thought it was a sort of torture I'd heard about."

"Nothing that I've ever heard," Bear said at last.

"So do you think that had any meaning?" Rose pushed him with her foot to make him stop laughing.

"Yes," he said. "It means you're seriously demented."

"Bear!" she cried, kicking him fiercely. "Stop it!" But he now was rolling on the floor, guffawing helplessly. She jumped up and began beating him on the head with a sofa cushion. He grabbed at her ankles, growling playfully, and she shrieked and tried unsuccessfully to leap back onto the couch.

"Blanche, help!" she cried.

Blanche merely grinned. "That's what happens if you corner a bear."

"Oh, nice—sit there and watch while he eats me!" Rose whapped Bear on the head again until he finally released her with a pretend whimper.

Rose collapsed onto the couch and said, "Well, do you want to hear my recurring dream? I'll tell it so long as you don't hoot at it like you did at this one."

"Is this the one with the blood?" Blanche asked, pulling up her knees with a shiver.

"Yeah." Rose turned to Bear, who was now lying on his back beside Blanche, and explained, "I've been having it since I was oh, six years old. I don't know why. It's one of those riddles of my life."

"What happens in it?" asked Bear, trying to regain his composure.

"It's pretty simple, usually. Sometimes it's just this dream, and sometimes a dream I'm dreaming turns into this one. I keep wondering if I'm making it up." She tucked her feet more comfortably under her. "Sometimes in the beginning I'm scared, running away from something, like a tiger. Then, other times, I'm just at home in Warwick, eating supper with our family. And it's early evening. Then I say, 'Oh, I've got to pick the roses,'—or sometimes my mom asks me to go outside and pick the roses, and I go outside and start picking them, tearing them off with my hands, and because I'm in such a hurry and too stupid to go back inside and bring out a scissors to cut off the thorns, my hands are getting all torn up. So, I'm there picking the roses—I'm always in a hurry—I think I'm supposed to pick them in order to make a wreath for the table or something—that's it, because we're having company come over, and my mom asks me to pick roses for the table.

"Then I look at the road and it's all full of red water, like blood. And the sun is really weird, too. And I think, the sun's going down, and the water is just reflecting it. And the road, this is the weird thing, the road leads back to the country, and all of a sudden I'm wading in this red river and I'm singing. And then all of my family comes out and yells at me—'Come back here! Get out of the water!'—but I just wave and keep walking down the river. And it's like blood. That's the freaky part. But for me in the dream, it's normal and I'm happy as I'm walking away, and I know all of a sudden that I'm never going to see them again. But I don't care. It's a very weird feeling, but I like it."

She ended and looked at the two faces looking at her silently from the carpet. "You see why I asked you if you can interpret dreams?"

"I see," Bear said slowly. "Perhaps you're going to be a martyr."

"I've thought of that," Rose said. "That's what I think, but I don't know." She looked at him. "What about you, do you have any weird dreams?"

"Always," he said lightly. "Horrible ones. So bad, I go to great lengths to forget them. You're lucky you don't have to try to forget your dreams."

"Oh, I do, sometimes, but even my scary ones are like stories, and I sometimes lie awake, wondering what would have happened next if I hadn't woken up," mused Rose.

"What about you, Snow White?" Bear leaned back to look at Blanche, who colored at the name he'd started using for her recently.

"Why do you keep calling me that?" she asked, a bit annoyed.

"I'm just saying your name in English. Blanche is French for 'white.' Right?" He gazed at her, a faint smile on his face.

"Then why don't you just call me 'Whitey?'" she asked, resentfully. *Snow White was a stupid name.*

Bear snorted. "Oh, Snow White sounds much better. It fits your skin tone, too."

"Thanks," she muttered, fiddling with a hole in her sock. *If he only knew.* She rested her chin on her knees, letting her hair fall all around her, obscuring her face.

"That's a compliment," Bear tugged at a strand of her hair. "Just so you know."

"I said thanks," she said, tossing her hair out of his reach.

"Don't you think Blanche has beautiful skin? I think that it's so senseless that tanned skin is supposed to be attractive. If Blanche lived in the Victorian Age, she'd get the admiration she deserves," Rose said, staunchly defending her sister as always.

"And it would probably go to my head, too." Blanche blew a strand of hair away from her eyes.

"So tell us about your dreams," Bear said to her.

"Me?" she said. "I don't have dreams."

"Oh, come on. Everyone has dreams."

"I don't," Blanche insisted. "You can ask Rose. Or at least, I never remember mine. I either sleep too deeply to dream, or I don't dream at all."

"Well, everyone dreams. But you never remember yours?" Bear murmured. "That's very strange."

"I suppose," Blanche fixed her eyes on the colored titles on the bookshelf as she spoke, "that there are so many fears I have during the day that God feels sorry for me, and never gives me nightmares."

"What about just plain dreams?"

"Things seem very real for me," Blanche spread her hands helplessly. "Sometimes it seems to me that every word that we speak—even the words on advertisements—has meaning, that even the most stupid little detail is terribly, terribly important—like the universe is written on stone and nothing is ever left to chance. And then some days, nothing seems to mean anything, and I feel as though the whole cosmos is shaking and collapsing. Sometimes I think

I'm hallucinating. Maybe I do. But I never remember my dreams, if I ever have any. There's too much that goes on during the day."

There was a pause, and Blanche again blushed, this time feeling she had said too much.

Bear was silent. "There is one dream I could tell you about," he said at last.

"Tell us." Rose looked at him, curious.

Bear leaned back and frowned at the ceiling. "It still gives me the creeps," he said, although he looked more serious than scared. "When I was younger, my kid brother and I used to go roller blading in Central Park. That was back before it became really popular. We must have spent all our free hours at the Park, whizzing around the paths. We used to think we were real hotshots. Actually, one time, there was a gang of boys who decided to try and beat us up for our skates. But we just got on the path and started skating, and we outdistanced them in no time."

He grinned at the ceiling in memory. "Man, I remember the look on their faces. We were just flying. Anyhow, we thought we were big stuff after that. Boy, we didn't know anything." He sank into silence for a minute.

"Where'd you get the roller blades?" Rose asked, curious.

Bear shrugged. "My dad got them someplace. It was his going-away present to us. He gave them to us and then told us that he was divorcing my mom. We never saw him again."

"Do you know where he is?" Blanche asked, feeling a sudden gap in her chest.

Bear laughed sarcastically. "Actually, yes. Do I care where he is? Frankly, no." The bitterness in his voice stung them both into silence.

After a pause, he said, "Anyway, in the dream, my brother and I were roller blading and this gang was chasing us. But this time, we weren't skating fast enough. You know how it is in dreams? It was looking pretty bad for us. The gang caught us, and they were hitting us with iron pipes and sticks. Then, all of a sudden, they vanished, and there was this guy standing in front of us. A big guy, with a cross around his neck. He was the one who scared them away. He helped us to our feet and we went someplace with him. There was a lot of other stuff that happened next that I can't remember. Most of it probably didn't make sense. But we were with this guy, and I was starting to feel better. We were walking someplace, and all of a sudden, we fell into this pit. I couldn't move, and I started screaming because I thought I was paralyzed. And then everything went black."

He hesitated. "Now, you're going to think this is funny, but in the dream, it was really, really scary. I saw these little shapes moving around my body. They looked like little men. They were little black dwarves, and they were cutting pieces out of my clothes and hair and taking them away. I realized that they had already eaten the guy with the cross, and my brother, and they were going to start eating me next, little by little. And then I woke up."

"Ugh!" Rose and Blanche both shivered.

"I had it a long time ago, but I can't forget it. I always seem to start thinking about it when I'm in a small, dark place," Bear confessed. He rolled over onto his side and stared at a color plate of the Bayeaux tapestry.

"Did you know the guy with the cross?" Blanche asked, to distract herself.

"Yes, actually," Bear said. "He was a good friend of mine. Sort of my substitute father."

"What happened to him?" Rose wanted to know.

"He was killed in a robbery—the thief shot him," Bear said briefly. "I'd rather not talk about it."

"You know, you're always saying that . . ." Rose tried to make a joke, but her words trailed off into nothingness.

There was a silence, and Blanche felt the darkness of the March night crawling inside the house.

"Thanks for telling us about your dream, Bear," Rose said, after reflecting. Blanche was glad that her sister could find something to say.

"Yeah. Now you too will start seeing little cannibalistic men in the shadows every time you go into your room after dark," Bear said with a ghastly smile.

"No, I'm serious. I think it takes guts for a man to admit that he's scared of—of a dream."

"Pff! I'm scared of lots of things. Not just dreams, either." Bear stood up and stretched himself from head to feet. "I should go."

He scratched under his dreadlocks and stared thoughtfully at the door. "You know, I don't know how much longer I'll be able to keep visiting you so regularly. I'm just getting to be too busy, and I'll be having to work more in the evenings."

"Oh no!" both girls exclaimed in dismay.

"Oh, I'll be back again," Bear said hastily. "Don't worry about that. I just can't come as often."

"Well, come by whenever you can!" Rose urged. "You're practically our only friend!"

"We'd miss you a lot," Blanche said in a small voice, strangely disconsolate.

Bear laughed. "I will be back at least a few times this month," he promised. "Thank you." His eyes had returned to their usual teasing warmth. He picked up his coat from the stand and said good-bye, leaving the girls to gloomily imagine life without their odd friend.

"Dull, dreary, dark, and depressing," was Rose's verdict as they went upstairs to bed.

"Dead," was Blanche's sole comment. She wouldn't say any more.

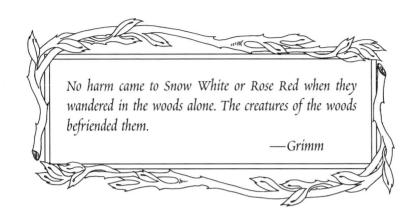

No harm came to Snow White or Rose Red when they wandered in the woods alone. The creatures of the woods befriended them.

—Grimm

Chapter 7

MONDAY NIGHT, Bear didn't come by, and Tuesday Rose was depressed at school. Even Rob's teasing couldn't get her out of her blue funk. He dogged her footsteps in the hallway when she passed his locker before lunch, singing her name to the tune of a popular song. She gave him a half-smile and ignored him.

He grabbed her by the shoulder and spun her around, startling her. She gazed in surprise at his blue eyes, which were very close to hers, and wondered in shock if he was going to kiss her right in the hallway, with everyone watching.

But instead he said, "How'd you like to go to the senior prom with me?"

So it was real. It was happening. It had happened. "Yyyess—" she stammered. "I think so—I'd have to ask my mom—"

He looked a bit miffed. "Still tied to the apron strings, huh?"

"No, not really," she said defensively. "But I would have to ask her."

"So ask her," he shrugged. "It'll be a blast."

"Thank you," she said, not sure how else to respond.

"No problem," he said lightly, moving away. "Just let me know."

Rose could hardly wait to see Blanche. She finally saw her sister right before her last period class. "Blanche," she bubbled over with excitement, "Rob asked me to go to the prom with him!"

Blanche stopped, and stared at her. "Rob?" she asked.

"Rob Tirsch, of course!" Rose bounced up and down. "I'll have to ask Mom, but I'm so excited! We'll have to go look for a dress and everything. Can you believe it? Rob Tirsch asked me!"

"That's great. That's just great," Blanche said mechanically. She looked suddenly upset, and turned away. "I'm going straight to the library after school, so you don't have to wait for me to walk home with you."

"I have violin lessons, so I'll be late anyhow," Rose argued.

"It's my term paper on Vincent van Gogh. I'll be there until dinner time," Blanche said stiffly, and gave a small smile. "See you later, then. I'm happy for you."

She hurried off, leaving Rose standing there in dismay.

Stupid, stupid, stupid! Rose chastised herself angrily as she walked home after her violin lesson. The day was foul and cloudy, and Rose's mood was equally foul. She felt a kinship with the weather, the wind that was complaining that spring was here before its store of chilliness was exhausted. There was no rain, and it wasn't cold enough for ice, but everything was wet from the morning's rain that refused to dry and refused to freeze, but remained in sour puddles on the pavement and grass.

I should have thought that Blanche might be jealous of my going to the prom. Why didn't I think before I burst out with my news like an idiot?

"But I was just so happy," she protested to herself, banging her violin case against her legs as self-punishment. "How could I know she'd be so upset?"

She badgered herself for not being more sensitive to the little signs that told her that her sister was unhappy—her reluctance to talk with Rose about Rob, the stiffness that crept into her face whenever Rob's name was mentioned. Rose had assumed it was just because Blanche didn't like Rob—he called her the "Immaculate Complexion" like all the other kids did. But all along, perhaps, it was because Blanche was feeling left out with Rose getting all the attention and favors.

"Oh, maybe I just won't go with him," Rose said aloud to nobody. That would pacify Blanche. But Rose felt like crying. Oh, she would miss the unknown thrills and terrors of going to a prom. Going on a real date somewhere with a nice guy. She moaned and shook her head. It was too much to give up.

These were the times she wished she could talk to her father again. He was just like her—quick-tempered, red-headed, easy-going, eternally optimistic. Her soul mate. Perhaps because she felt so much like him, she rarely missed him. It was only when she felt uncertain of herself—when she disliked herself—that she began to wish he was still around to let her know that things in the universe were really okay in the end. Dad always knew just how she felt.

Rose hadn't been there when he died, but Mom had told her all about it, how she had been sleeping in his hospital room when he went into sudden cardiac arrest. Even though he'd been in acute pain, he died with a smile on his face. Rose could imagine that last smile with almost mystical clarity. Things were all right with him. She knew that, almost the way she knew how to breathe and how to walk. Without thinking. Just knowing.

There was a large park near their neighborhood, and Rose went to find some solitude there before it got dark or began to rain. For a while, she wandered along the cold, black cement paths beneath barely-budding trees until she came to the pond. There, despondency came over her again, and she scowled at the water, her hair blowing out of her thick brown coat hood. *Why couldn't God make things equal, equally nasty or equally easy for everyone?* It really was unjust that she should be so lucky while her sister was neglected and persecuted. "By all rights, Rob never should have asked me to the prom," she grumbled. Oh, why were things perpetually simple for her? She didn't like it at all.

Feeling melodramatic and just plain rebellious, she put down her knapsack and took out her violin. Pushing back her hood, she tucked the hard plastic cup of the instrument beneath her chin and began to play. The low strings quivered through her jaw as she ran the horsehair bow up and down, stretching and groaning the strings with the wind. She was making up the tune, but it reminded her of something from Wagner. The violin's voice was dark, ominous, not as thundering as the bass or cello, but still black in its own way. Up and down the scales, warning the universe with palpitating anger, up and down. Eyes dilating, staring out at the rippling waters, squeezing down painfully hard on the strings, pressing down the bow as if to crack it, forcing note after deep note out—Rose worked out the pulsing fury within her, gradually releasing the tension and rising a few notes up on the scale. She climbed her way up, the song growing louder, more insistent, still jarringly minor—now it sounded like Debussy. Birds hurtling themselves across the sky, screaming—Why? Why? Why? Dizzying note upon note, faster, faster, faster, in an accelerating canon chasing its tail in hypnotic repetition, faster, faster, why, why, why—

Rose sustained the last quivering note, and sent the final one singing higher up the scale than she had yet chosen to go, a distant, bold note flying high as a bird to the clouds, for no reason at all. It hung there, doubting, descending, surging up again and down, finally swooping down to the low notes she had begun with, down dark, then rising a half step, hopeful, subdued, final.

She lifted her bow from the strings in the silence of the rushing wind, her ears racing from the sound. There was a slight cough beside her and a voice, "Bravo."

She turned, and saw a thin, young man with long scraggly hair propped up against one of the trees. He wore a thin jean jacket, a scarf, filthy jeans, a dirty shirt, and a flat grey cap. His light brown hair hung around a face which was anonymous behind its black glasses. A few crack vials were smashed into the ground around him. Rose instinctively drew back.

He spoke. "Do I look like a dangerous character?" His voice was amused.

"Yes." Rose didn't take her eyes off him.

"Well, you need have no fear of me. I'm too tired to mug anyone, even if I did that sort of thing. And I won't try to sell you anything. I haven't got anything anyone would be interested in buying, anyhow." He shifted himself and put his hands behind his head. "You play very well. Are you a professional or something?"

"No," Rose said, still guarded.

"Just sort of playing for therapy? Letting off steam?"

"Sort of," Rose admitted.

"Classical music does wondrous things for the human passions. Oh, I'm Fish, by the way."

"I'm Rose," she said before she thought, and then wondered if that had been a wise move. Probably not.

Fish, as he called himself, scratched underneath his flat cap. "So you're ticked off? Or is that too personal a question to ask a young girl like you?"

He couldn't be much older than Blanche, but he talked as though he were much older. It was curious. Rose said at last, "It's just a little thing. My sister's mad at me."

"Ah, sibling rivalry?"

"Not really. It's because I was invited to the senior prom and she wasn't."

He chuckled. "Oh, that old thing. I should have guessed. Well, your sister is feeling left out. Naturally, you want to be sensitive. But there's only so much you can do. You can't help how she feels."

"But she's my sister!" Rose argued. "I don't want to do things that make her feel bad!"

"Well, you can't help that, can you?"

"I don't think you understand." Rose tossed her head angrily. "My sister's feelings are more important to me than going to the prom. If I had to choose between her and this guy, I'd choose her. It's just—just hard, that's all."

"Well, maybe you won't have to choose," he said after a pause. "Maybe she'll get adjusted to the situation. Give her a little space, and time."

"That's true," Rose said, remaining silent for a minute. "But what if she doesn't?"

"Then you'll have to choose according to your convictions, won't you?" the youth said mildly. He gave her a crooked smile.

"You're very comforting," she said stiffly, opening her violin case and putting her instrument away.

"God isn't fair, is he?" Fish gave a melodramatic sigh.

"Of course He is!" said Rose indignantly. "He's a just God."

"In theory, yes," Fish nodded. "But in what seems like reality . . ." he cocked his head, "you'll find He deals out some odd judgments."

"Well, that's fine with me. I still believe in Him, and I'd follow Him till death!" she contested him hotly.

"Amen, sister!" he said, amused instead of chastised. "I didn't say I don't believe in Him. I just mean He doesn't often make sense to me." That strange contorted smile flitted over his face again. "You'd better get home now. This park isn't safe after dark."

"Thank you for your advice." Rose thrust her chin in the air and marched home, not looking back. She was almost sure she heard him laughing softly behind her.

When she got home, the house was dark, except for a light shining in the upstairs hall. It came from under the door of their bedroom. She went upstairs slowly and opened the door. Mother was sitting on the bed, stroking Blanche's head, which was buried in her lap.

Rose felt a pang inside her and quickly knelt down by the bed. "Blanche, I'm so sorry. I'm such an idiot," she whispered.

"It's not your fault," Blanche's voice came muffled. "I'm the one who's—being so silly."

Rose wanted to cry, but Mother put a gentle hand on her head and smoothed back her hair.

"It's hard sometimes to be happy for other people's happiness," Mother said softly. "It just takes time."

Blanche lifted her head and rubbed her red face with her hands. "It's just that I've always wanted to go to a dance, and now I'm a senior and I'll never get a chance to go to a prom," she muttered. "It's stupid."

"No, it's not!" Rose cried. "It's your prom! You deserve to go—not me!"

"So, what are you going to do—ask Rob to take me instead?" Blanche blew her nose on a tissue Mother proffered.

"I could ask him," Rose said staunchly.

Blanche chuckled. "He'd only laugh in your face. Spare yourself."

She got up on the bed and hugged Rose. "Rose, it's okay. I'll be fine. I'll even go look for dresses with you if you still want me to."

"But now I feel miserable!" Rose collapsed on the bed. "I don't want to go any more."

"Shut up!" Blanche said vehemently. "You've got to go. You can't be always bothering about me!"

But she looked so woeful that Rose burst out crying.

Mother laughed at her distraught daughter. "It's all right, Rose."

"I'll get over it," Blanche insisted.

"Oh, sure you will!" Rose sobbed.

"By the time I'm sixty, at least."

"There will be other dances—in college, definitely," Mother said soothingly.

"Yeah, dances I probably won't get asked to," Blanche cracked a smile.

"You never know," Mother said, putting her arms around her and squeezing her. "You never know."

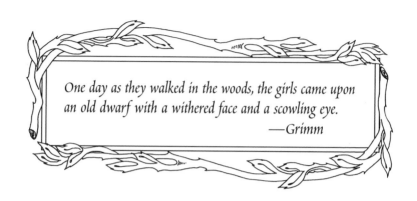

*One day as they walked in the woods, the girls came upon
an old dwarf with a withered face and a scowling eye.*
—Grimm

Chapter 8

"SO WHERE ARE WE going to find a prom dress?"
Blanche asked her sister a few Saturdays later as they
left the house. It was a bright day, and spring had decided
to make an appearance at last.

Rose paused on the steps to lovingly stroke the rosebushes in the window boxes, whose thorny stems were green
with tiny leaves.

"I looked up the addresses of a bunch of thrift stores in
the phone book," Rose said, hopping down the steps. "We'll
take the subway downtown and check them out."

"You may only find old wedding dresses," warned Blanche.
"That's all they had at the thrift stores back home."

"So I'll dye a wedding dress blue and wear it. Nobody
has to know," Rose countered. "I'm sure I can find something. It's a wonderful advantage to know how to sew."

Into a forest of possibilities. . . . Blanche fingered the
ten dollars in her pocket as they came up from the subway.
The morning sun brightened even the dingy city streets.
All the stores were open. There were black men from the

Caribbean with their wares laid out on colored carpets on the sidewalks: leather purses, woven handbags, sunglasses, belts. So many were on one street that Blanche felt as though she were in a Mid-Eastern bazaar.

But Rose steered her past all of them. "Thrift stores," she directed. "We dare not be distracted."

Blanche obediently followed her sister's lead.

The first thrift store they came to was a narrow shop squeezed between a drug store and an "accessories" store, with huge boards hung with rows and rows of barrettes, hair scrunchies, hats, necklaces, scarves, bandannas, earrings, and bracelets, in red, purple, royal blue, and gold jutting out from the narrow doors. It was such an eye-catcher that even Rose paused for a moment, fingering a pair of gold hoops on a card, and the little Chinese proprietor came out of the store, smiling at them. Rose quickly darted into the thrift store, and Blanche stood blushing for a moment, shook her head "No, thank you," at the man, and followed her.

Inside the store, a mannequin with a jazzy dress and bracelets on stump styrofoam arms hovered on a table overseeing a tumbled pile of shoes. That was the sole attempt at interior decorating. The rest of the store was crammed with clothes—African prints, polyester dresses, designer rejects, name brands, Woolworth's specials, formal dresses, satin bathrobes, denim skirts, sixties fashions, the widest hodgepodge of garments cramped into the smallest space imaginable. Rose chose a rack and began to paw through, grabbing whatever she thought looked interesting off of the racks and throwing it across her arm. Blanche was more cautious. She walked throughout the store, inching her way around other customers through the barely-visible aisles.

"Blanche, look!" Rose hurried over, sporting a black knitted swing coat. "Look!" It had long knitted strips attached to the sides of the neck, and Rose threw them around her neck like a model. It was a built-in scarf.

"Nice," was Blanche's comment.

Rose gazed at herself in the mirror, and wrapped her head in the black strips, like a movie star. "All I need is shades. Gosh, I feel so much like Audrey Hepburn that I could die. Isn't this an awesome coat?"

"How much is it?"

"Uh—" Rose fumbled for the tag. "Twenty dollars."

"You came for a prom dress."

"All right, all right, don't hassle me, I remember." Rose slowly unwrapped the luxurious coat and slid out of it. "Boy, I want this so badly. It only has one moth hole."

Blanche returned to the rack of blouses she had been going through. She needed a shirt to wear with the new plum skirt she had made. A simple white or ivory one would do. Here was a nice-looking oxford shirt—size 3. No. A nylon blouse in her size had a stupid bow on the neck. Never. A striped polyester number, a nurse's uniform shirt, a cotton peasant blouse with embroidered flowers round the neck—the last one halted her, but the flowers were orange and bright blue, two colors she detested. No.

"Blanche, look!"

She sighed and turned. Rose was grinning out of a long blue fur coat with unbelievable light blue fur fringe. "Isn't this cool?"

"Rose, you look like Cookie Monster."

"I've never seen a coat like it before!"

"That's because they keep it in a store like this, out of sight of the public."

"It's wild! Can you see me wearing this to school?"

"Rose, take it off. It's an abomination."

"I wonder how much it is?"

"Rose! Your dress!"

"*Fifty-five?* Is this a thrift store?"

"They know how to keep dangerous garments off the streets. Take it off."

Rose went back to her search, heaving the sigh of the censored. Blanche came to the end of the blouses and started on sweaters. There was one white sweater with glittery thread woven through it. No. A cashmere pullover with a hole on the sleeve. A light blue cardigan, also too small.

"Isn't this a neat vest?"

Rose was holding out a suede purple vest stitched with black.

"Yes, very Edwardian." She wished Rose would focus on prom dresses.

Now, here was a challis off-white blouse that looked interesting. Blanche examined it for stains in the sleeves and back. No holes, no flaws. And, it was a brand name. The price decided her—five dollars. At last, something to try on.

"Blanche!"

"What now?"

"Look!" Rose exclaimed, exhilarated. She flourished a hanger with a blue-green sequined and satin dress dangling from it.

Blanche came over and examined it. The bodice was covered with blue-green sequins, and the long, full skirt had petals of dark green chiffon overlaying the underskirt of teal satin. "It's beautiful," she said, running a finger down the long gleaming folds of the skirt. "Try it on."

Rose folded it lovingly atop the huge pile of clothes over her arm. "Come with me." She looked at Blanche's one blouse. "Is that all you have?"

"Yes."

"Here, let me grab some things for you to try on." Rose grabbed a red satin dress from the rack and added a paisley print jumper from another to her pile. "It's no fun unless you try something on that you know you won't buy."

The dressing room was one long closet, like a gym locker, where you sort of had to undress in front of whoever else happened to be in the room. The room was empty at the moment except for a white-haired old Hispanic lady over sixty trying on a smock, who beamed a smile at them as they came in.

"Oh, forget it," Blanche said upon seeing it. "Suppose a guy comes in?"

"Come on, we've got to risk it," Rose argued. "Besides, I like this dress."

"With our luck, a man will come in while we're in here," muttered Blanche, standing in a corner with her back to the door. She nervously buttoned up the blouse, then turned to face the mirror. Yes, it fit.

"What do you think?" Rose was engaged in the complicated exercise of undressing while keeping her coat draped over most of her. "Hm—nice blouse. Hey, try that with that paisley jumper. Here, can you zipper me?"

Rose turned around for Blanche to fumble with the tiny nylon snake of a zipper. "There. Ooo, spectacular, huh?" The teal dress fit Rose's slim figure well, although the satin skirt was a bit long. "Oh, this is terrific. I think I have a dress."

Blanche stood beside her sister in blue-green and noted

that the dress matched her sister's eyes. A small knot of jealousy twisted inside her. "It looks beautiful, Rose," she said again. "You look like a jade princess."

Rose was happy and swayed about the room, pretending to dance a waltz. "Where's the tag?"

Blanche found it dangling from the armpit and gasped, "Hey, this is only eight dollars!"

"Cowabunga! This is it!" her sister laughed, exhilarated, and spun around, rippling the skirt. "And to think that Jennifer Draper is spending over a hundred dollars on her gown!"

"You need to find shoes."

"Next job. Okay, unzip me. I want to see how these jeans I found go with that vest. Why don't you try on the jumper?"

"Rose, it's a maternity jumper."

"So what? You'll need one some day, won't you? It'll match your blouse."

"Let me try on that vest first."

"Okay. Try on that red dress I brought in for you."

"No thanks." Blanche was buttoning up the purple vest over the blouse. She had hoped it would fit, but the vest's arm-holes were narrower than the sleeves of the blouse, and bunched it up in a funny way. She sighed.

"Why don't you try on that red dress?"

"I'd rather not try on a formal dress today," Blanche said coldly.

Rose was nonplussed. "Okay, I will, then."

Blanche slipped out of the vest and was unbuttoning the blouse when she noticed the black velvet jumper someone had left hanging on a hook in the dressing room. It looked interesting, so she slipped it off the hanger and wiggled into it. It was velveteen and a little tight, but she pulled down the blouse beneath it and it fit. She gazed at herself in the mirror. A perfect match.

"Hey, you look like someone out of a fairy tale—that's neat," Rose said.

Someone out of a fairy tale—yes, the jumper with its tight bodice and narrow straps and full skirt looked like something that a fairy tale maiden would wear. It made her look like a little Tyrolean shepherd girl, like one of those foreign dolls. She liked it, but where in the world could she wear it? A dress like this would never fit in with the modern fashion scene. Not unless she were to wear it without a blouse (the neckline was so low she shuddered at the thought). She'd be scared to wear it to church, for fear of standing out. She could wear it at home, and pretend to be a shepherd girl, or peasant maid, if she wanted to.

But that was silly. Why should she want to do that? *Because,* something stubborn inside said.

She remembered that once, when she was a little girl, she had seen a pretty young woman with golden hair down to her knees in a long flowered dress, and had said to her, without thinking, "Are you a princess?" The girl had laughed very kindly at her and asked her what her name was. Blanche remembered going away from her, led by her mother's hand, thinking to herself that the girl really was a princess, but in disguise. And she had re-solved that someday, she would dress as though she were a princess in disguise.

Huh, she thought to herself, gazing at her uninteresting figure in the mirror, her pale face even whiter above the black jumper, *fat chance of me ever looking like that girl.*

A lament of horror came from Rose, and Blanche jumped. "What's wrong?"

"Blanche, look!" groaned Rose.

Blanche looked and saw her sister standing in front of the mirror in a red satin dress with purple sequins wrapping the bodice and encrusting the swirling petals of the short skirt.

"What's wrong?"

"I like it!" Rose buried her hands in her face. "What should I do?"

For crying out loud, Blanche thought. "How much is it?"

"Eight dollars!"

"Well, decide which dress you like better!"

"Which one do you like better?"

"The jade one. The skirt is longer and more modest."

"But this one is a fun one, Blanche. And the skirt reaches the knee. That's Mom's rule."

"*Just* reaches the knee. Well, then get this one if you like it."

"But the other one *is* more modest!"

Blanche stood beside her and attempted to be helpful. "Look, some of the sequins are detached here," she pointed out.

"That's easy to fix. The other one has the same problem."

Silence. Rose spun around, and the skirt flared out. It had a black crinoline sewn beneath it, so it didn't matter. "I like it," Rose emitted another sorrowful sigh.

"Why don't you wait and see what kind of shoes you can find?"

"I'm getting black patent leather heels. That'll go with either one."

Silence.

"Maybe I'll just buy both," Rose said finally.

"Both?"

"Well, then you can wear one in case someone asks you to go. Or we can save them for the next dance."

The next dance. That was Rose for you. "Yes, but I don't like both of them. I only like the jade one."

"Well, then I'll buy the jade one for you and just in case I decide not to wear the red one."

"Rose, that's a lot of money."

"Hey, these prices are phenomenal. Two dresses for sixteen bucks—is that exorbitant? When have you seen such a deal?"

Blanche threw up her hands. "Okay, it's your money." She started to unzip the black jumper.

"Are you going to get that?"

"Nah." Blanche wiggled out of it, and strung it back on the hanger.

"Why not? It was cute."

"I'd never wear it any place."

"Wear it when you sit around at home and play piano."

Blanche was struggling back into her sweater. "I think I'll look around some more."

"Hey, do you want to try on these jeans? I can't buy them, but I think they'd fit both of us."

They were light blue. "Okay." Blanche began undressing again. Rose was trying on the paisley maternity jumper, which was like a tent on her. "I could live with someone in this dress and no one would know," she remarked.

"Well, that was a good day's shop," Rose said gleefully as they left the store. She hugged her two bags to her chest, dreamily imagining herself in a long, rainbow colored dress combining the best characteristics of both gowns she had bought. The city streets, bright with the color and noise of hundreds of various shoppers and sellers, complemented her mood. She felt like singing.

Blanche walked quietly beside her. She had bought the white blouse and (at Rose's urging) a pink and blue kerchief on display at the counter for fifty cents. Rose wondered if her sister was still feeling jealous, and decided to exercise her energies in cheering her up.

"Why don't we go to that flea market we saw on the last block?" she asked.

"Okay," Blanche said, a bit interested. When the girls had lived in the country, one of their favorite places to browse were flea markets.

They soon found the market on a blocked-off street and immersed themselves in the crowds going back and forth in packed masses among rows of wooden tables where antiques, jewelry, old books and records, and paintings were being examined, haggled over, and sold.

"Hold onto your purse," Blanche murmured in Rose's ear, and Rose slid hers beneath her sweater to keep it safe from pickpockets. She held onto her sister's hand, and they wove among the dealers and buyers with eager excitement.

They spent a good deal of time admiring glass-topped boxes full of silver rings and necklaces, and then Rose saw a table full of old books. "Let's go over there," she suggested. So they shouldered and excused their way through the crowd until they were able to squeeze into the bookseller's stall.

The owner, a long haired blond lady in dark glasses and

an Indian sari, sat on a camp stool reading Nietzsche. She mumbled something about negotiable prices at them when they started to look, but otherwise paid no attention to them. "I wonder if she has any Chesterton?" Rose mused to Blanche.

"These look like Hindu books," Blanche said. "I doubt there's anything we'd like."

Just then, Rose recognized the other person in the book stall with them, a short thin figure in a hat and raincoat, several packages and an open book in his hands. "Mr. Freet!"

The figure started, dropped several packages, swore, and stooped to the ground.

"Oh, I'm sorry!" Rose gasped as she and Blanche rushed to help him pick them up.

"Damnation!" Mr. Freet swore, looking down at the street where there was a drain covering, "I've lost my keys down this grate!"

"Oh, and it's all my fault!" Rose cried penitently.

"Don't just stand there—you've got small hands—use them to get my keys instead of using your tongue!" Mr. Freet snapped.

Rose got on all fours and tried to fish for the keys, which were lying about six inches below the grate. She tried, to no avail.

"Blanche, see if you can get it. Your hands are thinner than mine," Rose suggested after a minute.

So Blanche tried, with no luck. But before Mr. Freet could spout out more expletives, she took out a crochet hook from her purse. "This might work," she said.

She managed to snag the keys with the very tip of it. Carefully she eased them through the bars of the grating, and handed them to Mr. Freet. "We're awfully sorry we startled you," she said.

He didn't thank her for the keys. "Older people startle easily. You should know that," he grumbled, looking about for the book he had dropped.

"What were you reading?" Rose asked, inquisitive as always.

"Some piece of Eastern mumbo-jumbo," Mr. Freet said, picking it up. "It's everywhere, these days. New Age gibberish." He sniffed disparagingly. "About the only thing I find remotely intriguing are the pre-Christian Gnostics. But you can't find them in a place like this."

"I like G. K. Chesterton," Rose volunteered, thinking that the air was ripe for a good conversation.

"Chesterton? Highly overrated," Mr. Freet snorted. "A good stylist, but too air-headed. Spouting simplistic platitudes. Read Shaw. At least he had his head on straight." He made as if to leave, but suddenly stopped, as though something had caught his eye on the other side of the street. He leaned forward, a look of avid interest on his face.

Rose looked around, trying to figure out what he was looking at. But she saw something that made her forget about Mr. Freet. She clutched her sister's arm. "Look! Isn't that Bear?"

On the other side of the street, facing them and talking to an antique dealer, was a tall, burly figure in a black trench coat whose dark dreadlocks were covered by a leather motorcycle hat. He wore shades and had a tough-guy expression on his face, but Rose recognized him at once.

Freet pushed out of the booth past them and disappeared into the crowd.

"Look, what's he doing?" Blanche exclaimed in a low voice.

Bear, talking to the antique dealer, had taken out something he had hidden in his trench coat. Gold glimmered in the early spring air, glancing out at them from across the crowd. Rose recognized the shape. It was a chalice, the kind priests used during the Mass.

Apparently Bear was trying to sell the chalice, because when the dealer said something and shook his head, a grimace flashed over Bear's face and he thrust the chalice back under his coat and turned away.

"Let's go talk to him!" Rose said eagerly. Her sister's face was frozen.

"Rose, suppose he stole that from that church he took us to?"

"Oh, come on, Blanche!" Rose pulled her sister into the crowd and started making for the booth.

She caught a glimpse of Bear striding away, fast. He hadn't seen them. She tried to run, but the people of the market pushed around her and blocked her way. After a few minutes, she realized that it was probably impossible, but she kept doggedly in the same direction.

Blanche, holding all three shopping bags, panted to her sister, "Rose! Stop!"

"I'm just trying to get to that open place ahead. Maybe we can see him!" Rose called back.

Blanche said something Rose couldn't hear. But in a moment, she had arrived at the open spot, a corner of the block at one end of the market. She looked around and saw what she had hoped not to see—Bear disappearing down a side street the next block over.

"Hurry up!" she shouted, plunging back into the crowd.

"Rose! You're going to get us killed!" Blanche cried to no avail.

The crowds were thinning out, and Rose was able to run, still hanging on to Blanche and dragging her along. In a moment, they had reached the side street and Rose dived down it. It was mostly deserted, but none of the few people visible were Bear.

In the middle of the block, Blanche said, "It's no use. We've lost him." She sounded relieved.

Rose begged, "Let's just try a few more streets."

There was no sign of Bear anywhere amid the rows of crumbling tenement buildings.

"Let's get out of here," Blanche finally mumbled, looking around.

"Okay," Rose agreed reluctantly, and they tried to trace their way back to the market street. But they seemed to have lost it.

"Where are we?" Blanche asked.

Rose studied the two street signs on the corners closest to them. "Uh, actually, I have no idea."

"Great, just great," Blanche heaved a sigh. "Let's ask for directions to the nearest subway."

"Okay," and Rose crossed the street with Blanche in tow. She approached a cigarette-smoking woman in a tight skirt who was standing there.

"Excuse me, can you tell me how to get to the subway?" she asked politely as the woman looked at them curiously. Rose had never seen someone wearing so much makeup.

"Sure honey. Just go around that corner and take a right. You'll see it up on the left." The woman motioned with her cigarette and turned to smile at the man walking past them.

"Thank you!" Rose called as she and Blanche walked

away quickly. They found the subway and got onto the train that would take them home.

"Rose, do you know what that woman was?" Blanche asked in a low voice as the train began to rumble beneath them.

"No—should I?"

"She was a streetwalker! Didn't you see her looking at the men?"

"Oh," said Rose in surprise. "No, I guess I didn't pick that up."

She was silent as the car roared on towards their neighborhood stop. "Well, she did give good directions," she remarked.

"All the same, next time let's ask a policeman."

Snow White was the meeker of the two, and would remain at home, engaged in quiet pursuits.

—*Grimm*

Chapter 9

ROSE STARED at herself in the mirror in fascination. Perhaps she had turned into a fairy. She certainly didn't look like the redheaded girl who usually stared out of that shining surface. Now, the reflection gazing back at her was a sprite with hair piled atop her head—thanks to her mother's artifices—her enigmatic eyes darker and more mysterious, highlighted with a dash of shadow and tasteful mascara, and her slim form encased in red satin and purple sequins. Whenever she moved, something glistened. A splendid and many-colored creature. No, she did not look at all like ordinary Rose Mary Brier.

"How do I look?" she asked Blanche, when she dared to speak at all—lest the vision vanish.

Blanche stood beside her, frowning. "I wish you'd worn the other dress. The skirt on this one is too short."

"I sort of like it that way," Rose murmured. "It's daring, isn't it?"

Blanche didn't answer.

"I can't believe that it's really prom night—at last," Rose

123

said. She felt that she was making Blanche feel bad, but she simply had to say something.

"I'm sure you'll have a good time," Blanche said, toying with the jewelry box on the bureau.

Their mother came over. "Let me spray your hair one more time, Rose."

Rose shut her eyes gently, because of the mascara, and basked in the pungent rain of scented alcohol. The smell was invigorating. It meant she was going out.

"Did you use to do your hair like this when you were a teenager?" she asked her mother after she'd opened her eyes and examined her gleaming hairstyle one last time.

Mom laughed. "Yes, something like it. But my older sisters and aunts were a little more wild in their hairstyles—teased and fretted beehives! I'd watch them do up their hair that way, and they taught me. This hairstyle is pretty conservative by comparison."

"I like it," Rose breathed a deep sigh. She liked to think of her mother as a teenager, being laughing and stylish and giddy. These days, their mother tended to be pretty sober most of the time—she'd been that way ever since Dad died. Rose smoothed back the tiniest hair that had escaped the twist and sprayed it. For some reason, wearing her hair like her mother gave her a sense of continuity with the past. She liked that.

Once again she ran a light finger over the twisted knots and loops of hair pinned firmly on her head, just to luxuriate. She hoped it would stay up during the dancing. "Thanks, Mom." She caught her mother's eyes in the mirror and smiled.

"You look lovely, Rose." Mother bent down and kissed her. "I wish they wouldn't have called me into work tonight.

It makes me nervous not being here when you're out. I almost think I should have volunteered to chaperone."

"But Mom, I'm only going to a banquet hall, and then back to school for the after-prom. There's nothing really to worry about," Rose protested.

"I'd feel better if I knew this boy. You'll be out so late—" Mother ran a hand down her braid and frowned. "Suppose something should happen—"

"What could happen? I know your number at the hospital. I'll call if anything is wrong." Rose was becoming slightly irritated. Mom's agitation made her jumpy.

"Well, come straight home from the after-prom. By one o'clock. And call me at the hospital when you come in."

"But, Mom, suppose Rob wants to leave early to go to a party at his parents' house? He said something about that."

Mother hesitated. "If his parents are there, that's fine. But I still want you home by one. Is his number in the book?"

"I wrote it on the refrigerator for you. I'll be all right, Mom, don't worry," Rose begged.

"Well, I'm a mother—I'm paid to worry," her mom sighed. "Please call me or Blanche if there's any sort of trouble."

"Yes, Mom." The doorbell rang, and Rose leapt downstairs like a scarlet rabbit to answer it.

"Hi, Rob!" she exclaimed delightedly.

"Hi." Rob was holding an umbrella, since a shower had started. He was wearing a white tux with a black bow tie, like a casino dealer. His hair was shiny with gel, flopping over his face, and he looked uncomfortable. And handsome.

"Are you ready?" he asked.

"Sure am," Rose said cheerfully. "Come in?"

"Uh—the others are waiting in the car . . ."

"Okay." She changed her mind about having him meet Mom. "Hold on, I'll be right out." She ducked back inside to get her coat. But her mother opened the door wide, exposing Rob to the light.

"Well, hello there, Rob," her mother said.

"Hi, Mrs. Brier."

"Come in, won't you?" she invited.

"Okay," he said, a bit unwillingly. He set the umbrella down in the entrance way and stepped inside the house. Blanche saw his eyes rove around the living room uncertainly. She wanted to hide, but instead she stood there, acting nonchalant in her jeans and flannel shirt, holding Rose's best coat.

"Mom, this is Rob. Blanche, you already know Rob." Rose reintroduced everyone, and felt awkward.

"Rob, I've told Rose that she needs to be home by one. You can go to the after-prom party at the school from midnight till one, but then I'd like her back here. All right?"

"Sure, Mrs. Brier. No problem." Rob seemed a bit taken aback. Rose could sense he wanted to go, so she didn't linger.

"Good-bye Mom, good-bye Blanche," she said, pulling on her coat. Her hands were shaking. She was leaving home, to go out on a date. Her first real date.

"I wish I had a camera," Mom said regretfully. "Have a good time!"

"I'll call you when I get home," Rose said quickly, kissing her mother good-bye lightly, not wanting to smear her lipstick.

Rob bounced on his foot, twirling the umbrella. Rose could hear the engine running. She quickly grabbed her purse and carefully ran down the stairs as fast as she dared in her high heels.

"Have a good time!" Blanche called out as her younger sister got into Rob's father's Oldsmobile and they pulled away. The car sped smoothly down the shining black street, freckled by the light patter of rain. She watched at the door until it was gone.

"Well, there she goes," Mother said, a little hopelessly.

Blanche leaned on the door jamb and wondered idly what it was like for a mother to watch her daughter go off on her own into the world for the first time. She wished she could offer her mother more support. But after all, she was only two years older than Rose, and she didn't feel very grown-up at all. Not tonight.

Mother turned back into the room, but Blanche remained behind for a second, watching the cars go by at the end of their street. At last she closed the door silently and went inside.

An hour later, Blanche sat alone at the kitchen table, listening to the rain chatter on the roof. Mom had left for her emergency shift. Rose was off on her fairy tale adventure with Rob. There was nothing left for her to do, except sit and listen.

I have been reduced to the status of an ear, she thought. Which reminded her that there was her report on Vincent van Gogh to work on. "But if I do, I might end up feeling suicidal myself," she murmured. Crossing into the living room, she threw herself down on the couch to stare at the ceiling.

"It's not as though I really wanted to go with anyone

from school anyhow," she muttered to herself, and sighed. With a listless hand, she picked up her library book. She was trying to read, and avoid thoughts that would make her sorry for herself, when the doorbell rang, startling her. She flew off the couch and bounded to the door in half-fright. Once she had opened their apartment door she peered out the peephole of the house door to see who was outside. It was Bear.

He had never come to the house when she was alone. She cautiously opened the door.

"Hiya, Snow White," he grinned at her. "Can I come in?"

"Sure," she said hesitantly, "I guess."

She let him brush by her and sit down on the couch, shouldering off his wet coat. As she re-bolted and locked both doors, she realized that she had lost her solitude in his coming. The thought made her a bit resentful, although three minutes ago she would have been glad for company.

"Where's Rose?" he asked, leaning back on the couch.

Why was her tongue sticky? "She's at the prom."

"Prom? What prom?"

"The senior prom. Don't you remember?"

"Oh, yeah, that's right." Bear squinted at her. "I thought she was a junior."

"She went with a senior."

"Ah. Who?"

"Rob Tirsch."

"Oh, yeah. The smart-talking guy on the subway."

Blanche smiled. "That's the one. He's really kind of nice."

"When will she be back?"

"There's dinner and dancing, and then an after-prom

party from midnight till eight in the morning at the school. But Mom said she had to be back by one."

"So where's your mom?"

"She's working till three o'clock this morning. This should have been her night off, but they needed her unexpectedly."

He whistled. "That's lousy."

"One of the other nurses is sick."

"Thank God I'm not a nurse. I don't know how your mom does it." He leaned his head back to touch the wall and stared at the underside of a picture frame. She leaned on the back of the rocking chair, biting her nails and staring at the floor.

"What are you doing home?" she heard him say.

"Doing my term paper."

"You're a senior, aren't you? Why aren't you at the prom?"

Did he have to sound so *patronizing?* Blanche thought. Wasn't it obvious why she wasn't there? But she merely shrugged, as though to say she didn't care.

Bear must have seen her eyelashes fluttering, though. "You don't feel bad about not going, do you?"

Did he expect her to deny it? She was silent, studying the edge of the chair cushion.

He heaved himself forward and leaned on the cushion of the rocking chair, looking up at her, thrusting his face into her vision and smiling. "Hello? What's going on in there?"

She just stared at him. Finally she said very softly, "Why don't you just shut up?" She turned and walked upstairs to her room. Now he would leave.

She had buried her face in a pillow when she heard him knock on the bedroom door. She froze, pretending that she was ages away from here, light-years away, on a leaf on a frozen pond in a far-off field on an asteroid floating through outer space, hearing nothing, seeing nothing but white ice and white sky, feeling nothing.

Stillness.

She heard his heaviness creak on the board before her door and then nothing. It was impossible to tell if he had gone down the hall or down the steps to the living room or out the door. She didn't move, just allowed the pillow to fill in the crevices of her face and keep the tears inside. Her insides were totally still. Perhaps her heart wasn't even beating.

Softly the murmur of the piano crept through her pillow, into her consciousness. A distant melody, as though someone were caressing the keys. Was someone outside playing the "Moonlight Sonata" on the radio?

A jarring lower note roused her. That was no professional pianist. Was it . . . could it be her piano?

All at once she sat up, listening. The progression, the last rising scale—She slid to her feet and stole across the room, straining to decipher the notes which were trickling away as she moved—

She opened the door. Silence, except for an echo. By the time she reached the living room, the last note had vanished, but the walls rung with an invisible motion. Bear was lying on the sofa, watching her.

"Blanche, why don't I take you to the prom?"

It was impossible to dissuade him from the idea. "It's your prom, you should go," he kept saying. At first she said, no thank you, then, "I don't have tickets."

"We'll just go to that after-prom party you said they were having at the school. That starts at midnight, right?"

"I don't have a dress."

"Oh, come on," he said. "I know you girls have stuff."

She didn't have any shoes. "So what? Wear sneakers. We'll go casual."

What was he going to wear? "Leave it to me, I'll find something."

"But there's not enough time—"

"It's almost ten. We have until midnight. That will give us both enough time to get ready."

Only once she said, "But I don't mind not going." He just looked at her and said flatly, "Liar." She didn't try that one again.

Slowly he worked on her: she would go and get ready and he would be back in an hour and a half to take her. It was no use trying to discourage him. "Okay, Cinderella, I'm going to get something to wear—you get into your glass slippers and I'll be back by 11:30."

He was out the door into the rain before she could say no again. She stared at the still-vibrating door.

The closet door slid open, and the light found the dress. The sea-green one Rose couldn't help buying. The satin showed through in places where the sequins had unraveled, but it was still pretty. Blanche, dripping from the shower, studied it on the hanger, and a pit grew quaking in her stomach. She wasn't going to admit it to Bear, but she had never been to a formal dance in her life. Once she'd been to a fancy wedding in eighth grade, and had worn her mother's mauve silk dress, but that was four years ago. That was kid stuff, anyhow. Prom night was the night everyone dressed in the latest styles and drove in limousines. She was sure that a home make-over and a thrift-store dress would never cut it.

It is quarter to eleven now. I should just tell Bear I can't go. Sorry. I'll make you look stupid. Sorry. I just don't want to. But he was being so nice . . .

Her stomach turned over. The girls in class would look at her with their black-lined eyes and smile sardonically, thinking: *There's Blanche, trying to fit in.* No way! She rebelled. Why should she go and make herself a target to those leering looks, those rolling eyes?

But then there was Bear, coming back soon, ready to take her—he wanted to take her. He didn't know she was so terrified of Lisa and Eileen. All he knew was that he didn't want her sitting home and crying on her prom night. Maybe he just wanted to do something for her in return for her family taking him in—like a clumsy uncle who forgets how old you are and buys you a Barbie doll on your sixteenth birthday. You have to remember it's the thought that counts and tolerate the gift.

Well, if it would make him feel better. . . . With shaking hands she reached for the dress dangling from the wire hanger.

When it comes down to it, all you really need to do to get ready for a dance is put on the dress, if the dress is fancy enough. She found it easy enough to repair the raveled sequins with tiny safety pins—Rose had done the same thing. Then, after she struggled for five minutes desperately to zip the dress shut, almost dislocating her shoulders to grab the tiny zipper—God forbid Bear should come before she was in it!—and finally mastered the last quarter of an inch of the zipper—there really wasn't time to fret over any other details anyway. Hair—she blow-dried it, brushed it down, and decided she couldn't really do anything else with it, unless she were to curl it and spray it for three hours. That was the good thing about having boring hair—it could look simple and dramatic. Her golden locket necklace and her Sunday watch would be sufficient jewelry, and she didn't dare to experiment with any makeup—she might smear something and end up having to rub her face red trying to get it off. Nope, just blush (a necessity) and lipstick. Nervously she applied the lip color and re-applied it, and thought that it looked too dark. Finally she wiped almost all of it off and decided she'd go plain-faced.

Shoes she agonized over. Her black flats looked too drab and her brown flats looked dumb. Finally, she took out her Chinese slippers and put them on. They had blue and pink flowers with green leaves embroidered on the toes, exactly the color of the dress. Blanche thought she looked silly in it, but it was a lovely gown.

She jumped when the doorbell rang and nervously went to answer it. It was Bear, wet from the rain, but in a tuxedo.

"Where in the world did you find a tuxedo at this hour?" she asked, flabbergasted.

He grinned at her over the white shirt front. "A buddy of mine has an uncle who used to own a tuxedo shop. His uncle gave him this suit. I thought it might fit me."

"It looks great," Blanche said sincerely. Unfortunately, his dreadlocks still looked dreadful. He'd tied them back, but they looked like a fuzzy mane.

"Does my hair look gross still?" he asked, catching her glance.

It did, but she could never say that.

"Can you grease them back?" she asked hesitantly. "Rose has gel."

"Nah. There's not much you can do with dreadlocks," he said, obviously not too concerned, and clearly happy with his prowess in attaining a suit. "Hey, you look great."

She blushed. "Thank you."

She swept the floor with the flowered tip of a shoe, not knowing what to say. Bear had tried his best, but he still looked hairy and wild. She had hoped somehow that evening clothes might transform him, but no. This would certainly be a Beauty and the Beast night. *As if I'm Beauty,* she scolded herself as she went to get her coat. Well, they would still be themselves—her in Chinese shoes and him with the dreadlocks.

Suddenly, in a sweet breath of excitement, she didn't care a bowl of sugar. It would be an adventure, going out with Bear. Who cares who sees us or what happens? Resolutely she put on her Sunday coat, but suddenly teetered on the verge of a decision. Mother's Irish cloak was in the back of the closet. It was grey tweed, but it would cover her dress perfectly and would be good in the rain. Besides, her Sunday coat was tight in the sleeves. She shrugged it off and threw the cape around her shoulders. The hood almost blinded her, but she didn't care. Feeling more comfortable, she ran to get her purse (and the blush) and went to meet Bear, who was waiting by the door.

"Shouldn't you call your mom?" he asked her.

"Oh—yes." Hurriedly she went to the phone and dialed the number for the hospital. Her mother came to the phone quickly.

"Mom, it's Blanche. There's nothing wrong. It's just that Bear came over and he wants to take me to the prom." She talked rapidly, thinking how bizarre this was.

"Bear? Oh, that's wonderful, Blanche. Certainly. That's very kind of him."

"Yes."

"What time will you be back?" Mother asked.

Notice: "What time will you be back?" Not: "Be back by this hour." Mother trusted her more than she trusted Rose. Maybe there was a difference between eighteen and sixteen after all. "I'll ask him," Blanche told Mom.

"What time will we be back?" she asked Bear.

"Any time you want to leave the dance," he replied solemnly.

That might be pretty soon, she thought. "He said any time I want to go," she told Mother.

"Well, I'll trust him to get you in at a decent hour. Tell him Rose is supposed to be home by one. Good news: they might let me go home early, so maybe I'll be home when you and Rose get back."

"Good!" Blanche exclaimed. "Well, I'll see you then."

She hung up the phone with a light heart and turned to Bear, smiling. He grinned back. She wondered for a moment if she should leave a note for Rose. *But I'll probably see her there*, she thought in a rush of excitement. With Rob. And all the other popular crowd. Suddenly her insides trembled again. Maybe it might not be so nice, if Lisa and Eileen saw her with Bear and decided to make fun of him, too . . .

Don't think about it, she told herself fiercely as she went back to the living room to leave.

Outside, the rain shook out of the sky like pepper and the city danced excitedly. Bear dragged her along, swinging her over the puddles that were too big to jump over. "We'll take the bus," he said. "It's too far to walk at night."

"I have money," she said, fingering her purse.

"Keep it. My treat," he grinned at her.

They came to the main street, and half ran to the bus stop. The cape flew out behind her, and she couldn't help laughing as she tried to keep her dress and shoes from getting wet. It was the silliest thing in the world—taking a city bus to crash her own after-prom party in the company of Mr. Grunge. But she was doing it, and that gave her a terrified courage.

"You're drinking in the joy of life," Bear told her when she tried to explain why she was laughing. "There's so much opportunity for drinking deeply of it, and we very rarely do it. When you do, it makes you feel alive all over."

"I do feel alive," she told him.

"You look alive," he said to her, looking at her flushed cheeks and smiling. "You didn't even need to wear blush."

"My skin's too white," she said.

"Says who, Snow White?" he asked, touching her cheek lightly with one hand.

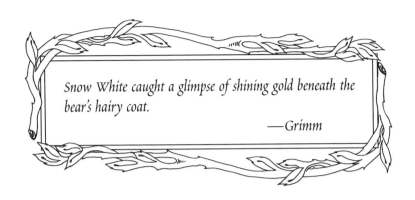

Snow White caught a glimpse of shining gold beneath the bear's hairy coat.

—Grimm

Chapter 10

THEY GOT OFF at their stop, and the bus rushed on its way with a roar through the rainy night. Bear continued talking as they walked down the glittering sidewalk. "Every once in a while you just have to decide to go out and do something very crazy and very right—just to dare yourself to live. I don't mean doing something stupid and destructive—just something fun and good and beautiful. Otherwise, you'll be a drone like everyone else, following the crowd instead of joining the Great Dance of Life. We're in the Dance right now. Consciously. Can't you feel it?"

"Yes," she said in a small voice.

He paused in the dim spot between two street lights and looked at her. "You look almost elven in that grey hood," he told her.

Something quickened in Blanche—she *felt* elven. She drew closer to Bear with a sudden, child-like trust.

They were approaching the school grounds. The after-prom, the party sponsored by the parents to keep kids from going out drinking, had just started, and the parking lot was full of rented limousines dropping off kids in tuxedos and gowns. Some of them stood outside around the entrance smoking beneath umbrellas, making an odd picture in their satin gowns and bow ties. Blanche was glad that Bear was next to her as they walked through the crowd.

Inside was a roar of noise and a thundering beat of music. The chaperone by the door eyed Bear warily and asked for their prom tickets. Bear argued with him that they'd missed the prom, and the chaperone let them in after seeing Blanche's student identification card, which she'd remembered to bring with her.

"I'm glad they let us in," Bear shouted in her ear, as he helped her take off her cloak and handed it to the teacher manning the coat room. Without the protection of the heavy tweed, Blanche felt naked and vulnerable in her flimsy sequin dress, discreet as it was. She couldn't meet the eyes of the kids who stood chattering in the hallway. Bear took her by the hand and led her into the darkened gym where the dancing had started.

The strobe lights in the gym made the walls pulse and gyrate with color in the semi-darkness. White cross-hatched trellises dotted with tissue flowers lined the gymnasium, with a huge artificial fountain at one end. Tables with floral covers dotted the sides of the hall. Couples leaned against the walls or sat at tables, talking. The dance floor was crowded with pulsing dancers, and more people were coming in all the time. The beat was so loud it shook the floor beneath their feet.

Blanche had been wishing that it wasn't so dark so that she could find Rose, and now she was wishing that she hadn't come at all. She noticed that the other kids passing them turned away and steered clear of Bear.

Did they know something she didn't know? Her tentative trust in him was shaken, and her feelings of uncertainty came sweeping back.

Bear himself seemed to have lost his confidence, and stood hesitantly, looking at the churning mass of people. Blanche didn't see anyone she recognized.

"Do you want to sit down?" he yelled in her ear.

She nodded and he led her over to an abandoned table. He sat down and put one arm across the back of her chair. It was an odd sensation to have him so close to her, but reassuring.

It was too loud to even consider talking. The crowd of people thrashed about to the music, jumping and shaking. Almost nobody was smiling. They all had either tight-lipped looks of grim concentration on their faces or fake smiles—everyone was playing a role, even those who seemed so scornfully unconcerned about what others thought of them.

Bear was surveying the scene critically. She wondered what he thought of it. Somehow, it didn't seem like his idea of fun.

"Are you happy?" she thought she heard him ask.

"What?"

With a crash and a rumble the stereo cranked into a slow swoon song with a pulsing beat. The rioting subsided and couples began to melt into each other's arms. Everyone seemed to be with a partner, although some dissolved from the group and gathered like sediment on the walls of the gym. The head cheerleader and a dark-haired husky young man were heavily involved with each other, but even they were aware of who was watching.

"Would you like to dance?" Bear shouted above the

bellowing singer, and Blanche nodded and rose, nervously throwing back her hair. She was glad she'd worn it down as it seemed to give her some protection. The song was one she didn't recognize. It was something too old or too new, and either way she felt uncomfortable. Bear put his one arm on her waist and held the other out in a surprisingly gracious manner. At first, she thought he was being funny.

"What, is this a waltz?" she asked.

He didn't say anything, but abruptly put his arms in a half-hug around her waist that was more in conformity with the rest of the crowd. Keeping a comfortable distance from him, she put her arms around his neck, and they began to dance. Somehow, this was more uncomfortable, because she had to look in his eyes or at his throat, and she couldn't do either. So she looked to the side, watching everyone else dance. He did the same.

The girls from class were there, wrapped in embraces with their dates. Eileen Raskin was wearing an unbelievably short black dress with ropes of pearls dangling down the low-cut back. She had her hair up and looked very chic. Blanche didn't recognize the guy, and supposed he was a college boyfriend.

Lisa was in red velvet mini-dress with ruffles. Somehow she'd managed to look even more made-up than usual, and Blanche thought she looked like a snake. Her date, Lester Johnston, appeared more brutal than normal, if that was possible. Bear and Blanche brushed by them and Lisa gave Blanche a narrow, questioning look as though she didn't recognize her.

There was no sign of Rose or of Rob. It was as though

they were in a crowd of strangers. No one talked to them. The girls who usually sat near Blanche either avoided her or were nowhere to be seen. The guys, on the other hand, kept throwing glances at Bear, and she saw gestures and muffled laughter. She looked at Bear, who was stolid, not looking at them.

"What's their problem?" she asked.

"Just ignore them," he said.

After two songs, Blanche still hadn't seen Rose and concluded that she must have gone with Rob to a party at his house after all. She managed to say hi to one or two girls from English class, and finally felt comfortable enough to face the crowd in the bathroom and replenish her blush.

She didn't recognize anyone right away, and slipped into one of the stalls. As she did, she overheard some conversation that made her heart jump.

"Did you see that guy who walked in with Blanche Brier?" she heard a shrill voice say as the door banged open. Lani Ferguson.

"Yeah. He's probably some distant relative she dug up to take her to the prom," Lisa said pithily, and someone snorted.

"Tom said he knows the guy. He's a dealer who hangs out around here sometimes."

"I wonder if Blanche knows what she's gotten herself into—probably so desperate for a date she didn't care." Lani clicked a lighter and Blanche smelled cigarette smoke.

"Is this guy the same one who cheated Tom out of fifty dollars last week?" Eileen was interested.

"No, that was some other guy they both know. But Tom swore he's mad enough to call the cops on this guy."

Blanche was frozen, but Eileen laughed. "Tom? Tom's

close enough to getting kicked out of school before graduation as it is. He'll talk like that, but he's too scared to do
anything that would ruin his chance of an athletic scholar-
ship. Did Shannon tell you what happened to them last
night?"

It seemed as though the girls remained there, talking
and smoking, forever. By the clouds of smoke rising to the
ceiling, Blanche knew they were planning on hanging out
there for a while. Dear God, what if something happened
to Bear while she was still in here, a trapped eavesdropper?
Should she just walk out? That would make her look like
a fool, for certain. But suppose that boy did call the cops
on Bear. . . . Her throat went dry. Suppose they were making the phone call now?

She had to decide. *I know Bear is not into drugs,* she told
herself fiercely. *I know it.* Hands on the latch, she prayed
an entire "Hail Mary," then opened the door and walked
quickly to the sink.

Eileen and Lisa looked over, and watched her, silently.
She could see their reflections looking at her in the mirror.
Her own reflection was bright red. Hardly breathing, she
fiddled for a paper towel, hearing them savor the silence. In
her imagination, she could see their black-rimmed eyes
boring into her so potently that they left marks on her
skin.

Finally, Lisa spoke, "Hey, Blanche—" but suddenly the
door banged open and a girl outside hissed, "Teacher!" sig-
naling the three girls to duck into the stalls and flush their
cigarettes down the toilet. They pushed past Blanche out of
the restroom, Lisa breathing, "Watch your step, Immaculate," as her red lips passed Blanche's ear. A moment later
a suspicious chaperone peered into the restroom and sniffed.

Blanche wasn't smoking, but all the same, she received a searching look before the chaperone closed the door.

Blanche was fighting tears and anger as she burst out of the restroom and made her way back through the crowds to find Bear.

She found him drifting along on the outer fringes of the crowd by the gym doors, but before she could say anything to him, he steered her back inside. He took her out onto the dance floor, elbowing through the commotion to the far side of the gym, away from the chaperones. She wondered if something had happened, but he said nothing as they began to dance.

The song was a silly one from the sixties, and Blanche felt that her awkward attempts to dance to it weren't very successful. But what else could she do? She couldn't dance in front of Bear the way the girls around her were dancing with their dates. It was a wretched situation, and she decided that she wanted to go home.

"Bear," she said at last, but she hadn't spoken loudly enough and he didn't hear her. Just then, the song ended, and a completely different beat began. It was an oldie—a song she faintly recognized.

> *Say, it's only a paper moon,*
> *Sailing over a cardboard sea,*
> *But it wouldn't be make believe,*
> *If you believed in me.*

There were groans and a general exodus of kids from the dance floor. It wasn't the heavy-handed beat they were used to—it had a swing beat. Obviously one of the chaperones had requested it.

Yes, it's only a canvas sky,
Hanging over a muslin tree,
But it wouldn't be make believe,
If you believed in me.

It sounded like a decent song, but Blanche had no idea how to dance to it. Some of the athletic types were still on the floor, bopping around, and a few of the chaperones were cutting loose on the sidelines. But most of the crowd had stopped dancing, and were talking loudly, hoping that the DJ would change it.

She saw Bear staring at the dance floor, an angry look on his face. Suddenly, he grabbed her hands. "Come on," he said, "follow me," and pulled her out into the middle of the gym.

He faced her, putting one hand on her waist and with the other held her hand while he stood still, feeling for the beat. The next minute, he pulled her towards him and began swing dancing, carrying her with him.

It felt so natural even though she had no idea what to do. Amazed, she yielded to him and let him do what he wanted. "I'm going to spin you," he said in her ear, and the next second he pushed her away from him and let go of her hand and she spun around, her satin skirt rippling marvelously around her legs. Next instant, he had pulled her in, whirled her out in the other direction, and spun her again. It was so exhilarating she almost laughed.

Without your love,
It's a honkey-tonk parade,
Without your love,
It's a melody played in a penny arcade.

The crowd on the sidelines gaped at the long-haired rat in the tux dancing the jitterbug with all the flair of a veteran. And the thin girl in his arm became an iris of swirling color with every motion of his arms, as if he were working some kind of spell.

> *It's a Barnum and Bailey world,*
> *Just as phony as it can be,*
> *But it wouldn't be make believe*
> *If you believed in me.*

When the song was done, Blanche landed exhausted in his arms and he dipped her dramatically, and drawing her up, kissed her on the forehead.

"You were great," he told her. "For five minutes, you were the envy of every girl in the gym. You could see it in their faces."

Blanche was in a daze as they walked back to their seats, but still exhilarated. He had kissed her. On the forehead, well, sure, but it was a kiss. Her first. And she had never danced like that before. She felt a lightness inside, as though all of her dark angry thoughts had spun away with that miraculous dance.

"That was the first time I actually liked dancing," she burst out to him.

He grinned at her, "That's because that was *real* dancing."

She stared at him in awe and with a new respect. His long hair seemed poetic instead of pathetic now. First the Sonata, and now this dancing—"There's something strange about you—" she started to say.

"Oh, well, thanks!" he chuckled, his brown eyes twinkling at her.

"No, I mean—" her thoughts trailed away as Dr. Freet, the principal, loomed into their vision. He looked like his artistic brother, but taller and balder. Right now, his face was hard.

"Young man, I'd like to speak with you."

Bear argued that hey, man, I'm not causing any trouble, but the principal was adamant. "Get out of here, before I call the police. Get off the school grounds altogether. We don't want any trouble here."

"Listen, I was just taking my friend here to her prom. Is that a crime? What, are you going to embarrass her by kicking her out of her own prom just because you don't like the way I look?" Bear said angrily.

"It's not because of how you look, it's because of who you are," the principal said coldly. "She can stay, if she wants."

"No, thank you, I'll go," Blanche said quietly, and gripped Bear's arm to tell him that she was serious. She just wanted to get out.

The principal escorted them to the coat room and Bear apparently decided to unnerve the man by helping Blanche on with her coat and opening the door for her with the smoothest gentility as they left the building. They walked out of the school silently.

Bear steered them through the shadows of the now de-serted parking lot. The rain had paused, and the sidewalk shimmered with beads of oily rain.

"Blanche, I'm sorry this happened," he said quietly, still sounding angry.

But she clung to his arm. "Bear, I had such a wonderful time," she said, sighing.

He seemed surprised. "Really?" he asked.

"Really!" She met his eyes, and saw them kindle with renewed warmth.

"Great!" he said exultantly, and lifted her up over a puddle. She laughed, and he accidentally missed and set her down in the middle of it with a splash. She gasped at her wet shoes and then burst out laughing, hugging him.

"Forget it, just forget it!" she gasped.

He held her too, looking into her eyes, and she suddenly began to feel very shy. But all at once Bear stiffened and whirled Blanche behind his back. She peered around him and saw three boys.

They were standing there, watching them. One of them Blanche recognized as Tom.

"What do you want?" Bear said after a pause, in a voice Blanche had never heard him use before, slow and dangerous. He still held her hand tightly.

"That's what we're wondering about you, junkie," the biggest boy said, with a grin on his face. "We were wondering if you happened to bring back the fifty dollars you ripped off from my buddy here last week."

"You're mistaking me for someone else," Bear said evenly.

"Yeah, sure. We paid one of your boys for four hits and when we got it, there were only two. What's up with that?"

"I don't mess with Shaky's stuff." Bear continued to stare at him levelly. "You take it up with him. It's not me."

"How can we believe that?"

"I don't think you picked the right time to talk to me." Bear had a warning edge to his voice.

"Oh, I think we picked the right time. Seems you'd be in a more generous mood now—anxious not to get into any trouble."

"I can get into trouble anywhere I want," Bear responded, growling. "I haven't got a reputation to whitewash."

Tom laughed, "Well, if it was your friend who gypped us, maybe you'd be willing to make up the difference."

"I haven't got any money. Even if I did, I wouldn't give it to you," Bear snarled. His voice terrified Blanche, but she stood still.

"Any money would be okay—" the boy's eyes landed on Blanche's purse, "Even your girl's cash would be just fine."

Bear snorted. "You're very funny, moron. Tell you what, you push off right now and I'll agree to forget you said that."

But the boy nodded to the others and all three of them rushed him. Blanche screamed, leaping out of the way as one of the boys staggered and reached for her. Bear shouted at her to run. She darted away, but one of the boys pursued her, snarling and laughing. The next thing she knew he had caught her, and grabbed her by the arm. She hurled her purse away with her free hand and kicked at the boy when he scurried after it. Then another boy shoved her, and she fell, the pavement biting her cheek. Suddenly there was a yelp and she heard the purse drop beside her. A body hit the ground with a crushing thud, someone was shouting for the police, and two arms were pulling her to her feet while the world swirled. She heard Bear's voice telling her to run, and heard someone else yelling Bear's name. Bear pulled her along, but the air was growing black, darker than black normally seemed—

There was an ugly sound of a curse word and suddenly Bear was gone and she heard the sound of more fighting. She tried to move away but caught her shoe in a grate and staggered forward. Someone caught her, someone smaller than Bear, but with Bear's voice. "I've got you. Hold on, now. Chin up," the voice was saying, and through the moisture in her eyes she could see a face with eyes like Bear's swimming in the blackness before her, glimmering like the reflection of the moon in the river, and then the depths swallowed him up.

The thin boy grabbed Blanche and half dragged her along with him while Bear dispatched the punk who was still wrestling him with a thump on the head. His assailant crumpled to the ground and Bear ran to the thin boy and gathered Blanche in his arms.

"She's blacked out!" said the thin boy.

Bear moaned, searching her pale, blank face. "Get a taxi. It's going to be pretty hot around here soon."

"Righto." The boy jumped into the street and signaled a passing yellow cab. It pulled over obligingly.

Bear gave the driver Blanche's address, then sank back into the cushions. "What's up now?" he asked the thin boy.

The boy's face was pained. "It's trouble. I can't tell you here."

"Right." Bear stared ahead as Blanche's street came in sight, but when they turned onto it, there was a police car parked in front of the Brier's house.

Bear blinked, licked his lips. He glanced at his companion, and saw the same consternation on his face that he had felt at the sight of the patrol car.

"Driver," Bear said suddenly. "Change of address. We're going to Manhattan."

The driver turned around, squinted at them suspiciously,

then shrugged and turned away with a grunt. He didn't want to get involved.

The cab passed the police car in front of the Briers' door, streaked down to the end of the block, turned right, and was off again into the night.

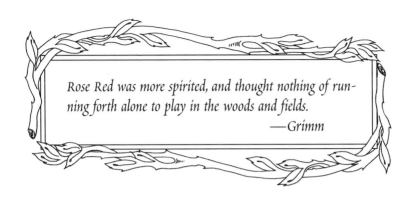

Rose Red was more spirited, and thought nothing of running forth alone to play in the woods and fields.

—Grimm

Chapter 11

AS IT TURNED OUT, Rose's evening was somewhat different than she expected. When she had left the front door, she had found that Suzanne from her chemistry class and Rob's friend Franklin were waiting in the back seat of the car. They said hello to her as she slid in the front seat. Rob had gotten in the car and threw it in gear. Next thing she knew, they were skimming down the rainy streets to the prom.

Rob turned up the rock song on the car stereo after asking her if she minded. She did mind, but said she didn't, just to be polite. Her fingers kept pinching the satin of her dress and rubbing it together, to feel its slickness. Rob talked, raising his voice over the stereo, about small, unimportant things like the weather and the baseball team's lousy season. Franklin and Suzanne were talking in low voices in the back seat. Rose tried to come up with other topics of conversation, but felt at a loss.

The best part of the whole night was when they were walking up the steps to the banquet hall and Rob remembered to open the door for her, and gave her his arm. Timidly she took it, and came into the restaurant on the arm of the most popular guy in school. She saw heads turn, whispers, nods. An awareness of her suddenly enviable status was like a current of electricity coursing through her.

They went into the softly lit banquet hall to the beat of the slow rock song playing in the background. Guys and girls drifted around the tables, talking, drinking, preening, flirting. Everyone seemed more sophisticated and grown up in the plush atmosphere. Rob found the table they were sharing with his friends and their dates. He pulled out the chair for Rose and seated her. She sank into her seat, smoothing her skirt over her legs.

"We're cutting out of here early," Rob said in her ear as he sat beside her.

"Why?" she asked.

"These things get old real quick. We're going back to my house for some real fun."

"Will your parents be there?" Rose asked guardedly.

Rob grinned sarcastically, "What? You can't go anywhere unless there's a parent present? Are we still in kindergarten?"

"No," she said, miffed, "it's just that—"

"Sure, my parents will be there," Rob said, putting his arm around her.

There was a buffet supper with dessert afterwards. Rob and his buddies talked about baseball and cracked jokes about various couples passing their table, while the girls made small talk, and flirted with their dates. It was fun, but not terribly fun, Rose thought.

"Is my hair starting to fall down?" Suzanne asked her in a low voice when the guys had gotten up to get more drinks.

"It looks fine," Rose said. Suzanne's brown curls were pulled into a French twist at the back of her head.

"Your hair looks stunning—where'd you have it done?" Suzanne looked envious. "The hairstyling place did mine, but I think it looks gross."

"My mom did it," Rose admitted. She'd never thought of going to a hair salon.

"Really? You'd never know. Where'd you get your dress? It's cute."

Rose had been admiring Suzanne's sophisticated (but too short, she thought) black velvet. "Oh, at a thrift store." She hoped it didn't sound cheap.

"Really? Wow. How are things going with Rob?"

"Good, I guess." Rose was puzzled by Suzanne's look. "Why?"

"Oh—you never know. He's a pretty cool guy, I guess."

Rose wondered, but the guys came back with the sodas just then. A few minutes later, the music became loud and fast. The lights dimmed. The prom had officially begun.

"Wanna dance?" Rob asked Rose.

"Sure." Feeling strangely uncomfortable with him, she rose. Rob took her hand and led her to the dance floor to the pulsing beat of the latest hit. The music was energizing, intoxicating. Rose felt the glances of other people and held her head high as she began to cut loose. This was going to be fun.

Rob treated the songs as though they were athletic exercises, making choppy motions with his feet so that he jerked back and forth to the music. Rose preferred to flow into it and let the beat take her where it would. Soon she realized that dancing with a person who can't dance, when you know you can, makes you very self-conscious. She had danced before at sleep-overs with her girlfriends in the country, when they had pretended to be in a TV dance contest. *But dancing in front of a guy is different,* she thought as she toned down her movements beneath his shadowed gaze. An uncomfortable feeling stole over her. She danced away from him a few steps and tried to dance next to a few other girls. But they seemed as self-conscious as herself. Rob continued to pulsate awkwardly away, and inside she knew that he wouldn't want to dance to any other fast songs.

The next song was a slow drawling love tune, and Rob pulled her to himself and wrapped his arms around her, which she found more hot and uncomfortable than romantic. Rob continued to make small talk which she couldn't find interesting. She wished he would at least look at her, but he didn't really look in her eyes, just over her shoulder. His hands were moving slightly over her back. For some reason, not being able to look him in the face made her nervous.

"Want to go see what else they have to eat around here?" he asked when the song was over and the beat picked up again.

"Sure." She followed him off the dance floor, glancing behind her a bit longingly.

They drank punch, and danced a few more times to slow songs. Each time she felt his hands moving across her back she wanted to squirm. She didn't like it. She wondered if she should say something, but everything she thought of sounded too dumb. After about seven songs, Rob looked at her and said, "Let's go."

"Where?" asked Rose, stupidly.

"Back to my house, like I said. Franklin and George and

their girls are coming. We'll have a little party by our-
selves."

Rose considered, and wondered what to do. "What are
we going to do?"

"Kick back, watch a movie, relax. There'll be other girls
there. Come on, be a sport."

Rose paused. "What movie?" she said at last.

"*Casablanca.* My folks have it. Ever seen it? It's a great
movie. One of my favorites. I'd like you to see it."

"Well, just for a bit. But I have to be home pretty close
to one."

"As if I didn't remember. Come on, let's go."

Rose sighed. So that was the prom. *Oh well,* she thought.
It wasn't that much fun after all. A little bemused, she looked
around for Suzanne.

Rob lived in an apartment building a few blocks from
the school. It was a nice place, modern and slightly classy.
There was no sign of Rob's parents, but Rob said they had
probably gone out to the store to get some more snacks.
Three other couples were there, all Rob's friends.

As promised, *Casablanca* was on the screen soon after
they got to Rob's house. But there was a stereo blasting in
the next room, and the one couple who stayed in the living
room were obviously more involved in each other than in
the movie.

Also, there was beer. Franklin went to the fridge as soon
as they came in and got out two six-packs. Rob offered her
some, but Rose, shocked, shook her head no. "Aw, come
on," he teased her. Then he said, "All right. Let's watch the
movie now. I'll be right over, okay?"

So Rose watched the movie while the others drank. She thought about calling home several times. "Who's driving home?" she asked Rob once.

"Oh, Manny is."

"Who's he?"

"The designated driver. Over there in the corner of the kitchen."

Manny was talking to a tall blonde. She didn't want to disturb them. *I should call home,* she thought. *As soon as this scene is over.*

But the movie, which she had never seen, *was* good. Fascinated by Ingrid Bergman, she kept telling herself that she would get up after the next scene, but she didn't. And pretty soon, Rob sat down to watch it with her. She thought that was kind of him. Even though he took occasional drinks of beer, he pointed out all the best lines, and after a while, she began to relax and enjoy herself again. It was a very romantic movie.

"How do you like it?" he asked during an interlude.

"It's fantastic," she said. "But I sort of wish they'd turn off that music."

"Why don't we go in the other room?" he said to her, "My parents have a TV that's hooked up to the VCR. It's quieter in there."

"What?"

"C'm here." He vaulted over the sofa, a bit unsteadily, and walked over to the first bedroom down the hallway. Rose followed him cautiously, stopping to take her purse for security.

He switched on the TV and *Casablanca* came on. "Pretty cool, huh?" he said, "We can watch it here."

A bedroom. "No thanks. I think I'll watch it out here," she said cheerily.

"Aw, come on! See, I set it up especially for you!" he grinned again. Normally, he had a nice smile.

"No, I don't think so—" Rose shook her head.

Rob interrupted her, his eyes on the TV screen. "Hey! You don't want to miss this. Look, this is the good scene where she pulls a gun on Bogart."

He took her hand and pulled her gently into the bedroom and sat down on the bed. "Just watch this part with me. It's good."

He had shut the door behind them. "Rob, I—" Rose's eyes darted to his and to the door, unsure of what to say.

Now he leaned back on the bed, a smile playing over his face. "Relax, won't you? Boy, you're tense. I'm not going to eat you."

"I just—"

"What's wrong with a little privacy? Sit back with me and relax for a while. We'll watch the movie. You'd really get distracted if we were out there in that crowd."

He patted the bed and gave her a puppy dog smile. Unwillingly, she sat down on the very edge of the bed. Rob leaned back beside her, but didn't touch her. Her eyes moved back to the TV screen as the music sang with tension. It was too easy to sit still and watch as Bogart faced Ingrid Bergman, his eyes taut with ambiguous thoughts.

"Sit back here with me," Rob whispered through Bogart's sarcastic retort.

She decided to pretend she didn't hear him.

"Rose—" Now Rob's voice dropped to an even lower whisper. "You're really beautiful, do you know that?"

She did, and he was distracting her. "Thank you," she said distantly, her eyes on Bergman's anguished face.

Rob put his hand on her shoulders, then began to pull her head towards him.

"What?" She tried to move away, disturbed. "What's wrong?"

"I want to kiss you," he murmured in her ear. "Come here."

Kiss him. The thought flashed through her mind, attractively, but Rose ignored it. "No, I don't want to," she said, pretending to be absorbed in the TV screen.

"Why not?" She felt him moving closer.

"I don't know you well enough," Rose muttered, and moved away. His arm caught her around the waist and stopped her.

Danger lights went on in her mind, and she quickly looked at him. His eyes were changed, and he suddenly looked different. She could smell the alcohol on his breath.

"You don't know what you're talking about," he said, and turned up the volume on the television set by the remote control very loudly with one hand while holding her with the other. Then he tossed the control aside and grabbed her with both arms.

His arms were strong. She tried to pull away, and realized that he could hold her and kiss her and there was nothing she could do about it, no matter how hard she might struggle. . . .

She put on a slow smile and deliberately calmed her racing heart. "This is so romantic of you, Rob. But first," she said quietly, offhandedly when his face was less than an inch from hers, "I really, really need to go to the bathroom right now." Eye color: guileless blue.

He looked at her in bewilderment.

"Is there a bathroom here?" she asked quietly.

"Right behind you," he said, a bit sullenly, and released her a bit.

"Excuse me," she said, and rose. He let her arms go, and she wondered if he could see her shaking as she reached down casually to pick up her purse.

Once inside the bathroom, she locked the door and sat down on the toilet seat, breathing hard. *Narrow escape, you fool.* The only way out of the bathroom was back into the bedroom with Rob, and she had no doubt that things would get out of hand if she went back out. She paused, and her mind darted over this escape route and that, and the more options she thought of the more she realized that she was flaming, raging mad. He had no right to trick her like this. And now he thought he had her trapped.

All right, so she had been trapped. Thank God he had let her go. Now what? She clasped her shaking hands and prayed hard. *Better do something fast, girl, before he gets suspicious.*

The window. She stood on the toilet and opened the curtains, praying that there were no bars on it. There were none. It was a small window, looking out on the back of the apartment building. She was on the second floor, and she estimated there was a good twelve-foot drop.

However, there was a balcony with a fire escape at the bedroom window. It was within an arm's length. She kicked off her shoes (wretched high heels) and, after a pause, flushed the toilet with her foot and pushed the water spigot with her toes so that the water came on. Then, after dropping her purse and shoes outside, she hitched up her skirt and wiggled halfway out the window. She could reach the fire escape with both arms, and pulled herself all the way outside, trying to get a good grip on the wet metal surface. For a terrifying moment she flopped between heaven and earth, her feet kicking about for a hold. Then she pulled herself up (eternally thankful for all those chin-ups in gym class) and got a leg over the fire escape rail.

The next minute she stood shaking on the wet metal balcony. Were the windows open? The shades were pulled, but the lights were on, and Rob might see a movement and guess. Thank heavens the TV volume was still turned up so loud.

"Here's looking at you, kid," Bogart was saying.

"I wish I didn't love you so much," Bergman replied.

Hurriedly she tiptoed over to the metal slide ladder and fumbled about in the dark for the metal hook that would release it. After what seemed an eternity, it creaked free, and Rose let it slide slowly down, catching it and setting it down so that it wouldn't clang on the pavement below.

In another moment she was climbing down and the next minute she was on the ground, sprinting down the alleyway to the street, her purse and shoes clutched in one hand. There was a chain fence, four feet high. Her stocking feet numb against the wire, she clambered over, tearing her tulle underskirt. Then she ran down the road, hoping for a taxi, praying for a taxi.

At last she stopped and debated about putting on her shoes. And darn, her coat was still at Rob's house. She noticed that her hands and arms were black with grime from the fire escape. *Just great.*

There were no taxis in sight, but there was a police car

parked by the side of the road. Murmuring a prayer for help and understanding, she hesitantly walked up and knocked at the window.

"Sir—" she managed to say to the black-browed officer sitting in the front seat.

"Yeah?" the officer scowled at her. He didn't seem friendly. "What's the matter?"

"I think I need help. I need to get home, and I don't have any money."

The policeman skeptically surveyed her torn dress, bare feet, and black-streaked arms.

"What happened?"

Rose paused, trying to phrase what had occurred in general terms. "I was out with a guy, and he tried to t-take advantage of me. So I ran away."

"You thinking of pressing charges?"

"I'd like to talk to my mother first—"

The man sighed wearily. "What's your name?"

"Rose Brier—"

The radio crackled and the officer picked up a receiver, muttered some numbers into it, then turned around and scrutinized her again. Rose wished that she had listened to Blanche and worn a longer dress. She felt so wretched outside, in the rain, in her stocking feet. Before she could stop herself, she sniffled.

"Wait a second. Brier. Doesn't your mom work in the emergency room at NYU?" the officer demanded.

"Yes, sir," Rose managed to say. "Her name's Jean."

"Yeah. Jean. I know her. Where do you live?"

Rose gave her address.

"That's not far," he mused. "All right. Get in the back.

But next time you go out, bring money for a taxi, okay? Police don't have time to do taxi service for every stupid kid in New York City."

Rose nodded gratefully, swallowed, and got into the police car.

When she got home, she thanked the policeman and got out. She ran up the steps and banged on the door, waiting for Blanche to open it. No one answered. Biting her lip, she knocked again and again, but no one came to the door.

Where was Blanche? As she stood there, trying to collect herself and deal with this new problem, someone shouted at her. She turned around. It was the policeman, who was still there.

"Isn't anyone home?" he yelled to her from the car.

"My sister's supposed to be, but no one is answering the door," Rose said, red-faced.

"Don't you have a key?" he yelled in amazed disgust.

"No." Rose truly felt like a fool. The officer put his hand over his eyes, muttering something.

Rose banged on the door again, but the house was silent. Silent.

At last the policeman said, "Come here."

As she carefully walked down the steps, he said, knitting his angry brows, "Where's your mother?"

"At work."

"What's the number?" He pulled out a car phone.

Luckily, Rose knew the number. She gave it to him, and he punched buttons furiously. Rose wondered if he had ulcers from his job.

"Emergency Room. Let me speak to Jean Brier. Jean?

This is Officer Cirotti. I've got your daughter Rose here. Yeah, she's all right. She doesn't have the key to her house . . . That would be very helpful, yes. I'll be waiting with her."

Officer Cirotti hung up and looked at Rose with that intimidating stare. "Your mother is coming home. You can wait with me in the car until she gets here."

"Thank you," Rose breathed, and got back into the car.

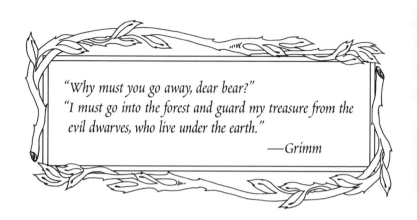

"Why must you go away, dear bear?"
"I must go into the forest and guard my treasure from the evil dwarves, who live under the earth."
—Grimm

Chapter 12

BLANCHE was swimming out of a river, slowly, and each stroke cramped her arm. Was it because the river was so black? It was draining her strength away, like a long illness.

But what she needed was sleep—long, white strokes of sleep. The black waves turned to white foam which drifted easily and carried her into light, to the shore, to the day—

Her eyelids fluttered open stiffly. There was grey before her eyes, and something like a snowfall—a cloud hovering over her, sifting out the sun. . . .

She stirred, and felt satin between her fingers. Sequins around her middle. The dress. But no, on top of that was something softer than satin, soft and unimaginably smooth. Puzzled, she stroked and squeezed it, and felt flannel and silk between her fingers.

Now, she was perplexed in her reverie. How had she sunk into silk?

She tipped her face up toward the ceiling. The air was chilly, but she was warm beneath her covers, in a bed . . .

A bed? Quickly she sat up. Bemused, her hair falling

over her face and obscuring her vision, she turned her head back and forth, trying to discover her sanctuary.

It was misty and dim, and the air yielded when she touched it. Then her fingers made contact with what she realized were cascades of lace curtain hung around the bed. The comforter she lay beneath in her satin prom dress was white quilted silk, so soft that it confused the fingertips.

Like a mermaid escaping seaweed, she unwrapped herself from her cocoon and parted the sheer curtains with a finger. Outside the world sharpened in focus: an ivory-and-grey papered room with three huge windows overlooking the pinkish grey skyline of the city at earliest morning. It was still raining.

Shivering, she stepped onto an angora rug at the base of the round couch of a bed. Her purse lay on her cloak, which was folded over the back of an elaborately padded and flounced ottoman of white satin. The wallpaper had stripes and garlands and tiny pink flowers on it, very suave Victorian. Pink silken balloon curtains sagged from the three windows, like heavy eyelids.

Wondering, she wrapped herself in the cloak and looked for her Chinese slippers. They were nowhere to be seen. She padded out of the room in her nylon stockings. She found herself on carpet in a darkly-papered hallway leading out into a living room with sweeping skyline windows. A creeping fear stole over her. *Where am I?* She glanced to her right, and saw a balcony. Tiptoeing close, she saw a curved staircase stretching down, curving around the outside wall of the room nestled in what seemed to be the center of a building. A majestic frosted chandelier dripping with crystal hung from the center of the domed ceiling. Shadows wreathed the room below.

There were two voices, talking. "Is Mrs. Foster okay?"

"Yeah, but she's real shaken up. I called Steven before I left, and he's coming down from the university tonight. The place was trashed, Bear. Completely."

"And it's gone," Blanche recognized Bear's voice, flat and tired.

"Yes. I could kick myself—and you. I wanted to move it to a safer place, but you just had to have it around to use as bait for antique dealers."

"It was worth a shot, wasn't it?"

"Not really, considering what's happened now. Bear, someone is onto us."

"Okay. So we'll go underground a bit further. I know."

"Bear, no more of this visiting stuff. We're in danger. Anyone who knows us is in danger."

"You're right," Bear said dully. "I should have never gotten started."

"Bear, how much do these girls know about you?"

"Not much. Look, I tried to be careful, okay? I didn't just blurt anything out—"

"Are you sure?"

Blanche heard the sound of someone jumping to his feet.

"Look, brother. If you're suggesting that the Briers were the ones who ratted on us, you'd better shut your big mouth right now."

"Take your paws off me, big brother," the voice said mildly. "My, quick on the draw to defend our ladies, aren't we?"

"Cut it out." A chair creaked.

"Look, no hard feelings. But no more fraternizing, okay?

I'm taking off. Get rid of that girl as soon as you can and follow me. Rendezvous number thirty-two. Got it?"

"Right."

"Man, oh, man. Steve's going to kill you when he sees his suit."

"If he doesn't kill us for anything else."

There was the sound of a door opening and closing quietly. Blanche saw a tall dark-haired figure in a tuxedo cross the room and come towards the steps.

Guiltily, she came towards him and stood at the top of the steps.

He looked up and saw her. His face was tired and his tuxedo was stained and torn, but his voice attempted to be cheerful. "You've arisen!" he said, coming up the steps to her. "What happened to you?"

"I just faint sometimes," Blanche admitted. "Mother says it's a stress reaction."

"Poor kid." Bear put a hand on her cheek. "Probably the last thing you needed was to end up in a fistfight."

"I guess I must have given you a scare."

"Well, yes. Especially when you didn't come to right away." The strain was creeping into his voice. "I was going to take you to the hospital."

"I think I fell asleep," she said. "I'm sorry."

He took her by the hand and led her down the steps. "Well, it's not as though you could help it."

They reached the ground, and Blanche looked around, shivering. "Bear, where are we?"

"No place important," he said brusquely. "Come on, you've got to get home. It's after three. Your mother must be freaking out."

"Well, Mom trusts me with you, so maybe it's okay," Blanche murmured.

"Yeah, but I better get you home. I don't know what your mother will think of me now that I bring you back all bruised like this."

"Bear, you're upset about something. What's wrong?" She halted, holding him.

"Look, it's nothing to do with you. Don't worry. It's just something I've got to take care of," he said, clamping his mouth shut. That stubborn look came over his face, and she knew it was no good pressing him.

"I'm going to see you get home, and then I've got to leave."

She wondered if he knew what she had heard. All of a sudden, she staggered and Bear seized her shoulders.

"You almost fell. Are you still dizzy?"

"I am," she admitted. "I'm sorry." Tears began coming. She hated being weak, especially at a time like this.

Without a word, Bear picked her up in his arms and carried her. "Just close your eyes and forget all about this," he said. "Forget you ever saw this place, just forget it and I'll get you home."

"Where are my shoes?" she whispered as he pulled the hood of her cloak over her face.

"I don't know. Maybe in the school parking lot," he said. "Just lie still and relax."

With her head against Bear's chest, Blanche shut her eyes. *When you were weak, you were weak.* She just had to accept it. But she didn't mind being carried, at least not by Bear.

She was distantly aware of entering an elevator and then being carried out of doors. She heard the faint noises of traffic, and saw the grey glow of early, early morning and smelled the City smell. Bear flagged down a cab and set her gently inside.

"You're coming with me, aren't you?" she whispered to him.

He paused, one hand on the door. It looked as though he were debating with himself, and she wondered if he was thinking of what the other boy had said about "no more visiting."

"Okay," he said finally. "I do want to make sure you get safely home." Getting into the cab, he told the driver where to go. She leaned against his side gratefully. Just a little longer. . . .

After awhile she asked in a low voice, "You're leaving us for good, aren't you?"

He looked at her in surprise. "Yes," he said. "I have to go away."

"We'll miss you," she said, suddenly shy again.

"Maybe we'll see each other again, some day. I hope so."

"Are you going to say good-bye to Rose and Mother?"

He stared straight ahead. "I think you'll need to do that for me."

"Okay." She looked at his profile. His eyes were half-shut, and his jaw was tense. His mind seemed to be somewhere else.

Her fingers felt for the locket around her neck. Dad had given it to her on her sixteenth birthday. Trembling, she felt for the clasp.

"Bear, I want to give you this," she said, letting the thin chain come off into her hand. "To remember us by."

He looked at the small golden heart she placed in his large hand and said nothing. Instead, he closed his hand over hers and squeezed.

"I'm sorry I made you go to the dance with me," he heaved a sigh. "It really turned into a disaster."

"I'm not sorry," she said. "But I—" She couldn't go on.

"But what?" He pressed her hand.

The taxi turned onto her street and came to a stop. He looked at her. She returned his gaze, and then quickly got out of the taxi, pulling her cloak around her. He followed her out as she ran up the steps to the door in her stocking feet and rang the doorbell.

"But what?" He repeated, hanging back by the taxi, hands in his pockets, looking earnestly at her.

"I—" The words wouldn't come. Could he tell? Someone inside was opening the door, and Blanche grabbed it and resolutely held it shut for a moment as she blurted, "I think I'm falling in love with you."

She hadn't meant to say that much. She saw his face for a second, dazed but elated, then she turned away from him, opened the door, and hurried inside past her bewildered sister.

Rose, wrapped in her bathrobe, stood in the doorway, gaping. Bear waved at her with a happy smile, then jumped back into the taxi. It pulled rapidly away into the dawning grey light.

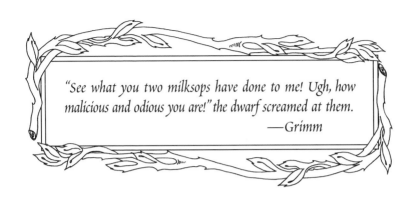

"See what you two milksops have done to me! Ugh, how malicious and odious you are!" the dwarf screamed at them.

—Grimm

Chapter 13

ROSE LAY drowsing in her bed Sunday afternoon, picking idly at the chipped polish on her nails. Climbing down a fire escape and over a fence had taken its toll on the burgundy enamel. Her cheeks colored at the thought of how foolish she'd been last night—her hair and makeup and nails had been sophisticated enough, but she'd left her brains behind, apparently. Why couldn't she be sensible and *aware* of things, like Blanche? Her older sister never would have gone to Rob's party, let alone be caught with him in a bedroom. Rose castigated herself remorsefully, and then forgot about it seconds later as another, more attractive thought entered her mind: the mystery of Bear. She thought it was wonderful that Bear had taken her sister out to the prom—although Blanche had been strangely reticent about the romantic possibilities therein. Blanche's story, narrated over a plate of pancakes cooked by Mother at four in the morning, had held Rose spellbound. Despite her weariness, she had hardly been able to sleep, mulling over the new paradox.

Rose yawned fitfully in her bed. "Are you awake, Blanche?" she asked.

"Sort of," Blanche said from her burrow of quilts and pillows. She continued to follow her own thoughts. *In a way, Bear leaving was a good thing.* After all, she didn't know what could have happened if he had stayed. She would have dated him, she supposed, but it would have been strange and uncomfortable and different. For now, she was safe. Though that was poor comfort as she lay curled up curled up in bed, wondering where he was and worrying about him. But it was the one dry crust she was offered.

"I just can't figure out how Bear got you into such a gorgeous apartment," Rose said, yawning again. "It boggles the mind."

"That makes two of us," Blanche said dryly. Both she and Rose discussed the mystery of the previous night over and over, but they couldn't come to any conclusion about it.

"Do you think we could figure out what street it was on?" Rose asked thoughtfully. "Maybe if we walked around some nice Manhattan neighborhoods . . ."

"I really have no idea. I didn't get a good look at where we were, and even if we found the right building, then what? It's impossible to find out who owns those kinds of places. Rich people buy those apartments on the top floors of buildings so they'll have privacy!"

"A penthouse!" Rose breathed, her arms folded under her head. "How in the world—"

"Maybe his brother owns it," Blanche had a sudden thought. "His brother was there."

"You know, he never told us much about his brother," Rose bit a half-colored fingernail. "Maybe their mother left him all the money without giving Bear a cent. Maybe that's why Bear didn't like to talk about him."

"No, wait. They didn't live there. They were talking about a Steve and a Mrs. Foster," Blanche mused, sitting up and stretching. "That's where they lived, I think."

"Hmm. Maybe we could look up 'Foster' in the phone book." Rose rolled off the bed and ran downstairs in her bare feet to get the New York City telephone book. Alone in the kitchen, she found the F section, turned some pages and groaned. There were three pages of Fosters.

"And at least ten of them were 'Steven Foster,' not counting all the 'S. Fosters,'" she complained, coming up the stairs.

"They're leaving the Fosters, anyhow," Blanche said, touching her cheek gently. She had a yellow bruise there from the fight in the school parking lot. "Well, I suppose it will remain a mystery."

At the word, Rose's eyes glimmered green. "Not if I can help it," she breathed. She stood up straight in her pink nightgown, one hand on her hip. "Watson, I think we have a case."

Blanche moaned and threw herself on the bed. "Just what I need," she murmured, pulling the pillow over her head.

Neither girl was anxious to go to school on Monday morning. "I can imagine what Rob must have told his buddies about what happened," Rose moaned as they walked to school. "He probably told some lovely whoppers."

Blanche was quiet. She desperately hoped the girls wouldn't tease her about "her boyfriend." Just now she was feeling very tender in that area.

As they walked up the steps to the main entrance of school, Blanche noticed a flap of tan cloth caught in the center door. "What's that?" she pointed it out to Rose.

"Looks like someone's coat," Rose said, intrigued.

She pulled the door open and the flap shot free. The sudden release propelled its owner forward. Both girls stared at the red-faced man on the floor.

"Idiots!" he screamed at them, scrambling to his feet.

"Mr. Freet!" Rose cried in regret. "I'm so sorry!"

"We saw your coat was stuck in the door . . ." Blanche ventured.

"Yes, and thoughtlessly decided to open it just as I tried to jerk it out myself!" Mr. Freet was dusting off his coat with quick angry movements. "Little imbeciles. Have you no idea what poor balance people my age have?"

"If we hadn't opened the door, you might have torn your coat," Rose felt compelled to point out.

"Therefore you decided it would be better for me to take a spill?" Mr. Freet's white hair was practically bristling with indignation.

"No, not at all," Rose pleaded. "We just thought—"

"You minxes don't think, or else you would have found a more civilized manner of dealing with the situation!" Mr. Freet bellowed, snatching up his umbrella and shaking it at them. "I'm beginning to think you two impudent schoolgirls are going out of your way to harass me!" He scowled and strode into the principal's office in a small white fury.

Rose heaved a sigh. "I must say, we do manage to get on his worst side all the time, don't we?"

"He isn't really a very reasonable person," Blanche agreed.

As it turned out, Rob had decided to ignore Rose, which was fine with her. Apparently he hadn't told anyone about their little adventure, and Rose hoped fervently he was repentant. But she suspected he was simply nursing wounded pride.

Since it was close to the end of school, the seniors had to be measured for their graduation caps and gowns. Between her afternoon classes, Rose found the hallway crowded with seniors standing around, talking and hanging out. Some of them had already been measured. Others were just killing time. Since she had a few minutes before her next class started, she thought she'd find Blanche. She passed the two Freet brothers in the hallway in earnest conversation. Mr. Edward Freet looked at her, glaring, as she passed, and Rose ducked her head, crestfallen. Down at the end of the hallway, she spotted Blanche getting something out of her locker. Eileen, Lisa, and Lani stood around her.

Sensing trouble, Rose hurried towards them in time to hear Lani say, "So have you had many hot dates with this guy, Blanche?"

"What's it to you?" Rose demanded, shouldering her way in beside her sister. Blanche's face was red, and she looked thankful for the interruption.

"Oh, it's Rob's new 'friend,' Rose Mary," Eileen said. Her eyes were slitted, and Rose fleetingly wondered how much she knew. "We were just wondering why your sister showed up at the dance with a drug dealer."

"He's not a drug dealer!" Rose said hotly. She didn't care how loud her voice was.

The three girls exchanged glances and laughed. "Now, I've heard of being naïve, but this is too much!" Eileen tittered. "So what does he do in the schoolyard—trade baseball cards?"

"I always thought he was a panderer," Lisa said slyly. "We thought maybe Blanche—"

Rose really forgot herself when she realized what Lisa was saying. The next thing she knew, Lisa was on the ground and she was standing over her shouting. There was an uproar going on all around her. Blanche had her hands over her mouth, and Rose thought she was laughing. Eileen was cursing wildly while Lani shrieked bloody murder.

The next instant, the principal was there with Mr. Freet at his side. "I want both of you young ladies in my office!" he said to Rose and Lisa, who was still gasping for breath. "You too!" he added to Blanche, recognizing her.

Five minutes later, Rose and Blanche sat next to each other in the principal's antique-filled office while Lisa, almost crying, described how viciously Rose had attacked her.

"She just laid back and punched me in the stomach," Lisa went on in a hurt voice. Blanche was amazed that such a tough-looking girl could crumble so easily.

"Excuse me sir," Rose said politely. "I only shoved her. She was being positively insulting to my—"

"Liar!" Lisa cried.

Rose looked at her with undisguised disgust.

"What provoked you to hit her, Miss Brier?" asked the

principal, leaning back in his Victorian armchair. His red forehead was creased and withered, but his eyes were less piercing than his brother's.

"She was tormenting my sister, the way she always does, and I couldn't take it any longer," Rose's words spilled out over each other. "She and her friends have been picking on her for no reason ever since we got here. For no reason whatsoever, just stupid cruelty."

The principal's eyes were impassive. "How was she tormenting your sister?"

Rose blew out all her breath in an attempt to calm down. "My sister went to the prom with a friend of our family's. This girl and her friends were making crass remarks—about his character." If she even thought about what Lisa had insinuated, she'd commit murder.

"Just who is this friend of yours?" the principal asked, eyeing the sisters.

Rose and Blanche glanced at each other. "He calls himself Bear," Rose shrugged.

The principal considered, then turned to Lisa. "You are not to go near either of the girls for the rest of the school year. I'd hate to have to deny you a diploma over a disciplinary incident. You may go." Lisa got to her feet muttering, cast Rose a dirty look, and flounced out of the office.

"Rose Brier, you have after-school detention for the rest of this week, starting tomorrow. And you are also not to go near Lisa or her friends." He took off his glasses and wiped them. "I feel I should warn you two girls that this character you call 'Bear' is a dangerous person. I recognized him the other night as a former student here, Arthur Denniston, who was arrested for trying to sell drugs. I don't know what type of association you girls have with him, but I'd advise you to end it. I say this as a school administrator concerned for your welfare." He gave them both a meaningful stare and dismissed them.

Rose wondered if Mr. Freet had told his brother about the episode with the coat this morning. Probably that's why the principal had treated them so sternly. "I just want to go home," Rose said to Blanche, holding her head. "I feel sick."

"Then let's go home," Blanche said soothingly. "I've gotten measured already. Mother can call the school later." She put a gentle arm around her sister and led her out of the school building.

"I just know Bear's not a drug dealer, I know it!" Rose said miserably after they had left the school grounds.

"I don't think so either," Blanche said courageously.

"It's just so confusing!" Rose wailed. "I want to believe Bear is who we know him to be, but—"

"Yes, I know," Blanche said gloomily. "My *feelings* say Bear isn't involved with drugs in any way, but as for what I know—it's sort of like the opposite of religious faith. Oh, let's not even talk about it."

"No, we've got to know the truth!" Rose insisted. She looked at her sister. "I was sort of kidding yesterday about investigating, but I really think we should."

"But why?" Blanche asked despondently.

"So we can know the truth," Rose repeated.

Blanche paused. "Suppose the truth isn't too nice?"

"Doesn't matter!" Rose answered passionately. "Truth is truth!"

"I suppose you're right," Blanche said dully. They continued walking in silence until they reached their block. "By the way, thanks for rescuing me."

"Any time," said Rose, flexing her muscles.

Mother had something to say to Rose about using violence to solve arguments, but she came down unfailingly on her daughter's side otherwise. "Let's just hope that this is the end of the matter," Mother finished. "It might be wise for you girls to stick together as much as possible until the school year ends."

"We will, Mom, we will," Rose promised.

"I only have four more days left before exams start, anyhow," Blanche said. "I'm glad for that."

When they woefully told Mother what the principal had said about Bear, she frowned. "Hm! That is disturbing. But after all, girls, Bear did tell us that he was arrested for using drugs."

"Yes, but why didn't he tell us he used to go to St. Catherine's? And why didn't he tell us his real name?" Rose asked.

"I'm sure he had his reasons," Mother said. "I don't know. I may be a cynic, but sometimes school principals don't know the full story behind everything that goes on in their own buildings. I tend to believe what I see, not what I hear. Bear seems like an honest boy to me."

"But the principal told us not to associate with him any more," Blanche pointed out.

"Well, we may never see him again," Mother said matter-of-factly. "If we see him again, maybe we'll find out the answers to your questions, but until then, we'll just pray for him and leave the mysteries alone."

Blanche and Rose looked at each other. Neither mentioned that Rose had no intention of leaving them alone.

"Let's begin at the beginning. Let's jot down everything we can remember about anything personal Bear ever said to us, and we'll go from there," Rose said that night in the bedroom, taking out a school notebook. They had gone up to their room early, telling Mother that they had extra work to do. She had said goodnight to them with a smile.

Blanche sat cross-legged on the bed, frowning. "Well, the first night he was here, he said he had a brother. And that they were both arrested for delivering drugs. Or something like that."

"Yeah. Mother would remember." Rose scribbled that down. "Did he say anything about where he lived that first night he came?"

"No, never."

"Hmm. That first night, we found out he liked G.K. Chesterton. I would guess that would make him Catholic for sure."

"Besides the fact that he went to St. Catherine's and was an altar boy," Blanche pointed out.

"He-heh. I forgot. Yes, besides that. Oh, I remember! He told Mom that his mother died of cancer. We should check the obituaries in the paper for a Mrs. Denniston."

Something clicked in Blanche's mind, and she stared. Suddenly she shouted, "A. Denniston! A. Denniston!" bouncing up and down on the bed.

"Shh! What's wrong? What?" Rose looked at her sister in amazement.

"Arthur Denniston is A. Denniston!" Blanche practically shrieked.

"What are you talking about?"

Blanche scrambled to her feet and seized her schoolbag. She rifled through her papers and pulled out one. "The poem we read! Remember—A. Denniston!"

"Bear is A. Denniston," Rose said mechanically. Her eyes kindled. "So he was Sister Geraldine's favorite student."

Blanche was practically crying with laughter. "The nut! We read him his own poem and he had to pretend that he didn't like it! He must have felt put on the spot! The nut! He must have wanted to die!"

"Oh, I don't think it's so hard to criticize your own poem. He probably couldn't stand it. I always think mine are wretched," Rose said.

"No wonder he was Sister's favorite," Blanche said. "All that poetry he's read on his own. He must have stuck out in class badly."

"Tomorrow," Rose pointed to her sister resolutely, "while I'm in detention, you are going to talk to Sister Geraldine."

Blanche opened her mouth to object, and realized there was no way around. If she wanted to see Bear's name cleared, she was going to have to get involved.

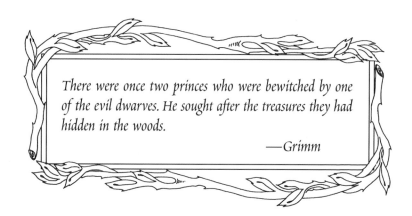

There were once two princes who were bewitched by one of the evil dwarves. He sought after the treasures they had hidden in the woods.

—Grimm

Chapter 14

ALL DAY LONG, Rose itched for school and detention to be over with so that she could hear what Blanche had found out from Sister Geraldine. But the day passed as slowly as a snail, and Rose felt she was going mad. That afternoon in chemistry lab, she was standing by the lab sink, praying obsessively that Sister Geraldine wouldn't have an unexpected stroke, when she realized that Suzanne was working near her. She hadn't talked to the girl since prom night, and the sight of her now brought back a stream of uncomfortable memories. Rob was still ignoring Rose, which was something to be grateful for. But she wondered how much Suzanne knew.

Suzanne looked up and saw her.

Rose decided to be friendly. "Hi, Suzanne."

"Hi, Rose." Suzanne seemed a bit uncertain, but still open.

"How's Franklin?"

"Oh, we're not dating anymore. We were never really serious." Suzanne fiddled with one of her dangling earrings, and then abruptly said in a low voice, "What happened with you guys the night of the prom? Rob said you took off."

"Yeah, I did." Rose suddenly found that her worn-down pencil point held a certain fascination for her. She picked at its edges with a fingernail.

"What happened? Nobody saw you go out."

"He was trying to pull some stuff on me. I told him to cut it out, and he wasn't stopping. So I left. I got a ride home." Rose decided against saying she had climbed out the window. She had hoped that Suzanne's memory of that night might be a bit hazy. Apparently, she guessed right, because Suzanne didn't ask her any more questions.

"Rose, I feel bad. Rob's done that to girls before. I should have told you, but I didn't know how serious you guys were."

"I wish you would have said something," Rose said. "I certainly wasn't expecting it. I wouldn't have gone out with him if I had known what type of guy he really was."

"Yeah, that's what I couldn't figure out—why you were going with him. Didn't you know that Rob and his buddies track down girls just to score off of them?"

Rose hadn't. Her face flamed in sudden anger. "Those jerks!" She could think of much worse things to say, but she confined herself to that.

"Yeah, they're pretty sick if you ask me. I'm glad you got him to respect you."

"I'm not so sure about that. I doubt very much whether he learned a lesson."

Suzanne's eyes widened. "Then he . . . "

"No, he didn't get a chance, thank God. Boy, that makes me mad!" She couldn't think of anything else coherent to say.

"Rose Brier, are you finished with your lab exercises?" the teacher asked from across the room.

"As a matter of fact, yes." Rose slammed the book and strode back to her seat, not looking at Suzanne again. She was going to have a talk with Rob.

She caught him in the hallway right after that class with some of his buddies. "I need to talk to you," she informed him.

He looked at her, a grin playing around the corners of his mouth. "Yeah? You want to say you're sorry about what happened on prom night?" he asked. His friends exchanged looks of muffled laughter.

Her face was flushed, but anger drove her on. All right, if she couldn't get him in private, she'd bawl him out in public. "Is it true that you asked me out just to see if you could score on me?" The ugly words fell from her lips distastefully.

Rob was taken aback for a minute. He stared at her, and at last came up with a denial. "I don't know what you're talking about."

"Because if that's true, you've got a lot to learn about what girls are for. And if you can't learn that, you're going to have an awfully miserable life."

"You've got it all wrong," Rob was saying, trying to smile, but still looking uncomfortable.

"I hope so." Rose looked him up and down and shook her head. "I thought you were made of better stuff, Rob. I'd like to think you're a man, Rob, not some little boy fooling around who doesn't want to grow up."

Rob's face went red, and Rose saw that she'd cut into his pride. Seeing she'd made her point, she turned on her heel and began to walk away. She heard a snort and one of the guys said, chuckling, "She's the one who doesn't want to grow up."

There was no way that she could let that go. She turned slowly, smiled in her most winning way, and went on: "Oh, by the way. That kind of love is sacred—something for real men who have the guts to make a lifelong commitment, not for short-sighted idiots like you guys." Eyes like flint, she looked each of them in the face. None of them could meet her gaze. "I pity you. I really do."

Slowly she turned away, and walked down the hall, head high, the blood still going dizzily through her brain. Yeah, she was scared. She didn't know what type of mess they'd make of her reputation now. But she didn't care. *Man, I live for moments like these,* she thought, pushing down the smile that kept creeping onto her face.

After school, Blanche approached Sister Geraldine as the old nun hobbled down the hallway, briefcase in one hand and cane in the other.

"Sister, I was wondering if—if I could talk to you for a minute," Blanche ventured.

"Certainly, Miss Brier. What can I do for you?" The frail old nun flashed her sharp blue eyes at her pupil.

"I wanted to ask you—about that poem that you gave me that day. The one by A. Denniston. Was that Arthur Denniston?"

"Yes, as a matter of fact, it was," Sister Geraldine said, surprised. "I haven't heard his name for a long time. How do you know about him?"

"He's a friend of ours, actually—my sister and me," Blanche said.

The nun paused and leaned against the wall to steady herself. "My goodness. If you please, could we go into a classroom and sit down? My knees aren't so good these days."

"So you know Arthur Denniston," Sister Geraldine repeated to herself in amazement after seating herself in a student desk. "Well, well. How is he?"

"I hope he's well. I actually haven't seen him for a few days. But we saw him quite a bit this past winter. He never told us very much about himself, and I was wondering perhaps, if you knew him well—"

"I must say I thought I knew him well, at one time," the nun admitted, her wrinkled face suddenly creased with sadness. "He was quite attached to a very good friend of mine, the late Father Michael Raymond."

"The one the school chapel's dedicated to," Blanche said softly.

"Yes, that would be him. A prince of a man. A kingly man. You don't often meet ones like him." Sister Geraldine looked older than ever. "He was chaplain for this school and pastor of the church next door, St. Lawrence. A remarkable person, he could talk anyone into doing anything. Could make friends with anyone. As you can imagine, those are wonderful talents in a pastor and administrator. He had his enemies—he was bull-headed, and, some would say, a stick-in-the-mud." She chuckled. "But more than anything, he was a good priest. Quite cultured, too. A wonderful influence on the young people."

"And he was friends with Be—with Arthur?"

"More than that, my dear. Arthur and his brother Ben were two of his converts. Yes, people he'd brought into the Church. He had met their mother in the hospital when she was dying of cancer, and she converted to Catholicism due to his influence. He was the one who convinced her to take her sons out of the preparatory school they had been going to—the family was wealthy, you see—and send them to St. Catherine's." She seemed to grow melancholy. "I often wonder if that was a wise decision Father Raymond made."

"Didn't they like it here?" Blanche ventured.

"Oh, well enough. I'm afraid they didn't quite blend in, with their cultured background and learning. I remember Benedict—Arthur's younger brother—wrote an article criticizing the sports program as detracting from the school's academics. As you can imagine, that made him very popular." She gave Blanche a wry smile. "Ben was the smarter one—mind like a steel trap—but Arthur was more talented. He wrote poetry, short stories—quite a musician, too, although he never did anything with it at school. This isn't the best Catholic school in the City, but I suppose the boys liked it well enough. They were Father Raymond's altar boys. Every morning before school, they'd serve Mass over at St. Lawrence and then come over here to school. I believe they never missed a day—well, until Father died."

"He was killed, wasn't he?" Blanche asked quietly.

"Yes," Sister Geraldine blinked. "It was a terrible tragedy. After he died, everything seemed to fall apart. He was the power behind the religion program here, behind the parish—so many things depended on him. Oh, nobody lives forever, but his going so soon—cut our legs out from under us."

"How did Arthur take it?"

"As could be expected. He and Ben were devastated. Father was—like a father to them, I venture to say—he meant far more to them than their real father did, especially after their mother died. As I recall, their father wasn't too happy that they wanted to go to St. Catherine's in the first place. I don't think they saw him at all after she died. It was a quite broken relationship. So Father was all they had in the world, and when he went—" Sister shook her head. "I never thought I'd see it happen to boys like them. But I'm told that losing parents can affect a young person deeply, and cause him to act in unforeseen ways. That's the only way I can explain what happened."

"But—how did Father die?" Blanche asked.

"There was a robbery at the church. Father Raymond heard the noise from the basement—he was working late at the church—and went upstairs to frighten them away, it would seem. He was a big man, and nothing scared him. The thief—or thieves—shot him." She blinked again. "I'm told he was actually strangled, too, though why I can't fathom."

"How horrible," Blanche murmured.

"I believe—and I'm sure this is the popular opinion—that drugs were involved. There's been a problem with drugs at this school for a long time. Only someone strung out on drugs could be that cruel. Those types do anything for quick cash. They cleaned out all the golden vessels from the sacristy closet."

She paused and coughed. "You see, Father Raymond had an unofficial ministry rescuing unused church vessels— chalices, monstrances, and so on. After the Second Vatican Council, many churches were getting rid of their 'extras.' The laity used to donate items like that to the Church all the time, so many of them ended up gathering dust some- where, or being sold, or, Father told me, even thrown out. He used to go around and buy them from antique shops and other places where they turned up. Once, he told me, he rescued a chalice from a bar, where the owner had it among his collection of beer mugs!" She shook her head wryly at Blanche. "So Father had quite a storehouse of old church vessels. Most people thought he was crazy. After all, most of them weren't worth very much. But Father believed 'holy things for the holy,' and he kept them safe and in good condition. He wasn't a reactionary or anything of that sort. He simply believed in showing reverence for all things connected with the Holy Mass. It was such a shame, everything that happened."

"What happened to Arthur and Ben after Father died?"

"I didn't see very much of them. They lost interest in their classes, they stopped serving Mass—well, then again, there was a good deal of difficulty finding a replacement priest, so perhaps that wasn't their fault. Then, the next thing I knew, the police held a raid on the school, and both of them were arrested for drug possession!" A look of pain shot over her face at the remembrance. "It just seemed so unlike them. But they did have the kind of money that could buy the enormous amount of cocaine they found on them. I suppose they could have been guilty. I myself just don't know what to think."

Blanche was silent for a minute, watching the elderly nun. Sister Geraldine sat, appearing to stare very hard at something a few inches from her face which she could not comprehend. At last, she roused herself.

"I'm sorry. You said you know Arthur Denniston? How is he? I haven't seen him at all these past few years—not since he went to juvenile prison."

"Well, Sister, I—" Blanche hesitated. But who could she tell about Bear, if not Sister Geraldine? She decided to relate the entire story. Beginning with his helping their mother with the groceries that far off night in January, she told her every detail she could remember about his relationship with their family. Sister Geraldine listened, entirely absorbed. She asked no questions, and barely moved during the entire narrative. Her face had a look of intense thought.

"What a very odd thing," she said after Blanche had finished with Bear's good-bye to her in the taxi. "It seems bizarre. He's changed—but yet, he hasn't changed."

"What puzzles me especially is why he would be trying to sell church vessels at an antique fair," Blanche said at last. "Especially if Father Raymond felt so strongly about keeping them for the Church—" She didn't dare suggest the lurid thought that had occurred to her: that Bear was somehow connected with the church robbery and murder.

"Yes, I admit that's the one thing that bothers me the most." Sister rubbed a veined hand across her temples. "Why would he be looking to sell a chalice?" She repeated the question to herself, then paused. All the color drained from her face. "Oh, my sweet Lord," she said softly.

"What?" asked Blanche, frightened by her expression.

The nun drew a deep breath. "I see what he's trying to do. He's looking for Father Raymond's murderer."

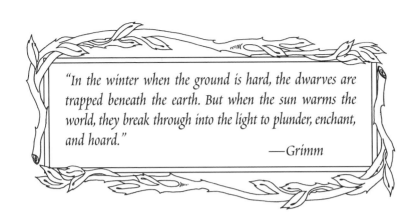

"In the winter when the ground is hard, the dwarves are trapped beneath the earth. But when the sun warms the world, they break through into the light to plunder, enchant, and hoard."

—Grimm

Chapter 15

"WELL, WHAT DID you find out?" Rose asked, bounding out of the detention hall to meet her sister.

"Hold onto your hat and I'll tell you," Blanche said as they walked out the door to the street. As she told her sister the substance of her conversation with Sister Geraldine, Rose's eyes got wider and wider.

"Holy candles, sister!" she breathed at last. "So that's it!"

"And I suppose now he's hiding, because the murderer—whoever he is—knows Bear is on the trail. That must have been Ben he was talking to that night in the penthouse, about the break-in at the Fosters' house." Blanche stopped at a crosswalk and waited for the light to change.

"Yes—that reminds me. The Fosters. I really think we need to find out who they are, and where they are." Rose paced up and down.

"Sister Geraldine didn't know the name. But she suggested we check in the old school yearbooks in the library. Perhaps we can find out more about the Denniston boys, too," Blanche said.

"That's tomorrow's assignment," Rose said with a grin. "Before school. I can't miss out on this part."

The next day was bright and balmy. They arrived at school an hour early and went straight to the school library on the top floor. No one was there except the elderly sister in black veil and white habit, who served as librarian. She and Sister Geraldine were the only nuns at the school who still wore their traditional garb.

"Sister Geraldine said you girls would want to look through some old yearbooks," the nun said fondly.

Obviously, she liked students who were interested in the past. She escorted them through the stately rows of encyclopedias and reference books to a shelf of faded yearbooks, a motley collection by comparison. "Let me know if I can assist you any further," the old nun said, nodding her head and walking away as silently as a mouse.

Rose lost no time. She counted down the years and selected five volumes from the appropriate classes. "Bear was here about four years ago, so we should be able to find something in these ones. Here, you take half and I'll take half. Check for anything that says 'Denniston' or 'Foster'."

They sat down at a table in the corner and began turning the glossy black-and-white pages. Naturally Rose, the quicker one, was the first to find something. She set aside one book and picked up another. "This would have been Bear's sophomore year, if my calculations are correct," she said, turning to the freshmen section. "Ha!"

She had her finger on a picture in the freshman section. Its subject was a young baby-faced boy with cropped hair, freckles, glasses, and a sour expression. The caption said "Benedict Denniston."

"That's Bear's brother," Blanche said. "Boy, he looks like he has a chip on his shoulder."

Rose stared at the photo and frowned, turning the book from side to side. "He looks familiar," she said.

"He looks like a thinner version of Bear," Blanche pointed out.

"Yeah, that's definitely true. Except for the freckles. And the lighter hair."

"We should look in back issues of the school paper for that letter he wrote about the sports program. I bet it was a kicker," Blanche said.

"Bear should be in the sophomore section," Rose said.

But no, he was in the "juniors" section, looking a bit bewildered, as though he really didn't belong there. He had thick, short, black hair and glasses, and his big shoulders almost filled the picture.

"He could have been on the football team, but he preferred to write poetry," Rose murmured. "I knew I liked him. I like him even more, seeing what he used to look like."

There weren't any other pictures of them in that volume. And strangely, there were no pictures of them whatsoever in the volume for the year after.

"They must have gotten arrested before the pictures were taken," Blanche said at last.

Rose shivered. "Poor guys. There's no mention of them at all."

Blanche took the volume from Rose. "Let me check the candid shots."

At last she thought she found one more picture of Bear. It was in Sister Geraldine's class, appropriately enough. She was teaching, a typical cynical expression on her face, while a burly student in the front desk looked at her. He sat up straight, but his face was turned from the camera, so that all that could be seen was his mop of hair. She showed it to Rose, who was busy scanning the other volumes.

"It's amazing how corny the hairstyles from a few years ago look, isn't it?" Rose remarked.

The only other thing Blanche could find that might be pertinent to the case was a picture of a student assembly, where a policeman was giving a presentation on the dangers of drug use. "I bet this was because of the drug raid," she said to her sister.

"Shh!" said Rose, holding up a hand.

"What is it?" Blanche asked, exasperated. Her sister was rapidly flipping pages in Bear's junior yearbook.

"Hold on . . . Yes!" Rose turned to her sister and gave a thumbs up sign.

"What is it, Sherlock?"

Beaming in triumph, Rose held up the yearbook and pointed to the picture of a smiling black boy. The caption said, "Stevenson Foster."

"I noticed that the seniors have all their addresses listed at the back," Rose said with exaggerated nonchalance.

The afternoon had turned hot and sticky, so Rose and Blanche changed out of their school uniforms into shorts and T-shirts before they went on their mission. Rose figured that the less official they looked, the better. On their way up to the Fosters' neighborhood, they rehearsed their questions. Blanche was unsure of how soon they should mention Bear's name. "Leave it to me," Rose urged her. "I'll just ask whatever comes into my head."

"That's precisely what worries me," Blanche complained in an undertone.

They found the street easily, but the house number was harder to pin down. The neighborhood was not exactly in the best condition, and some of the houses had no numbers. Many of the residents of the neighborhood were sitting on their doorsteps, chatting. A group of children screeched at each other, playing with water guns. At last, the girls located a house that seemed like the Fosters' place. An ancient air conditioner roared in the window next to the door. Rose had to knock twice. The door was cracked open, and a suspicious brown face looked out at them.

"Yeah?" a woman's voice asked.

Rose put on her most innocent expression. "Is Steven home?"

"And what if I said he don't live here?" the woman asked.

"We go to St. Catherine's high school, and we know he graduated from there a few years ago. We just wanted to ask him some alumni questions . . ." Rose tried to sound plausible without sounding suspicious, or lying.

"Who is it, Mom?" a male voice asked.

"Some girls asking for you," the woman said.

Rose saw another set of eyes look out, and then the door opened and a tall black youth in a sweatshirt, holding a basketball, leaned out the door.

"What's this about alumni?" He scratched his close-shaven head.

"We just wanted to ask you a few questions," Rose said, nervously.

"You're from the yearbook staff or something?" the youth said.

"Uh—" Rose floundered. "Sort of—"

"C'mon in if you want. It's roasting out here." The youth they assumed was Stevenson opened the door for them and they walked inside.

The front room was in a haphazard state. There were no pictures on the walls, and a slipcover in an African print covered the sagging couch. A heavy-set woman with tightly curled hair still looked at them suspiciously, leaning in the doorway to the kitchen. Behind her, Rose could see boxes with newspaper coming out of their tops. It looked as though the Fosters were moving.

The young man sat down heavily in a torn leather recliner. The girls sat down on the couch, and Blanche sat as close to Rose as she could. "Are you Stevenson Foster?" Rose asked.

"I am," the young man affirmed. He spun the basketball between his two hands. "Lucky you found me here. I just got back from college."

"What are you studying?" Rose asked, almost automatically.

"Engineering. So, what do you want?"

Rose glanced at Blanche, who nodded slightly, and began, "Well, actually, we're not with the yearbook. We were wondering if you might be able to help us find a friend of ours, Arthur Denniston."

Instantly, the faces of both man and woman took on a completely different expression.

"I'm not sure I want to answer that," Stevenson said slowly. The woman's face had gone from blank surprise to deeper suspicion, and, Rose noted, fear.

"But I know you know him," Rose said earnestly. "He knows you. He was worried about you and your mom, so I know he's your friend. And we've got to find him, somehow. Don't you have any idea where he is?"

"How do you know this Arthur Denniston?" the woman spoke up after a sharp silence.

"He's our friend. He helped my mom on the streets one night, and he visited our house a lot all this past winter. But then he took off, and we're really worried about him. All we want to do is send him a message somehow."

"Honey, you'd be better off not messing with guys you don't know too much about, and that's a fact," the woman said brusquely.

"But we do know a lot about him," Blanche spoke up, then lowered her voice. "We know he calls himself Bear, and that he's trying to find out who murdered Fr. Michael Raymond."

Again, both faces before them registered change, but this time it was slight. Apparently, both mother and son had decided not to reveal anything to these strangers.

"Sounds like a real kettle of fish to me," Mrs. Foster said at last. "You'd be better off not getting involved with folks like that."

"So you do know Bear?" Rose said eagerly.

"I didn't say I did." Mrs. Foster clammed up. There was an uncomfortable silence.

Blanche felt as though she had to say something. "Look, I know you must be terribly suspicious of us coming around, asking questions like this. We're just his friends. I mean, didn't he ever mention us to you, especially if he stayed here? My mom's Jean. I'm Blanche and she's Rose. He took us out to the opera once. He took me to my prom—maybe he borrowed your tuxedo," she turned again to Stevenson, who flicked his eyelashes suddenly. "I mean, you're about his size. Didn't he ever mention us to you? I can provide you with any details you want. You don't have to tell us anything that would get you in trouble."

"Let me ask you: just why do you want to know?" Mrs. Foster broke in. "Being nosy won't do anybody any good. Never does."

"Well, our school principal said he was involved in drugs. But that just doesn't seem like Bear. I know he hangs out in the drug areas and—well, he looks pretty scruffy—but I just can't believe he was selling drugs. You're his friends. Can't you tell us the truth?" Blanche pressed.

The son and the mother looked at each other uncertainly. Then Mrs. Foster said staunchly, "That boy and his brother never did any drugs. Never. Neither did my son, either. They were the cleanest kids in that whole stinking high school. Don't you believe that man, girlie. It's trash."

Stevenson was tossing the basketball from one hand to another thoughtfully. "That was a set-up if I ever saw one. Everyone at school knew it. It was ludicrous. But Dr. Freet believed they were guilty, and he's the important one." He looked hard at them. "You girls have any idea what Bear's doing?"

"Not much," Blanche admitted.

"Well, then that's how he wants it. If you keep snooping around, you could get into a lot of danger." He emphasized the last word. "Danger. I'm not fooling with you."

"Your house got broken into while he was staying here, didn't it?" Blanche said softly.

Stevenson looked angry. "That's right. Whoever it was totally trashed the place and almost killed my mother. She locked herself in the bathroom and he told her to stay there and be quiet or he'd set the place on fire. Bear and his brother had been staying here ever since they got out of prison. But after that happened, they took off."

"Do you know where?" Rose asked.

"Lady, I just told you I can't tell you that. I'm not even going to tell you if I know. He's gone." Again, he emphasized the words.

"If you girls are Christians, you can pray for him. If you ain't, then I can't help you," Mrs. Foster chuckled harshly to herself.

"How long was he in juvenile detention?" Blanche asked.

"Ten months. His brother was in for six months. It was real hard on both of them. Especially Arthur. That boy has got the most gentle spirit you've ever seen, and he was miserable." Mrs. Foster's eyes grew soft. "You never met a sweeter kid. That's why I didn't mind them two staying here. They were always over here with Steve when they were in high school, and when they got put in prison, their big-shot father didn't want anything to do with them. Threw them out on the streets. They're rich, you know, but they don't have a penny to their names now. Well, the surest way to send a kid back to prison is to wash your hands of him when he's down."

Blanche murmured an assent, and Mrs. Foster went on, "I raised my Stevenson right—that's why he's the way he is now. But I got friends who have kids in prison, and I know what a difference it can make to a kid to have an adult stand by him. Not that you say he's right when he's wrong—no ma'am! But that kid Arthur, he and Ben didn't do no wrong. Somebody set them up, that's for certain."

"But who would set them up?" Blanche asked.

"If any of us knew that, we wouldn't be sitting here with this room like it is, that's for sure," Mrs. Foster said.

Rose had remembered something. "Does any of this have anything to do with chalices?"

Mrs. Foster shook her head. "I wish I knew. Those boys were always trying to find someone who sold Catholic chalices and whatnot—" she caught her son's warning eyes and shut her mouth.

"You'd be better off not asking questions about that," Stevenson said briefly, in a manner remarkably similar to Bear's.

But Rose would not be deterred. "Was he trying to sell some of Father Raymond's old vessels? We know he collected vessels."

"I said, no questions!" Stevenson said flatly. "That's final!" At Rose's hurt look, he said curtly, "Arthur is one of my best friends. I can't afford to be giving out information right and left when I know he's in trouble. How do I know who'll you'll be talking to—accidentally or on purpose?" He caught Rose's protest and nipped it in the bud. "Oh, I know you girls don't mean any harm, but this situation is a bit more than you can handle. So just keep everything I said to yourselves, okay?" His look was adamant and harsh.

"Okay," Rose and Blanche faltered. He stood up to show them to the door.

"Thank you for all your help," Blanche said timidly.

He nodded and the girls filed past. As they reached the bottom of the stoop, Stevenson spoke again. "Hey look—it *was* my tuxedo he borrowed. He trashed it, too—the rat—but I know he had a really good time with the girl he was out with." He flashed a smile at Blanche and raised his eyebrows significantly.

Blanche blushed. "If you hear from him, please tell him to contact us as soon as he can. It's very important to us."

Stevenson and his mother looked at each other again. "I'm making no promises, but we'll do what we can," he said at last.

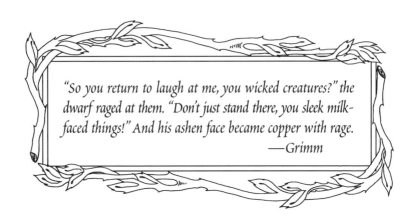

"So you return to laugh at me, you wicked creatures?" the dwarf raged at them. "Don't just stand there, you sleek milk-faced things!" And his ashen face became copper with rage.
—Grimm

Chapter 16

THE LAST DAY of regular classes they didn't have to wear uniforms, so Rose was going through her usual ritual of fashion indecision. Blanche noted in surprise that she appeared to have only tried on five outfits. At last, sighing, Rose decided on her royal blue tee shirt.

"Should I wear a skirt or pants with it?" she asked Blanche, who had dressed half an hour ago without ceremony.

"Skirt. That way I won't feel odd about being the only one in school wearing a long skirt," Blanche said. She was wearing the rose-colored calico jumper she had made for the white shirt she had bought at the thrift store.

"Do you want to wait for me to get out of detention?" Rose asked, taking out three or four skirts from the closet.

"I'd like to, but the seniors are dismissed at twelve o'clock and I was going to go home to work on my graduation dress," Blanche confessed. She had been attempting to make a dress of pale pink cotton for that event, which was this Saturday.

"Oh." Rose gazed sadly down at the paisley skirt she was holding to her waist and Blanche relented.

"I'll come by at three to walk you home. It won't take long."

"You don't have to," Rose argued unreasonably. "What about this peacock-patterned skirt?"

"Rose! You just asked me to meet you after detention!"

"Well, if you want. But you don't have to . . ."

Blanche groaned and walked to the mirror and ran her fingers through her thick hair. She couldn't decide whether to leave her hair up or down. She enjoyed wearing it down, but in this weather, it was more practical to wear it up.

Rose put on the peacock skirt and rummaged around in her accessories basket for the matching headband. "Blanche, you should try to wear stronger colors. That dark green skirt you had the other day really looked good on you."

"I don't want to find another outfit now," Blanche said. She wasn't a quick-change artist like Rose.

Rose fluffed up her bangs, checked her face, and moaned. "Oh, I'm glad I let Lisa have it, but boy, I hate going to detention!" She picked at a pimple with vengeance. "To do nothing but sit for a solid hour! Right now, it's like spinning wheels. Remind me not to do this again, Blanche."

Blanche sighed and gave her hair a last brush. "If you think before you act, Rose, it probably won't happen again."

As the girls walked into the crowded main hallway at school, which was buzzing with crowds of teenagers on the edge of summer liberation, they caught sight of Mr. Freet, walking swiftly down the hall towards them. He was scribbling something in a small appointment book while holding a brown paper package in one arm and a briefcase in the other. Just then, a shouting group of excited boys barreled down the hallway, jostling him. Mr. Freet started, lost his balance, and fell, dropping the package, which bounced on the floor with a heavy *thud thud.*

"Oh! Those boys!" Rose cried in anger and ran to help Mr. Freet up. Blanche bounded after the package and grabbed it. It was far heavier than she had expected.

Mr. Freet was red-faced as Rose dragged him to his feet.

"Are you all right?" Rose said anxiously.

Mr. Freet had said nothing, being speechless with wrath.

"Hellions!" he managed to utter at last. "You loathsome —females! Get away from me! Get away from me!" He swiped the package from Blanche's hands and as Rose cried a warning, aimed a blow at her head. Blanche dodged in the nick of time and fell back, astonished.

"If I catch either of you interfering with me again, I'll strangle you with your own hair-ribbons!" he ranted. "Get out of my sight!"

Blanche and Rose backed away from him, exchanging bewildered glances. Mr. Freet glared at them as if they had been personally responsible for his mishap. Then he turned and hurried down towards the principal's office.

"You'd almost think he was going to report us," Rose remarked, her face alternating between irritation and amusement.

"He had no right to treat us that way," said Blanche sharply. "By all rights, we should report him."

"Oh, I'm sure his brother would *really* listen to anything we delinquents said!" Rose tossed her hair over her shoulder. "Mr. Freet is definitely a troubled soul. It must be the unhappy dwarf in him."

"The what?"

"My theory. Remember? I think Mr. Freet is just a dwarf who's obsessed with the love of treasure. And of course, anyone who lusts after money is bound to be unhappy."

"I don't think he cares about money so much as he cares about art," Blanche reflected.

"Exactly. Gold and jewels and lovely things. He probably has a secret hoard in his basement."

Blanche giggled. "Rose, you're insufferable."

Rose remained melancholic over the state of Mr. Freet's soul. "I really do feel sorry for him. He must have a very sad life to be so cranky."

"Poor man," Blanche said lightly as they parted.

Detention is horrendous, Rose thought miserably, watching the hands on the clock inch slowly towards three. The rest of the school had been dismissed at two o'clock, since it was the last day of school. But the kids in detention had to stay until three. Rose was the only girl there.

A few of the guys in the room had been attempting to get her attention. True to form, she'd been ignoring them stolidly.

They probably wonder what I've done to be stuck in the room with them all week, she thought grimly. *I certainly don't look like their type.* She stared at the skull and crossbones on the back of the shirt of the boy in front of her.

At the center of the room, the monitor sat correcting papers and casting occasional glances at her charges.

There was a soft snicker behind her. She couldn't tell if one of the guys was trying to get her attention or his buddy's. Either way, Rose was not going to respond. She studied her nails and tried to think about something usual and boring, like nail polish colors. *Fifteen more minutes to go.*

Blanche looked up at the grandfather clock from her vantage point on the living room floor, where pieces of her graduation dress were laid out around her. It was a quarter to three. She had better go and meet Rose. She sighed, looking down at her sewing project. A premonition passed over her that she was not going to finish this dress by Saturday.

"But if I work on it from the time I get home until dinner, maybe I'll get everything done but the hem—" she argued with herself as she went out the door.

Three o'clock! Rose leapt to her feet, grabbed her near-empty backpack and was the first one out of the room. The guys all swarmed out after her and she decided to make a quick run to the lady's room to avoid their company.

In the bathroom she pulled a brush through her hair idly for a few minutes. She had been trying unsuccessfully not to think about Bear and his mysterious mission for the last hour or so, because if she did, she would only get more frustrated. There seemed to be nothing left to do but wait. And pray, as everyone kept telling her.

She cocked an ear to make certain that all of her fellow detainees had left. There was no sound of feet in the hallways now. The building was practically empty. But somewhere, two men were talking. She could hear their voices through the heating vent. Unconsciously, she moved a little closer to catch what they were saying.

In the middle of rebuking herself for eavesdropping, she heard something that made her freeze.

"A sixteenth-century ciborium," one of the men said. All thoughts flew from her mind and she strained her ears to keep listening.

Blanche always disliked walking alone in the City. Even now, in the broad bright light of a spring day, she still felt as though she might meet something sinister around the corner. Rose treated every excursion outdoors as a chance for adventure, the way she was always seeing dwarves or gypsies in ordinary people. Blanche thought there was some truth in Rose's insight. But the problem was, even dwarves could turn out to be nasty creatures, small but still potentially threatening to unarmed maidens alone in the woods. Or the City . . .

The problem I have with deeper meanings is that they make things more threatening, not less, Blanche decided as she kicked a small stone along the granite pavement. *Suppose I were to entertain these deeper warnings, instead of ignoring them the way I try to? Then the shadows of reality might grow bigger and bigger and overwhelm me with their realness. Truth isn't always safe.*

Smiling at her metaphysical reflections, she ran a hand absently through her loose hair as she approached a cross street.

A car roared past her in a terrifying wind and she jumped back from the curb as someone shouted something at her—her name? Insides quaking, she walked a bit faster.

That was just a freak thing, she told herself. The car just

swerved too close to the curb. It's ridiculous to think anyone is after me.

But her inner sensitivity was agitated. There were dragons in the area.

*Why not run, just to look as if I'm in a hurry? But that's
silly,* she told herself firmly. *No one's after me.*

Straining her ears as she walked forward, she thought
she heard car doors slamming behind her, and footsteps
running.

Should I look? I might as well look.

Keep walking. Everything is fine. There's no such things
as dragons.

"Blanche Brier!" someone shouted, and she turned to see
Lisa and Eileen hurrying towards her as the car they had
gotten out of sped away. Her stomach lurching suddenly,
she kept walking.

"Hey there, Blanche, how are things?" Lisa said, coming
up on her right side. Eileen came up on the other side of
her.

They had surrounded her. Blanche panicked and said
nothing.

"Don't be scared, Immaculate Complexion. We just want
to talk to you. Now that school's over, we'll never get to see
you," Eileen said in a friendly voice that didn't fool Blanche
at all.

"What do you want to talk to me about?" Blanche managed to ask, looking at her shoes. She could see on either
side of her feet, Lisa's sneakers and Eileen's tan feet in
leather sandals.

"You know what your problem is, Blanche? You never
hang out. We would have gotten to know you better if

you'd have given us the time of day." Eileen sounded offended.

"I'm always doing something wrong, aren't I?" Blanche heard herself say in a flat voice. "It's three o'clock, if you want to know."

Both girls laughed, and Eileen put a hand on Blanche's shoulder. "Let's talk for a minute."

Traffic sped by over the crosswalk. It was just Lisa and Eileen, hungry for some gratuitous verbal torture. Blanche took a deep breath and forced herself to look up into Eileen's tanned, thin face. "So what do you want to talk about?" she said in as strong a voice as she could. Eileen's face wore a sweetened smile, but her eyes were nervous.

Eileen sucked her lip and looked at Lisa, who silently looked back at her with dark cold eyes. Blanche saw Lisa squeeze her eyes half-shut. Eileen smiled again and said, "Well, actually, Blanche, I wanted to ask you about this boyfriend of yours."

"I just picked it up. Perfectly exquisite piece. I'd had my eye on it for years, and it just fell into my hands, yesterday. Isn't it magnificent?"

The voice came from the vent as Rose stood on tiptoe beneath it.

"It's lovely. So you got a good price," the other man said in a tired voice, as though not really interested. Rose recognized the voice of the principal, Dr. Freet.

"A good price indeed, brother. All that remains is for me to locate the last piece. If I can find that, then I'll have the entire set—chalice, ciborium, and paten."

"I really don't understand what you see in these old

church artifacts," Dr. Freet said. Rose heard the sound of a briefcase being snapped shut.

"That's precisely the difference between us, isn't it? To you, a mere museum piece. To me, a work of flawless craftsmanship and beauty. Perhaps that's why I am the flourishing gallery owner and you are the washed-out idealist bureaucrat." That disdainful voice undoubtedly belonged to Mr. Freet.

"That's about all of your sarcasm I can handle just now," Dr. Freet said shortly. "I have to get home."

"Well, I just wanted to let you know that I'm going to be leaving very soon on that overseas vacation I've been planning," the other Freet said. "I just have to finish negotiations on the last piece of the set."

"Congratulations. Send me a postcard."

Rose heard a door shut and the voices continued, but now muffled so that she couldn't make out what they said.

"Who?" Blanche said, blankly enough.

Eileen patted her shoulder consolingly. "You know, the one you went to the prom with. Cute guy. Quite a muscle pattern on him, hmm?"

"Why do you want to know about him? He's just a friend," Blanche said woodenly.

"Just curious. How'd you meet him?"

"Through my mom," Blanche said. *Let them figure that out.*

"You still seeing him?" Eileen asked, not missing a beat.

"Not lately." Blanche looked around in the bright sunlight flashing off of the windshields of the passing cars. She wished they would stop their game, whatever it was.

"Break up with him?"

"We weren't dating. He's just a friend." Blanche tried to sound more irritated instead of pathetic.

"Yeah, right." Eileen dug into her shoulder playfully. "That's not what I heard."

"I can't help what you heard," Blanche said.

"Heard you weren't as 'immaculate' as we thought," Lisa added, showing a shark's smile.

A flash of white anger came over Blanche, followed by cold disgust. But her retort was cut off by seeing Eileen give her friend a warning look.

"Lisa has such a sick mind," Eileen said, putting her arm around Blanche's shoulder. "She can't help it, really." She was looking daggers at Lisa.

Now this was curious. Why was Eileen so anxious to be nice? Something was aroused in Blanche, and she began to study her interrogators surreptitiously as they studied her.

Rose's fertile brain was whirling. *Chalices. Church vessels.* It might not mean anything, but then again, it might mean a good deal. It might be worthwhile to follow him to see if she could find out anything more. She debated with herself. If Mr. Freet had been so enraged by them this morning, who knew what he might do if she spied on him? But if she were very careful, he might not even know she was there. It was certainly worth the risk, wasn't it? After all, what could he do to her except call her names?

Rose went to the bathroom door and cracked it open. She saw Dr. Freet come out of his office with his briefcase and papers, followed by his brother, who was also carrying a briefcase and the famous brown paper package of this morning. *Ah*, thought Rose. *That's why he was so upset with Blanche for picking it up. He doesn't want anyone else to touch his precious vessels.* She marveled at the accuracy of her insight about Mr. Freet's dwarfish habits.

The two men walked down the hallway towards the side entrance. After they disappeared through the door, Rose walked into the hallway as casually as she could and strolled to the window overlooking the faculty parking spots. She saw Dr. Freet get into his car, but Mr. Freet set off down the street on foot.

Quickly Rose scanned the parking lot and the surrounding streets. There was no sign of Blanche. Probably her sister was buried behind the sewing machine and had decided not to come.

Well, that was probably better anyway. Blanche wouldn't like the idea of stalking an irritable old man. No doubt it was best for Rose to go on this adventure herself.

Rose raced down the steps to the door, then halted and walked outside casually. This whole thing might be a waste of her time and she could be worrying her sister unnecessarily. Still, there was always that chance. . . . Feeling the drumbeat of a quest beginning in her mind, she began to walk after Mr. Freet as idly as she could, while pretending to look for something in her purse.

"So tell me more about this guy. Is he a nice boy?" Eileen was saying.

Blanche said, "Yes," hesitantly, watching for Eileen's reaction.

"Does he call you a lot?"

"Uh, no—" Blanche made herself sound scared and uncertain.

"Where's he live?" Eileen asked nonchalantly. Lisa stared at Blanche intently.

So that was what they wanted to know.

"Why do you want to know?" Blanche looked from one to the other.

"Has he ever taken you to his home?" Eileen prodded.

"Why should I tell you?"

Eileen suddenly tightened her grip on Blanche's shoulder, making her wince.

"Didn't he tell you where he lives?" Eileen asked, as though nothing had happened.

Blanche struggled, but Lisa moved in on the other side and held her tightly at the elbow, jabbing her nails into Blanche's skin. The pain hardened Blanche's resolve to fight, but she played at becoming more frightened. Twisting, she complained, "Ouch! No. I have no idea. He always came to our house. What are you asking me all these questions for? Come on, let go!"

Eileen eased up. "So, where'd you go when you went out?"

"Why do you want to know?"

"Oh, come on, Blanche—where did you go?"

"Different places," Blanche said, stalling. Lisa was still digging into her.

"Like where?"

"We went to the Metropolitan opera once."

"Rob told us that," Lisa murmured.

Eileen ignored her. "Anywhere else?"

"Not really. Please, let me go!" Blanche had determined to say nothing about St. Lawrence church.

"She doesn't know anything," Lisa said.

"Shut up!" Eileen said to her abruptly, pinching Blanche harder.

"Please, let go of me!" Blanche made her voice more frightened than she actually felt, and Eileen released her. Lisa withdrew her claws, but still held onto Blanche's arm tightly.

She couldn't tackle Lisa in a fight, that was certain. Blanche looked up and down the street, wishing desperately that Rose would come by on her way home from school. But there was no sign of her sister. *Oh, where was Rose when you needed her?*

But before she could figure out what to do next, a car pulled to a stop right in front of her. Rob Tirsch was in the front passenger seat with two other guys, Tom and Lester.

"What's up, girls?" He leaned out the window at them, grinning. He looked handsome, wearing sunglasses and a sleeveless blue shirt.

"We're just talking with Blanche here," Eileen said.

"Want a ride?" Rob flashed a smile at Blanche.

Blanche ignored his charm. "Look, I have to go and meet my sister."

Rob shrugged. "So we'll give you a ride there—get in."

"C'mon, Blanche, let's go with them." Eileen took Blanche's arm. Rob threw the back door open, Lisa grabbed Blanche's other arm, and the two girls pushed and pulled her into the car. Almost before Blanche realized what had happened, they were in the traffic and accelerating down the main road.

Mr. Freet apparently walked a good deal, because he didn't slacken his pace for at least ten blocks. By that time, Rose was winded, but she didn't dare stop. She kept on, making certain she maintained a safe distance between him and herself. Goodness, in this blue and purple outfit, she would stand out a mile if he noticed her.

The neighborhoods they were passing were getting more and more upscale, which was some comfort. She supposed they were getting near his house.

The house. The house of a dwarf. What would it be like to enter the house of a dwarf?

Her quarry rounded a corner, and remembering how they had lost Bear this way before, she hurtled after him. Luckily, she had the sense to pause at the corner and look casually around it. Mr. Freet had climbed the steps of a tall old brownstone and was unlocking the door. Even as Rose watched, he disappeared inside.

She felt her adrenaline begin to pump in earnest now. What should she do? At last, crossing herself and murmuring a prayer, she walked slowly down the street, casting nonchalant glances at the houses on either side. Passing Mr. Freet's house, she noted that all the curtains were drawn and that there were bars over all the windows. An alley ran down one side of the house, and she could see basement windows, barred as well.

Uncertain of what to do now, Rose went stealthily into the alleyway, edged around the trash cans and recycling bins standing there, and looked at the windows. The first floor windows were too high for her to see into, and besides, they were covered by blinds. At her feet, the basement windows were curtained in black cloth. She heard a noise coming from the basement. Quickly she knelt down and listened at the window. Someone was in the basement, talking, but the voice was too muffled to make out.

Remembering a trick she had read about prisoners using, she went to the recycling bin and selected a tin can that seemed mostly clean. Then she huddled by the window, noiselessly set the can's closed end against the glass, and put her ear to the other end. The can smelled strongly of seafood, but at least it magnified the echoes so she could begin to make out more sounds.

Someone was speaking in a low, harsh voice. None of the words were clear, but Rose thought she caught "useless," "priest" and "easily." Then, a moment later, the words "Speak up!" There was the sound of a sharp thud, as though someone had hit a sack of grain with a stick. To her horror, Rose heard a response—a dull, inarticulate moan.

It sounded as though Mr. Freet was beating someone. Yes, that must be it. Rose heard his voice begin again, more insistently, angrily. Then, there was silence. More blows resounded through the can, and Rose heard again the indistinct, agonized groans beneath each one. Even though they were almost inaudible, each one resonated achingly in Rose's ear.

"So, what were you talking about?" Rob lounged back in his seat, looking back at the three girls over his tanned arm. "Girl stuff?"

"Blanche has been telling us about her friend, Bear, right, Blanche?" Eileen prodded her. Blanche's heart was beating quickly, and she could find no words to say. Was she being kidnapped? How did one behave when one was kidnapped? She remembered too clearly what had happened to Rose after the prom.

"Yeah, I'm interested in this Bear guy, too," Rob said, lighting up a cigarette. He smiled at Blanche. "You guys dating?"

"What's going on?" Blanche asked, finding her voice suddenly in a burst of panic. "I want you to drop me off right now."

Rob toyed with his cigarette. "Calm down. I don't think we can do that just yet."

"What do you mean, you can't? What's going on?" she asked.

Rob leaned forward, an earnest look on his face. "Well, it's very simple, Blanche. There's this guy—I don't know his name—who is paying cash for any information about an Arthur Denniston who calls himself Bear. The guy wants to get him a message or something. Now, we haven't been able to find Bear, but we all know that you know him. So, we just want you to tell us where he is."

"But I don't know where he is," Blanche insisted. They had to let her go—they *would* let her go, wouldn't they?

Rob shrugged. "We're perfectly willing to split the cash with you. It's a lot of money—and it's nothing illegal."

Would it help if she pretended to cooperate? "What's this message you're supposed to give Bear?" Blanche asked thickly.

"Well, now, I don't know if I should tell you that unless you're willing to tell me where I can find Bear. I sort of have an interest in this deal, myself, you know," Rob smirked.

What could she tell him and get off safely? If she told them anything, how much would she be harming Bear?

"Why does this guy want to know about Bear?" she asked, trying to think.

Rob shrugged. "I really don't know, but I doubt it's anything bad. You don't need to be afraid you're betraying him or anything." He waved his cigarette in the air, then tossed it out the window.

"Now, really, Blanche, can't we work out some sort of deal?" He took off his sunglasses and looked at her with serious blue eyes, their black lashes and dark brows a compelling contrast. He had never looked so handsome and earnest before to Blanche.

Thoughts flitted across her mind like butterflies. The deeper reality. What was *really* going on here?

The only thing she could say was, "You're an evil prince."

"What?" Rob gaped at her incredulously.

"You're an evil prince," Blanche said, shaking her hair back from her face. "And I'm not going to tell you anything."

Everyone in the car laughed at her. Rob's good looking face hardened into an unpleasant mask. "You're a real weirdo, you know that, Blanche?"

"She's always been weird," Eileen said contemptuously. Lisa was coughing and laughing at the same time.

For some reason, their jeers no longer bothered Blanche. She realized that she had ceased to care what they thought of her.

Rob kept staring out of the front of the car. Finally, he turned around and said to Blanche in a warning tone, "Look, Brier, we'll give you one more chance to come in with us on this deal. Otherwise, things aren't going to be so nice and you'll regret it."

She already knew that, but there was nothing else she could do. When she merely gazed back at him, he cursed and turned around. "Okay," he said to the driver, Tom. "Let's go meet the guy."

"What about her?" Eileen said.

Rob leaned back and surveyed Blanche with a shrewd

smile. "We'll just take her with us," he said. "Maybe he can make her talk."

Rose hunched down closer to the ground, continuing her secret eavesdropping. After an unbearable length of time, the beating stopped and there was silence for a while. Then the low voice said something about "ways of finding out." There was the sound of feet pounding up steps, getting softer and softer. After that, there was silence.

The front door of the house banged open, and Rose started, caught herself, and froze. She heard someone come down the steps and caught a glimpse of Mr. Freet passing by the alleyway, a hard, merciless look on his face.

Breathing as hard and softly as she dared, she crept out of the alley and peered down the street after Mr. Freet. He turned the corner and vanished.

She waited only a moment before she went to see if there was a door in the brick wall surrounding the back yard of the house. There was a high, ornate iron gate, but of course, it was locked. Inside the gate, she could see a small garden. Feeling fey, reckless, but strangely calm, she narrowed her eyes and gauged the height of the wall. It wasn't any higher than the wire fence around the town tennis court she had occasionally shinnied over back home.

Why am I doing this? she thought fleetingly as she hiked up her skirt, and put a foot in a small opening in the iron scrollwork. She didn't answer the question, because, being Rose, she was comfortable with letting those questions be. With practiced skill, she grasped the side of the doorpost, and pulled herself up onto the wall.

After a few unsuccessful tries, she got a leg over the

brick wall and scrambled down inside the garden, landing in a patch of thyme. The enclosed space seemed to be a cultivated mixture between English and Japanese gardens, with exotic bushes and peculiar herbs. Rose saw a miniature tree, a stone idol, and a Greek pillar as she looked around. But there was no time to explore. Lightly, swiftly, she ran to the back entrance, hoping without much optimism that it was open.

There was no knob on the door. Instead, a green light off to one side glowed balefully over a number code pad. It was one of those new computerized security locks.

Facing this technological dragon's eye, she paused, deliberating, cueing her own eyes to green as she did so. So there was a code—a riddle for the dragon. Very well. She licked her lips.

For a moment she floundered in the face of thousands of possible mathematical combinations. But, regaining her equilibrium, she forced herself to remember the larger picture. Mr. Freet was a dwarf—an atheist who mocked the Church, and all things holy. What sort of code might he use for his lair?

Striking out on an inspiration, her finger pushed the keypad three times—six, six, six. There was a brief click and the door swung open. Rose stared in astonishment, momentarily forgetting her crusade. *The unbelievable arrogance of that man!*

> "Whatever gets into the hands of one of these vile dwarves, does not easily see the light of day again."
>
> —Grimm

Chapter 17

INSIDE THE HOUSE, Rose caught a glimpse of dark, shadowed splendor. She cracked the door a bit wider. A large alabaster dog stood a few feet away, gazing at her. The room beyond was a carpeted, curtained parlor crammed with all sorts of ornamental statues and bric-a-brac. Yes, Mr. Freet was a hoarder, all right.

She paused on the threshold, trying to regather her store of caution. Ironically, she felt the same as she had in the doorway of Rob's parents' bedroom. *This could be a trap. A trap,* conscience warned.

But the situation at hand was completely different. She wasn't acting out of vanity, or refusal to think. She was entering what might be her river of blood—deliberately.

Her courage rallied, and without further question she stepped inside.

The sullen silence in the car continued. Tom, whom Blanche recognized as one of the boys who had attacked Bear on prom night, drove on moodily. They were still in the Bronx, somewhere near the Expressway. No one spoke as they turned onto a side street and headed for the industrial park cluster nearby. Blanche could hear Lisa swearing repeatedly under her breath. Eileen stared straight ahead with a fixed expression on her face.

Blanche still found it almost impossible to breathe freely. *Where were they taking her? What were they going to do to her?* She tried to rein in her terrified imagination, and felt that somehow things would be easier if she could simply acknowledge the fact that something horrible might happen to her instead of repeatedly insisting that she was still safe. She pulled the pink calico skirt of her jumper more tightly over her knees, glad for what she was wearing. She'd have felt far more vulnerable if this had happened when she was wearing her prom dress.

The car pulled into the deserted parking lot of a warehouse complex near the highway ramps. Realizing that her jaw had been clenched for the past ten minutes, she attempted vainly to relax.

They were in a narrow stretch between several huge storage buildings, blocked in on three sides. Directly ahead of the car, three closed doors looked out onto a raised loading platform, that stood prominently in the middle of the courtyard, like an executioner's scaffold. Blanche quickly glanced back at the open side and saw an empty field. Beyond it was the highway.

Tom stopped the car. "Should we get out?" he asked.

"Yeah, whatever," Rob said abruptly. "Bring her, too." The guys got out. Lisa opened her door, and pulled Blanche out, with Eileen, still keeping a grip on Blanche's other arm, following. Rob walked towards the platform and sat down on the edge, his back to the wall and legs hanging down. The two other guys lounged by the car, lighting cigarettes.

Rob smiled at Blanche as the girls brought her towards him, apparently having decided to keep up the facade of charm.

"Have a seat," he said to her, and Lisa and Eileen sat, forcing Blanche to sit between them. Rob lit up a cigarette and glanced at Blanche, sideways.

"Smoke, Blanche?"

She shook her head.

He smiled and blew smoke in the air. "Might have guessed. You don't do very much, do you?"

I guess not, Blanche answered him in her mind. *Not by your standards.*

"What do you do, sit at home all day, sewing?" Lisa asked derisively. "Give me the pack, Rob. I need a smoke. My nerves are shot."

"Relax, Leez. There's nothing to be uptight about. We're just going to give Blanche some higher education."

"I thought you said we're meeting someone here."

"We are. He'll do the teaching." Rob looked at Blanche calculatingly with his cobalt eyes and took another drag. "Do I scare you, Blanche?"

"Oh, she's scared, Robbie. You can trust the Immaculate Complexion to be scared. She just doesn't know anything," Lisa complained, blowing out smoke and coughing.

"Well, I think she does." Rob continued to stare a bit mockingly at Blanche.

Lisa was irritated. "This whole setup is so stupid. This guy'll give her the third degree for nothing, and then he'll have something to hang over our heads because *we* brought her here. Ever think of that?"

"Shut up, Lisa," Eileen said abruptly. The other girl had been keeping quiet, but she seemed to be as nervous as Lisa was.

"Leez, don't even try and think. It's bad for a brain like yours." Rob pulled his sunglasses back over his face and tossed the empty cigarette pack on the ground. "Besides, Blanche's sister owes me something. This will be a lesson for her, too."

Sister. Blanche felt a new pang of apprehension. *I wonder where she is right now*, she thought. And, glancing at her captors, she prayed, *I hope she's safely at home.*

What Rose needed was to find the door to the basement. She surveyed the two doors leading out of the parlor. Feeling as though she was having to choose between the lady and the tiger, she finally tiptoed through the right-hand one into a carpeted hallway. She passed a library room stocked with books. Next to it was a staircase. A life-sized stone boy, naked, with angel's wings stood in the stairwell. His hand held out an ashtray, and his empty eyes gazed at her sardonically. She inched past him, a bit unnerved.

The passageway ended in a narrow dining room. Stepping inside, she gaped at the high ceiling, which was covered with a canopy of what looked like a golden fishnet. Its ends came down one side of the wall in a graceful swag with silver weights dangling on the ends of ropes. There was a gleaming table with marble candlesticks set against one wall, and elaborate walnut chairs stood pontificating in each of the four corners. Through an archway, she could see the front room.

In that room stood a grand piano next to the entrance.

Golden candelabra stretched toward the ceiling on either side. A stone fireplace dominated the other end of the room, its mantelpiece crowded with golden statues, carved idols, and tall candlesticks. But there was no sign of a basement door.

She retraced her steps back to the parlor quickly, hoping that she could find the door before Mr. Freet returned. Time to try the second parlor door.

It led her into a small, dark kitchen, plain and drab by comparison, with walnut cabinets and a huge refrigerator. Stealing across the room, at last she located the basement door, almost hidden behind the huge painted face of a tribal mask. The only reason it caught her eye was because there were two heavy draw-bolts on it. Almost not breathing, she pulled them aside and opened the door. The dim light in the kitchen showed a few wooden steps going down into darkness.

There was no light switch.

Bold as she was, Rose hated walking into a dark place without any light. Mentally stretching a hand to God for guidance, she took a deep breath and stepped down into the musty blackness, holding onto the handrail for support.

After about thirteen cautious steps down, she reached a concrete floor. Once again she felt for a switch, and this time she found one. When she flipped it on, a small paneled room was illumined, with two doors. Both were locked. But before she could decide what to do next, she noticed another passageway which opened underneath the steps. Its door was open, and Rose felt instinctively that this was where her search would end.

Into yet another black place. Shivering, she felt again for a switch, and her fingers brushed a small one.

Gold. The warm honey glow from a hundred shining surfaces greeted her in that one click. Up and down the sides of the small chamber were rows of felt-covered black shelves, holding dozens and dozens of shimmering yellow vessels: chalices, ciboriums, patens, censers, cruets, goblets, and cups. Spots of cool emerald, fiery ruby, and icy sapphire glinted here and there, everywhere.

Even though Rose had preternaturally expected to find a treasure hoard in Mr. Freet's basement, its actual existence and stunning majesty dumbfounded her. Feeling a bit small and paltry in the face of such splendor, she timidly stepped forward to get a closer look at the vessels on the shelves.

Many of them were precious, but some of them apparently not. The less valuable ones, discolored or dented, were crowded on the lower shelves. She even saw some gold-flowered brandy glasses among them. But most of the vessels were in fine condition: tall high chalices decorated with silver overlay, vases inlaid with gems. There was a small table in the middle of the room where a matching ciborium and a chalice stood, more elaborate than all the rest, the king and queen of the collection.

A faint moan made her whirl around, and a shudder ran through her as she remembered her purpose in coming here.

The sound came from the far side of the room, still shrouded in darkness, where she could make out a pillar and a dark bulk at its base.

Rose forced herself to move forward one more time into the blackness, and stretched out her hands. After she had gone two steps, her hand touched a human cheek, and she stifled an involuntary scream.

The cheek was warm, and stubbled, and as her fingertips traveled down it, she felt a twisted piece of cloth where the mouth should be. Another barely audible sound came from the figure.

Now she knelt down and felt the form of the person with both hands. Her fingers brushed over damp flannel cloth and tight hemp ropes. Quickly she worked her way back up to the head and felt around the back of the head for the knot that tied the gag. It was difficult to undo the knot in the dark, but somehow she managed, leaning over with her face close to the dark figure, feeling his harsh, strained breath.

Once the gag was off, he coughed and gasped for a few minutes before anything else became coherent. "Who are you?" Rose kept asking.

At last he managed to speak. "I should ask you that," he rasped. Then, "The light's behind me on the pillar. Turn it on."

She groped, found a round button light, and pushed it. The light clicked on. Two large brown masculine eyes looked into hers. They were familiar, but unfamiliar. Their owner was young, long-haired, and his thin face was bruised, bloody, and very pale. Thick ropes tied him to the pillar as he slouched on a small stool. He looked exhausted.

"Hello again, violinist," he said in a hoarse voice. "Fancy meeting you here."

The group of teenagers continued to sit at the back of the warehouse, smoking, while the sun climbed across the sky towards the west.

"Is this guy showing up at all?" Eileen said at last. "This is getting to be a drag."

"How the heck should I know?" Rob sounded annoyed as

he lit another cigarette. Blanche was beginning to be afraid of what would happen when they ran out of cigarettes.

"Let's just take off," Lisa said.

"Look, I'm not leaving and I don't want to be stuck here with Blanchey girl," Rob said, aggravated.

"What, can't handle her? Then why don't we just tie her up and leave her here with you?" Lisa asked irritably. "This deal stinks."

Lester scratched the back of his head. "Not a bad idea. You could just say it was a joke if anyone else showed up."

Rob looked ticked off. "Look, all we've got to do is wait for the guy to get here."

"The guy is not here," Eileen said in a high voice.

"He will be."

"Hey, Lester, you got any rope?" Lisa asked.

"There's some in the car." Lester lifted his shades and fixed a pair of cruel eyes on Blanche.

"Cut it out!" Rob said. "No one's getting out of this!"

Blanche licked her dry lips. A thought occurred to her— if she dared to make a run for it, she might be able to get out of the courtyard and into the open field beyond, which was visible to the highway. Anyone could see her there, and she might be able to flag down a car.

I'd better do something soon, she realized. She couldn't tell if they were joking about tying her up, but if they decided to (and they very well might) that would end her chances of escape.

Hoping for just a scrap of courage, she began to pray.

"Fish?" Rose said, bewildered, finally recognizing the prisoner as the young derelict she had met in the park.

"Yeah, it's me. What the devil are you doing here, Rose?"

"I followed Mr. Freet home from school and—"

"Ah. Dangerous of you. He's coming back any minute. You'd better get out."

"But can't I—"

"You can try to untie me if you want. But I'm afraid Freet did a thorough job."

"It looks like it," Rose admitted. Fish's wrists were each tied separately around the pillar by ropes tied to the opposite elbows. His ankles were tied to the stool he was sitting on, and more ropes across his chest tied him to the pillar.

"Look, if you want to help me, untie my shoes."

"Why?"

"Just do it. Quickly!"

Rose hurriedly knelt and fumbled for the boy's shoes. He wore heavy sneakers, whose laces were tied in double knots. She undid them as quickly as possible.

"There!" she said. "What was that for?"

"It doesn't matter. Now just get out of here!"

She would have questioned him further, but just then, there was the sound of a door opening upstairs.

"Quick, hide! There's a place beneath the stairs. Wait, the lights!"

Mr. Freet seemed to be busy with something upstairs, so Rose punched the pillar switch and dashed across the room to flick off the other. Then she dove into the area beneath the stairs and huddled behind some boxes, her heart thumping wildly.

It was no use, she realized. Mr. Freet would see the open bolts on the cellar door and know he had been invaded. All she could do now was pray.

She heard his footsteps pause at the top of the steps for what seemed an eternity. Slowly, Mr. Freet began to come down the steps. Rose thought he would never reach the ground. Then she heard him beginning to walk towards their room.

Suddenly the lights on the rows of shelves came on, and Rose could see Mr. Freet's sharp profile against the glow as he stood there, his eyes gleaming like tiny gems. He held a gun in one hand with a silencer screwed on the muzzle. She did not dare to move, or breathe.

"Well, Benedict, I see you had a visitor," he said impassively.

There was a faint mumble from Fish.

"Someone talked to you, I see," Mr. Freet said, and for a moment Rose thought he had noticed the shoe laces. "They must have cared enough about you to risk hearing what you might have to say."

Fish laughed sarcastically, "Oh, you're wrong. Maybe I got the gag out myself."

"Don't lie to me, boy. Isn't that supposed to be a sin?" Still holding the gun, Mr. Freet walked towards him, scrutinizing the room around them.

"Whoever it was left, so you don't need to worry," Fish said.

"Ah. And who might it have been?"

"Could have been one of your drug flunkies. I wish he'd have untied me, but the guy just laughed at me and left. He didn't seem too surprised to see me," Fish went on, incredibly natural. "Do you do this sort of thing all the time?"

"As if I'd be such a fool," Mr. Freet said contemptuously. "I've already regretted half a dozen times since I nabbed you that I didn't strangle you right off. Kidnapping is far more trouble than it's worth."

"Far more trouble than robbery and murder, I suppose you mean," Fish said pleasantly. "Although you intend to end this episode with murder, I don't doubt."

He gave a sharp gasp and Rose guessed that Freet had grabbed a handful of his hair.

"Sooner than you think, altar boy, if you don't tell me the truth about what just happened."

"Fine. Don't believe me. I knew you'd only start torturing me again, whatever I said," Fish gave a strangled sigh. "You're a terribly suspicious man, Freet."

"We're too much alike, Benedict. That's why we've always hated each other."

"Yes," Fish coughed, and Rose hoped that Mr. Freet had let him go. Fish continued, "It was a shame I didn't have a more natural liking for you. I might have suspected you earlier. But out of some bloody spirit of charity on my part, I kept giving you the benefit of the doubt."

"You never suspected the degenerate atheist of murder? I find that hard to believe," Mr. Freet scoffed. "You're far too trusting."

"Yes. I had no idea your differences with Father Raymond went beyond theological arguments." Rose had a feeling he was trying to distract Freet, to give her the chance to get away. He went on, "If I'd had the least idea how much you disliked him, yes, we might have added you to the suspect list."

"Boy detectives," Freet taunted. "Hot shot rich kids. It was a pitiful effort on your part."

"Oh, I don't know. We got you scared, didn't we? We must have done something to deserve two eight-balls of crack in our lockers. Or was that your brother's doing?"

"My brother is an idiot," Mr. Freet said evenly. "He

didn't have the slightest notion of what I was up to—he still doesn't! All he cares about is politics, bureaucracy, degrees, and academic standards. He's still living in the sixties, trying to change the world. He has no idea what's *really* going on."

Freet went on, moodily. "My brother thought that Father Raymond was a backward medievalist priest. I knew better. I can spot someone with an eye for true beauty like he had. If it weren't for his superstitious preoccupation with religion I could have gotten on pretty well with him. But because of his pious obstinacy, he refused to sell his precious vessels to anyone who was not a priest. Maddening! But he wasn't as religious as he seemed. He used his devotion to the Church as a mask for his greed. Yes, he had the same desire I did—for gold, for rarity. He was just able to disguise it with some godly piffle about the 'treasures of the Church.' At least I didn't hypocritically hide my fetish for gold. So, we two hoarders had an inevitable gentleman's quarrel—a duel—over our private appetites. He lost, I'm sorry to say. And the duel would have ended if you two fresh-faced schoolboys hadn't rushed in to pick up the gauntlet."

"What else did you expect us to do?" Fish asked with subdued mirth. "It's amazing how much you understand, Freet, and yet how much you're deluded."

"Paugh! You're the deluded one. Do you think that your mentor's attachment to gold was anything more than the naked sin of greed? You probably don't recognize it, but I do. And you can't pretend that his affection for your mother extended further than monetary gain. Oh, now I've wounded your youthful pride, but it's true. I know how the clergy work. It's simply astonishing how many dying ladies end up signing over whole fortunes to the Roman Church due to some lily-faced priest they met before surgery. It goes on all the time. He got what he wanted out of your mother, don't doubt that."

For the first time, Fish sounded piqued. "You're wrong if you think so. My mother gave hardly a hundred dollars to the church before she died. And St. Lawrence never got the grants that she had planned to give, because of my dad."

"Yes, sensible agnostic that he is. He seized the purse strings, didn't he, when your little detective game fell through? Why did you keep up the pointless crusade? I suppose you still hoped to get back into Dad's good graces? It didn't work out so well, did it?" Mr. Freet chuckled unkindly.

"If you're trying to provoke me, Freet, it isn't working. I gave up on my reputation the moment you pulled the gun on me in the alley. The only thing I'm concerned about at this point is my soul."

"Still the saint, Benedict? Devout Catholics are so amusing. You'd be astounded at how much fun I have with them."

Rose had gotten to her feet and inched out of her hiding place. Now, she moved towards the door as quickly as she dared. Suddenly there was a whiz and a bullet ricocheted off the cement floor just in front of her, hitting a chalice on the shelf with a clang. She ran around the corner and tore up the cellar steps.

Mr. Freet was in close pursuit behind her. Breathing hard, she ran through the kitchen to the parlor and yanked at the door. It was locked and bolted. Out-maneuvered! But there was the front door.

She dodged out the other door as Mr. Freet barreled

into the parlor, sending another bullet after her from his silencer-equipped gun. Pelting down the hallway, she leapt into the dining room and was halfway across when she slipped. Stumbling to her feet, she caught sight of her pursuer in the doorway, giving the fishnet swag a yank.

Without warning, it rained heavy gold around her and she was crushed to the floor by the weight of the net. When she tried to leap to her feet, she was caught, tripped, and fell again, entangled in the meshes.

With a smirk on his face, Mr. Freet advanced towards her, still brandishing the gun.

"My, what a pretty minnow I've caught," he said. "Now sit still and tell me what you're doing here, or I'll put a bullet through your redheaded skull."

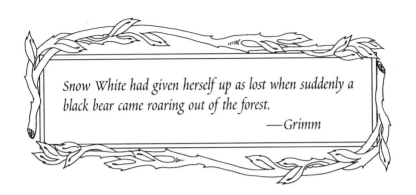

Snow White had given herself up as lost when suddenly a black bear came roaring out of the forest.

—Grimm

Chapter 18

TRAPPED, ROSE ceased her efforts to free herself and sat still under the net, watching Mr. Freet's face. The face was the same as it usually looked—withered, arrogant, but there was an unkindness there now, unmasked, that Rose thought she should have recognized before.

"Explain yourself," Mr. Freet repeated, waving the gun at her.

What should she say? Could she risk telling him the truth? Or would she be playing into his hands, giving him more of an advantage over Fish and Bear than he already had?

Taking a deep breath, she said at last, "I'm not doing anything, Mr. Freet. I just followed you home from school —on an impulse."

"Oh?" Mr. Freet squinted at her. She could tell he didn't believe her.

"Yes," Rose said simply. "I get these impulses from time to time, and I just know I'm supposed to follow them. I heard you and your brother talking about chalices through the heating vent, and I decided to follow you home."

Mr. Freet thrust out his hand and seized the back of her neck, pinching it tightly. "And why," his voice rasped in her ear, "were you interested in chalices?"

Rose struggled to maintain her composure. "It was a mad impulse," she said truthfully. "My sister says I am far too inquisitive. I suppose she's right."

He continued to squeeze her neck, as if trying to force the story out of her, but she let herself remain limp in his hands, enduring the pinch. It was probably better that he thought she was crazy than to discover her connection with Bear.

"How'd you get in here?" he demanded.

"I guessed your code," she admitted. "Six-six-six."

With a short laugh, he released her. "So, you are fey, then?" he said. "I could have guessed that about you and your milk-faced sister. Mooning around with your big eyes and prattling about Chesterton. You two are different from the typical adolescent imbeciles—unnatural changelings. I should have expected that you'd go out of your way to make trouble for me with your insane ways."

He began to yank a rope free from the net. "This divine madness of yours is going to cost you your life now, do you realize that?"

Rose gave a small sigh. "Curiosity killed the cat," she remarked, even as she wondered how quickly you died from strangulation and if it hurt very much.

Mr. Freet gave her a harsh grimace. "Those were my very next words. But unfortunately, I'll need you alive just a bit longer." He slid a hand under the net and jerked her wrists toward him. "Keep still," he warned her, tucking his gun under one arm and beginning to tie her hands with the rope. "You overheard my little conversation with Benedict. I need to interrogate him further, and you, my mad maiden, are going to help me. I'm afraid neither of you will enjoy it."

There was a pause in the conversation. No one was holding onto Blanche now. Lisa had her arms folded and looked angry. Eileen had closed her eyes. Blanche tried to figure out which of the guys was looking at her. As they were all wearing sunglasses, this was difficult. Was this the moment? Should she chance it?

At last, Lester lay down on the other end of the platform and shut his eyes. Rob asked Tom for a cigarette, and both of them started fiddling in their pockets for a lighter. She sprang to her feet and ran.

She heard shouts as she dodged around the car and ran like mad for the gap between the two buildings. She felt footsteps pounding after her. She saw the gap, coming closer, closer—

A hand—two hands—caught her around the shoulders and yanked her backwards. She kicked, fought against the two arms desperately. It was Rob. She screamed.

"Yeah, real cool, Blanche. You're going to get it now." He twisted her arms behind her back. Recklessly, she dug her nails into one arm and he yelped and let go. But the next minute he had grabbed a handful of her hair and jerked her head backwards. She screamed again.

"Shut up!" he fumed, starting to drag her back towards the car. She fought him, but he managed to keep moving back towards the others. "You're going to get it now," he repeated. "I'll tie you up myself!"

Suddenly he yelled in a different voice, "Hey, you guys! Come here, will you?"

Realizing that the others weren't coming to help him, she seized the time and began to kick viciously at his legs. He cursed her roundly, and then twisted back towards the car. "What's the matter with you jerks? Come here!"

Blanche heard the sounds of car doors slamming and an engine gunning. She tried to bolt, but Rob locked an arm around her neck and squeezed.

"Where are you going?" he howled at his friends. Blanche gasped for breath, twisted around, and numbly saw someone running across the field towards them. She barely had time to recognize who it was before he was upon them.

Mr. Freet dragged Rose back into the treasure room by her bound wrists. She caught a glimpse of Fish's face, and, though he gave her a crooked smile, his eyes were grim. Before Rose could even acknowledge it, Mr. Freet snarled and slapped her on the side of the head with his gun.

The unexpected blow made her stagger and fall. As she lay there, her temple smarting, she vaguely heard Fish cursing Freet.

Mr. Freet laughed. "So you're one of those boys whose manhood is wounded by the sight of suffering females? Just as I thought. That smack I gave her was to punish you for trying to evade my questions."

"That's how cowards operate," Fish snapped, but Rose could see his face was white. "If you want to hit someone, hit me."

"Oh, I can see that hitting her will be much more effective for getting an answer out of you," Mr. Freet said, dragging Rose to her feet. Dazed, she became aware of something wet trickling down her cheek and wondered if it was blood. Mr. Freet shoved her into a chair and began to tie her down. Fish was looking at her with an odd expression, breathing hard. She realized that, despite his stoicism, he was frightened of what was going to happen to her next. For his sake, she attempted a reassuring smile, and felt her own apprehension lessen.

Rob found two huge hands clenching his shirt collar and Bear's face a nose away from his. "Let go of her," Bear snarled.

Rob obediently let Blanche crumple into a painful heap on the ground.

Bear's face was red with rage. "I could thrash you within an inch of your life," he growled into the other boy's terrified face. "But you almost aren't worth it."

With that, Bear hurled him onto the ground. Rob landed with an "oof!" as his friends roared out of the parking lot in their car, not looking back.

Blanche found herself once more wrapped in a pair of arms, this time far more tenderly. She felt Bear's hand press her head against his chest.

"How'd you find me?" she asked, still panting.

Bear was stroking his fingers across her cheek. "I saw them shove you into the car. I just couldn't follow you fast enough on foot. But I know the meeting place these creatures use, so I made my way here as fast as I could. Not very fast, but fast enough, apparently."

He stiffened and let go of her suddenly. "You—stop right there!"

She turned to see that Rob had started to skulk away. But under Bear's finger, he froze, quivering, and sat on the ground.

Bear's anger was still blazing as he loomed over the boy. "So are you going to explain this stunt to me—kidnapping and all—or will I have to throttle you a bit first?"

Rob looked as though he were going to cry. "It wasn't my idea, honest!" He swore a bit, morosely, and was silent.

"You'd better explain."

"He said there was a man paying for information about you," Blanche interjected in a low voice, afraid of what Bear might do to Rob if Rob didn't talk.

"And I suppose you thought that picking on Blanche would get you a little extra cash—is that it?" Bear asked.

Rob protested. "All the guy wanted was to get you a message—"

"He's the same guy who was paying for information?" Bear asked.

"Well, yeah, and we thought Blanche might want to go in on it. So we took her for a ride to talk about it. I offered to split the money with her. That's all."

"And she turned you down, didn't she?" Bear shot a grim look at Blanche. "So what's the message?"

Rob kicked at the ground he was sitting on. "It was just that you're in trouble with someone who's been talking with your brother, and he wants you to drop off package number three at St. Lawrence's tonight."

Blanche saw Bear's face grow ashen. He said nothing for a long minute. Then at last he said ominously, "What else?"

"Nothing, I swear. I've never seen the guy. Never really

saw his face. A short guy. He had on a hooded sweatshirt and shades. That's all I know. I swear."

Bear reached down to the ground and picked up something—Rob's sunglasses. He looked at them in disgust and threw them at Rob's feet. "Get out of here."

Rob got to his feet and was halfway across the field in the next minute.

Bear turned to Blanche. His face was taut, and he looked much older. His voice was brusque. "Blanche, I've got to go take care of this business at St. Lawrence. I need you to do something very important for me."

"Anything, Bear," she said softly, fearful at how he looked.

"Good. Do you have money for a ride home?"

"Yes."

"Let's get to a street where I can call you a taxi to make sure you get home safe." He began walking very quickly towards the highway. Blanche hurried to keep up with his stride, her head whirling with relief and a new anxiety. In a few minutes they reached the highway ramps. Bear held her hand as they crossed the traffic and reached the sidewalk beyond, where a strip of stores began.

"Either a taxi or a pay phone will do for me right now," he said.

"What's going on, Bear?" she ventured to ask.

"Don't worry about it," he said gruffly. "It'll be over soon. Everything will be fine."

They found a pay phone at a corner store, and Bear dialed a taxi service. Then he drew her close to him, slipping a hand beneath his light jacket. As he hugged her, she felt him press a package against her hands. It was heavy. "Put it beneath your jumper right now and keep your hands over it. I don't want anyone to see it."

Fear shot through her. "It's not—drugs, is it?"

He kissed her forehead gently. "No, Snow White, it's not. It's nothing illegal at all, just something that's very special to me. It was special to Father Raymond, too. I heard from Stevenson that you know all about him now."

Blanche slid the package through the wide armholes of her jumper and held it there with her hands. "But I don't understand what you're doing—"

"Good. That's how I want it. Now, chin up. It'll be over soon," he smiled at her. Then unexpectedly pain flashed over his face and he hugged her fiercely. "Don't worry about me at all."

She found her lips trembling, "But I am worried!" she cried.

He laughed and rocked her gently to and fro against himself. She clutched the dead weight of the package in her arms and buried her head in his arms. He was saying something softly, " 'All shall be well, and all shall be well, and all manner of things shall be well.' "

There was nothing more to say. At last he let her go, and resumed his abrupt manner. "Look, I don't want you to hold onto this thing any longer than you have to. Put it in a safe deposit box or something. Or, better yet, mail it to someone you can trust who will keep it safe. It's—well, it's pretty valuable."

"I could mail it to my mom's sister in California," Blanche said, trying to play a thinking part.

"Good. Better yet, don't tell me where you're sending it. Just get it out of your possession and into some secure place. If worse comes to worst, you can send it to the Pope in Rome."

"But won't you want it back?" she couldn't help saying.

His eyes flickered. "Ah, maybe. I'll let you know." He looked past her. "Here comes your taxi."

He waved to the driver, opened the door for her, and gave the man the address. Then he leaned over to Blanche. "Pray for me," he said, his brown eyes burning with strain.

"Bear, can't you stay with me? I'm just terribly afraid," she whispered, holding the package tightly beneath her jumper.

Bear put his large hand on her cheek and looked into her eyes. Softly, he repeated,

> *"The men of the East may spell the stars,*
> *And times and triumphs mark,*
> *But the men signed of the cross of Christ*
> *Go gaily in the dark."*

He straightened up and stood as tall as he had stood that one night when he had taken them to St. Lawrence church. As the cab pulled away, he was still standing there, watching her go. She turned around and followed him with her eyes out of the rear window. As he receded in the distance, she saw him turn around and start to run. He was on his way to his appointment at St. Lawrence.

"Now, Benedict." Mr. Freet's voice came through the gloom. He had turned off all the lights except for one. It was between Rose and Fish, so they could see each other. But Mr. Freet was hidden in the shadows. "We've been over this many times before, and it's time you answered me: where is the paten?"

Fish was silent.

"You know that it's the last piece I need to complete the

set. I have the chalice and ciborium Father Raymond gave you. All I need is that one last piece. Where is it?"

Fish refused to speak.

Mr. Freet repeated the question, and again, Fish gave no answer. Rose saw his breath was coming in short spurts.

Suddenly, a heavy clear plastic bag was whipped over her face and twisted tightly around her neck. It was almost impossible to breathe. She saw Fish flailing in his bonds on the other side, shouting something. Then all at once, the bag was gone and air rushed into her lungs. She gasped in the air and sagged against the ropes tying her to the chair.

Dimly, she heard Fish saying, "Yes, that's the truth. It's around Bear's neck in a package. That's where he keeps it. That's where it was last time I saw it. Damnation, that's the bloody truth."

"You'd better not be lying, Denniston," Mr. Freet's voice threatened.

"I'm not hiding anything," Fish said in an insistent voice.

"I had no idea you were going to prove such a nerveless creature, Benedict. I should have brought a girl along before," Mr. Freet cackled.

Fish's eyelids lowered. "Unlike you, I have some morals."

"Which is why I am getting the better of you now. It's one of the reasons I make it my policy to have none." Mr. Freet came forward, still twisting the plastic bag in his hands. "Where can I find your brother?"

"I don't know," Fish said guardedly. "Don't you touch her again, Freet. I mean it. Bear probably took off when he discovered I was missing. I haven't the least idea where you can find him."

"I'm afraid that's not good enough," Mr. Freet said softly.

"Try St. Lawrence Church. He has the keys for it, just like I do. Or the old warehouse on Inwood Avenue. But more than likely, he's wandering around checking out all the drug hideouts to see if I'm there. That's where you'd find him," Fish said, his voice filled with disgust but his face exposing his anguish.

He's betrayed Bear to save me, Rose thought, and tears suddenly came to her eyes. "Fish, I'm so sorry!" she wailed.

"It doesn't matter," Fish said evenly.

"Oh, he's not telling me anything I don't already know," Mr. Freet sneered. "The keys to St. Lawrence are in my possession now, and I've used them well. What you may not know is that I also have the keys to the tunnel connecting the church with the school. That came in handy a long time ago, when Fr. Raymond was polishing his treasures in the sacristy one night. It might come in handy for trapping your older brother as well."

The silence was broken by a faint beeping sound. Rose turned her head and saw Mr. Freet kneel down beside a suitcase in the corner and open it. He took out a radio device and showed it to Fish, smiling.

"You see, I've done to St. Lawrence what Fr. Raymond should have done a long time ago—set an alarm system on all the doors. Apparently Bear has gotten the message I've been passing along through my various drug channels to meet me in St. Lawrence tonight."

Before Blanche realized it, the cab had halted in front of her house. She paid the driver. Getting out of the cab, her knees felt shaky. She stumbled up the front steps and opened the door with difficulty. Laughing numbly, she thought, *at least I'll have a story to tell Rose.*

But when she opened the apartment door and called, there was no answer. The apartment echoed strangely, and suddenly a wave of fear swept over her. She ran upstairs, downstairs. No one was there.

There were no messages on the machine, no notes. Feeling more and more doubtful, she grabbed the phone and dialed the number at the hospital. She asked for the emergency room and stood, twisting her fingers in the cord anxiously.

"Is Jean Brier there?" she asked the nurse who answered.

"Sorry, ma'am—she just left. Not more than a minute ago."

"Oh," Blanche trembled. She wanted to ask the nurse to run out in the parking lot and find her, to make sure that Mother came straight home instead of going out to do her usual errands. But—

"Sorry, ma'am," the nurse said again.

"That's okay," Blanche said. Maybe it was something silly—Rose had run out to the store and had forgotten to leave a note. She hung up the phone and collapsed onto the couch.

Her eyes fell on the package Bear had given her, which she had left carelessly on the table, a package wrapped in duct tape. She seized it and held it, for fear it would vanish in thin air. *What was it?*

Bear hadn't said she couldn't open it. Shaking, she picked at the duct tape. It had been wrapped a long time ago, and she had a hard time getting the tape off. She ripped off piece after piece. Eventually, she heard the sound of paper tearing, and peeled faster. There was brown paper under the tape, and then plastic bags—

Furiously she dug her way through the grey plastic mass and at last her fingers touched metal. Then, quite easily, a heavy, round, golden plate slid into her fingers.

She blinked and rolled it from hand to hand. It was incredibly magnificent, glistening and sparkling, engraved all over with the most intricate designs. In the center of its bowl was a lamb, inlaid with ivory and silver, with blue stones for eyes, and a halo of tiny rubies around its head.

She continued to roll it from one hand to another, marveling at how it caught the light and threw it back on her face with holy laughter. She found herself smiling in strange amusement as she turned it over and around, feeling its heavy, splendid weight, drinking in its beauty. One of Father Raymond's treasures.

Now she held it still, gleaming and responsively warm in her hands. This must have been the treasure that Father Raymond was killed for.

All at once, the fears she had temporarily forgotten in her childish play came rolling back over her. Bear. *Oh dear God, what horrible errand did he have at St. Lawrence's?*

Rose couldn't move. She felt sweat crawling along her bare arms down towards the ropes on her wrists. Fish sagged against the pillar, looking drained, sucked dry. Apparently he had lost hope for Bear now. More than anything, she wanted to cry.

Mr. Freet rose. "Well, while it would be useful to keep one of you alive in case I need to do more interrogation, I'm afraid two prisoners is simply more than I can handle."

He looked from one to the other, musing. Her throat going dry, Rose guessed what he was going to do.

"If you have to kill one of us, kill me," Fish said, with an edge to his voice.

"Naturally, that's how you'd feel, Benedict," Mr. Freet said mildly. He pulled out a pair of leather gloves and began to put them on.

Rose said nothing, afraid of influencing Mr. Freet the wrong way. She moistened her lips, and waited.

"Freet, you'd better not touch her," Fish said wildly as Mr. Freet took a step towards Rose.

"It's all right," Rose said softly. If she hadn't been there, it would have been Fish whom Freet would have killed. Mr. Freet picked up a roll of duct tape and began to toy with it musingly.

"Come on, Freet, I know you've been dying to get rid of me. Think how happy it'll make you. You hate me so much," Fish said coaxingly, but Rose could see the sweat standing out on his forehead.

Mr. Freet ripped off a piece of duct tape and advanced on Fish with a grim smile. "Exactly," he whispered as he pressed it over the boy's mouth.

Then he turned, picked up the plastic bag, and walked over to Rose.

Fish yelled something incomprehensible through the tape. Rose looked into Freet's eyes once more, and saw that Freet seemed strangely agitated by her gaze. Not wanting him to change his mind, she bowed her head. She heard the rip of duct tape being torn from the roll. His leather-covered fingers pressed the tape over her mouth, and she yielded, taking a deep breath. There was a pause, then he pulled the plastic bag over her head and began to tape it around her neck.

But the men signed of the cross of Christ go gaily in the dark . . .

She dimly heard Fish screaming against his gag and tearing at his bonds as Mr. Freet left the room and pounded up the stairs.

The bear, snarling, rushed on the dwarf and attacked him.
—*Grimm*

Chapter 19

BLANCHE SAT on the couch, staring blankly at the white light of the living room window, unable to think or pray. Bear must be at St. Lawrence by now. What could be happening to him?

If only Mother would come home. She was strong. *If only Rose would come home.* Her sister was full of fire and courage. She'd know what to do. She was the active one. All Blanche could do was sit still, and fear.

She had no idea how long she sat there, her body poised in the act of waiting—for someone to come. For anyone to come.

The jangle of the phone shocked her body into leaping to its feet. Her brain was still murky. She realized she had been in a stupor almost like sleep for at least a half hour.

Shaking, she reached for the phone on the coffee table. "Hello?" she said cautiously.

"Is this Blanche Brier?" a man's strange voice said.

"Who is this?" She was instantly terrified.

"Your friend Bear and I are at St. Lawrence. Bear's decided it would be better for all of us if you brought the package he gave you over here after all."

Blanche could not mistake the threat behind the words. All the breath was knocked out of her.

"By the way, he made this decision when he realized that I have your sister, Rose, in a safe place. I think you'd better bring the package over here right away. Oh, incidentally, don't try calling the police. If anyone else but you comes to the church, things could become very unpleasant for your sister."

Blanche struggled to say something, but no sound came out.

"I'll expect you to leave it in the church vestibule within the next fifteen minutes. If there's any conflict—well, remember what happened to Father Raymond."

A dial tone rang loudly in her ear. Blanche sank to the floor, holding onto the coffee table with both hands. She mustn't faint now, she couldn't!

When at last her head cleared, she looked at the face of the grandfather clock. Her mother wasn't yet home from her errands. Who knew when she would be back?

There wasn't time. There simply wasn't time. With shaking hands, Blanche picked up the paten and pushed it back inside its torn wrappings. There was no time. She felt as though she had dropped out of that whole continuum as she mechanically went to the door, opened it, and shut it tightly behind her.

Mr. Freet was no sooner out of the room when Fish had begun kicking at his untied shoes. In a few seconds he had one off, and began wriggling his foot loose of the ankle bonds. With his free foot, he clawed at the other shoe, kicked it off, and tried to yank his second foot free. He glanced at Rose. She was very still, and seemed to be doing her best to hold her breath, but he knew she would run out of air soon.

At last Fish had both feet out of the ropes. He braced himself against the pillar and kicked at the stool until he succeeded in shoving it out from beneath him. He stood up, and as he had hoped, the ropes around his chest were looser. Apparently they'd been coming loose from all of his struggling. Breathing hard, he began to saw up and down on the ropes, yanking them tightly as he dared. At last, to his relief, he felt them slipping down his arms. One knot must have come loose! Thanking all the saints and angels, he shrugged his shoulders, trying to force one arm free.

His wrists were openly bleeding but Fish struggled with renewed vehemence. Blood was coming into Rose's face as she was forced to take in more air. She wasn't struggling, just sitting calmly, as though waiting for him. Or for death. Fish didn't want to know which would come first.

At last, one elbow was free, and he jerked his arm up, almost dislocating his wrist. *Calm down, get at the knots.* He tried getting his face down to his wrist and nearly had a stroke in the process. *Try again.* This time, he was able to grab the edge of the tape across his mouth. He yanked hard, and with a blistering rip, the tape came loose. Now he seized the knot on his wrist with his teeth and jerked, painfully wrenching his back. The knot loosened. Two more yanks with his teeth, and it came undone.

Desperately Fish used his free hand to pull off the ropes, but still he was tied to the pillar by one arm. Feverishly he worked at the last knot. His fingers seemed to stumble now, as he saw her head drop down, saw her shoulders heave. She was beginning to struggle for breath. *Forever. Forever.* The knot would not yield. Sweat was running down his face freely. "Oh, come on!" he begged the knot. "Come on!"

Suddenly, as though yielding to Fish's voice, the knot gave. He pulled the last rope loose and sprang across the room to Rose, stumbling as he went. In terror, now, seeing her face was blue, he seized the plastic bag and tried to rip it open. His nails were too dull—he couldn't make a tear in it. He seized the corner of the bag with his teeth, and tore off a piece, biting a few strands of hair with it in his fury. He shoved his fingers inside and ripped the plastic bag in two, pulling it off her face.

Her hair and face were damp from her near-suffocation, and her chest heaved even after she was free, as she tried to fill her lungs with air. He ripped off the tape from her mouth, wrapped his arms around her, and pushed her chest in, forcing her lungs to work. She choked, gagging, and finally slumped forward, breathing normally at last.

Fish now had trouble untying the ropes on her wrists and ankles, but eventually the last bit of cord came loose and she collapsed onto the floor. He gathered her into his arms, gently comforting her.

"Are you all right?" he asked her anxiously.

Her eyes focused on him, and she nodded slowly. His tightly drawn lips relaxed a little. They stung, and he realized some skin had come off with the tape.

She looked at him in bewilderment. "You escaped?"

"I'm not called the Fish for nothing," he said with his crooked smile.

With a sigh, she closed her eyes and let her head drop into his lap. Fish looked around the cellar, and said, almost to himself, "I hate to say it, but we're as good as dead if he comes back here."

The paten was in Blanche's hands. The sun was half-sunken in darkening clouds. She walked. The world continued to stand still around her. The darkness had swallowed Bear. And Rose. Mother was not here. There was no one left but her.

Blanche walked straight ahead. There was only one thing she must do, and that was to leave the paten right inside the church doors. The paten that Father Raymond had died to protect. And maybe Bear, now, too. She was going to give it to the man whom they had tried to protect it from. She would do that. After that, nothing else mattered.

Oh God, she called out softly inside. *God.*

She continued to walk.

The men signed of the cross of Christ go gaily.

In the dark.

The shadows were getting longer, even though the sun was far from setting. She walked.

I'm just a china doll. I can't do anything

Her heart had frozen long ago and turned her flesh to stone.

I can't move or I'll break.

It would be very simple. All she had to do was leave the paten and walk away. She never needed to go back.

It was too frighteningly easy.

The towers and spire of St. Lawrence separated themselves from the other buildings around it. She could see the square ugly block of St. Catherine's blotting out most of it.

Go gaily in the dark.

I can't smile. How can you go forth gaily if you can't smile?

She crossed the last street.

She walked past St. Catherine's. She reached the doors of the church and stopped. She looked up at the spires, black against a cloudy sky.

Oh God I can't. Not even this. Please, send someone else.

There is no one else.

She continued to stand there, frozen, as all the fears she had ever experienced in her life came rushing down upon her. She swayed, stumbled, and steadied herself.

It would be easier to faint.

It was wrong, it was wrong. The universe was grossly unjust. Father Raymond had tried to do good, and he was murdered. Bear and his brother had tried to protect the treasures, and they were lost. Rose—where was she? Was she still alive? Why were things this way? You tried to do good and were slapped in the face.

Rose was wrong. If life was really a fairy tale, it was a sick one. Where the ogre gobbled up everyone in the end. She clenched the paten in her hands and felt nauseous.

I have nothing. I have nothing.

She trembled there, feeling her utter insignificance against the dark evil inside the abandoned church. It was wrong of God to let her be the only one left. Why not Rose? Rose would have gone into the church singing in the dark.

She took a step, and realized she had decided.

But I am going into the church, too.

She was going in, but not to surrender. Yes, going into the church was one thing, the only thing she could do.

Rose regained consciousness with a jolt and lifted her head. Fish instantly supported her shoulders.

"Are you feeling better?" he asked.

Rose leaned on him and climbed to her feet unsteadily. "We've got to get out of here. Bear—"

"Yeah, I know." Fish scrambled up and helped her stand. "Can you walk okay?"

"I think so—" Rose took a step and leaned against the pillar for support. "So you're Bear's younger brother?"

"I am," he acknowledged. "By the way, who are you?"

"Rose Brier."

"Ah, one of my brother's lady friends. Yes, I guessed that."

Rose wondered what he meant by that, but there were more pressing things to think about at the moment.

"He's got locks on the cellar door," Fish said. "It's probably hopeless."

"Doesn't he have any tools down here?" Rose cast a glance around at the chalices and treasure.

"I doubt it. He wouldn't be so silly as to leave us a screwdriver or a lever."

"Then there's nothing we can do?" Rose blinked back tears suddenly and felt as though she were going to collapse back onto the floor. For a moment, she actually gave up.

"Hold on, don't faint or anything. Just sit down again." Fish dragged forward the chair she had been tied to and made her sit down. "So how'd you find me here anyhow?"

She knew he was trying to distract her, and she let herself be distracted. "I followed Mr. Freet, like I told you before—" Her voice was shaking and she rubbed away tears from her eyes and tried to calm down. "I listened at the basement windows and I heard him beating someone—"

Something changed in Fish's expression. "There are windows in this basement?"

"Yes." Rose looked around at rows of shelves, suddenly doubtful. "At least on the outside—"

"He's probably just blocked them off, but if you could hear through them, they must be here somewhere." Fish leapt to his feet and began feeling along the walls.

Blanche's hands looked very small, grasping the wrought iron handles. The doors looked as though they were locked. But when she pulled, they opened.

She stepped inside the vestibule, and crossed herself out of habit. After all, it was a church. The heavy door swung shut slowly, and the bar of dim light from outside grew thinner and thinner until it vanished into the grey.

She took another step into the dark and found the doors to the main body of the church. She pulled them open.

According to the murky walls, the sun was as good as down. Inside was a forest of shaded pillars, ghostly outlines of marble statues. The somber light above sent down faint beams through the far-off windows. But most of the church was overborne in black reverberations and emptiness.

Blanche walked forward, the huge canopy of the hollow building stretching over her. Row after row of empty pews passed her by. She continued on, unsure of what to do, moving in and out of the shadows cast by the columns in front of the stained glass windows, with white light shining here and there through missing pieces like broken teeth. Each sound she made was distorted by the echoes.

She reached the sanctuary and stood in front of the marble altar rail. There in the obscure interior of the holy place was something ebon and hulking. At first, her heart stopped in fear, then she recognized it.

"Bear?" she whispered, her voice shaking with panic.

There was a rumble, and a movement. Something clinked against the marble, and the ragged shape raised its head.

"Who's there?" his voice was low, strained. She saw his face, grey and fuzzy in the semi-darkness, with an inky stripe of blood on one cheek.

She went and knelt in front of him. "What happened to you?" He was lying on the floor of the sanctuary with his hands handcuffed around the marble post of the altar rail. His shoulders were sunken, and his eyes were glazed, almost subhuman. She scarcely recognized him.

He stared at her woozily, like a drugged animal. "You shouldn't be here. Go away." The words were only sounds, with no meaning.

"Who did this to you?"

"Black dwarves," he said thickly and buried his shaggy head in his arms. "Go away. I told you to go away."

"Bear—"

There was a subdued snicker from behind. Blanche turned and saw the phantom outline of a man coming towards her. His hand held a gun that gleamed in a patch of light.

"He's suffering from a slight concussion, as you can see," a harsh voice said. "But he won't be suffering much longer."

Rose pushed as hard as she could, while Fish dragged one of the shelves away from the wall. She was amazed at how much of his vitality had returned, even though he was obviously in worse shape than she was, after his imprisonment.

"How are you feeling, Fish?" she asked.

"Not good, but that's a lot better than dead," he answered. "Ah! Yes, you're right—there's windows."

He pulled on something, and there was the sound of tape ripping. Suddenly the failing evening light poured into their cell from a small rectangular pane that had been hidden by black cloth and padding taped to the wall.

"But there's bars on them," Rose reminded him, her sudden hope quickly dying.

He looked at her with an amused expression. "Yes, I noticed that."

Blanche straightened herself and tried to force her eyes to see the man in the dingy light. But he remained a blur, except for the gun, which was terribly real.

"There was no need for you to come inside. You might have spared yourself this," he said.

"I had to come," Blanche murmured. "There wasn't any other way."

The man laughed. "You're made of the same stuff as these crazy boys, I see. No wonder they gravitated towards you and your sister."

With a sickening jolt, Blanche remembered Rose. "Where is she?"

"Do you believe in the afterlife?" The voice in the dark was mocking. "If there was an afterlife, perhaps you'd meet her there."

Blanche heard the words, but all she saw was Rose, singing as she walked down a river of blood.

"She decided she'd rather die than see me kill the other boy. But, like the fatuous Christian martyrs, hers was ultimately a pointless sacrifice. After you give me the paten, both boys will die. And you, too, I'm afraid."

Blanche said nothing.

"You are terrified, aren't you?"

Blanche still was silent.

"Good." The man stepped forward, a faint shimmer of light illuminating his creased, cold face. Blanche recognized him. "Then this will be easy."

While Rose watched, whispering a prayer, Fish examined the chalices on the shelves. At last he selected a heavy one and pulled aside the curtains from the cellar window. "Rose, get me a rag or some kind of cloth," he directed her in a composed voice.

She found a polishing cloth on one shelf and handed it to him. "Good enough," he remarked, wrapping it tightly around his hand. Then he picked up the chalice, and smashed it against the basement window. The glass cracked and he pounded it again. Rose winced at the racket it made, although theoretically she knew it would be good for them to make noise.

Now Fish was picking away at the glass from the window.

"But what about the bars?" Rose persisted.

"Have a little confidence in me, okay?" He shot her an ironic glance, then cupped his hands and shouted out the window, "Help! Murder! Police!"

Mr. Freet was coming towards her. Her eyes were fixed

on the gun, its muzzle enlarged by a silencer, heavy in the muted light.

"Give me the paten," Mr. Freet was saying in a calm, reasonable voice.

The gun was flecked with black. The flecks swelled into spots, which began to fill her eyes. Blanche shook herself, and the engorged inkiness fled. She felt her head careening.

"You're ill, I see. Come on now, give me the paten." Mr. Freet continued slowly up the aisle, his hand outstretched.

Blanche held on to it tenaciously. "I can't give it to you. It's not mine to give."

There was a harsh laugh. "You can't keep it from me!"

For an instant, unconsciousness threatened to overpower her again, and again she forced herself to fight through the fog. Quickly making up her mind, she turned boldly towards the altar and stumbled up to it before her will could forsake her.

She lifted up the heavy golden dish, set it down on the bare surface, and let it go. She turned back to the dumbfounded Freet. "Take it from there if you want it."

With a gravity she was not aware she possessed, Blanche stepped off of the platform and walked towards Bear. He was crouched on the ground, his chained hands hugging the pillar, his eyes sharp like a wild animal's as he watched Freet.

"Idiot!" cursed Freet. But his attention was consumed by the paten. Keeping his gun trained on Blanche, he stepped greedily into the sanctuary towards the altar. The floor creaked warningly beneath his weight.

Blanche almost didn't see what happened next. With a roar, Bear swung his foot around and swept Freet's legs out from underneath him. Freet fell forward heavily, his gun arm crashing through the rotted boards of the floor. Bear leaped towards him as far as the handcuffs would allow and kicked at him furiously. Freet struggled in the hole, twisted on his side and fired. Three bullets tore up through the floor, blasting splinters of moldy wood into the air. Bear shouted and fell, his arm erupting in a spray of blood. Almost before she realized what she was doing, Blanche seized the brass candle-lighter from against the wall and aimed a blow at Freet. He fell back again, and she heard the boards below him give way. Freet disappeared through the floor as abruptly as if the ground had opened to swallow him alive.

It seemed that Fish and Rose were shouting at the window a long time before someone took notice. A Hispanic man in painter's coveralls rushed down the alley towards them.

"What is the shouting for?" he asked them.

"Call 911. Tell the police that there's a murder about to be committed in St. Lawrence Roman Catholic Church. They better get over there right away!"

"St. Lawrence," the man repeated. "Right." He ran back to the street and shouted something in Spanish. Fish turned to Rose with a dire expression, his eyes doubtful.

"Let's pray they get there in time," he remarked.

Blanche and Bear clung to each other in the darkness of the church beside the gaping hole. She couldn't move, and Bear was still handcuffed, his arm bleeding profusely. But he had regained his human form, and was speaking coherent, soothing words. "All shall be well—didn't I say that? Blanche, it's all right."

But the last vestiges of her strength had collapsed, and she was sobbing openly.

"Peace. All shall be well," he said again, kissing her forehead. She leaned against his shoulder and tried to calm herself.

"God was here," she said at last.

Bear put his lips against her tangled hair. "I know," he said. "He lives in weakness."

Suddenly there was the sound of a ricocheting bullet. A piece of pulpy wood hanging over the gap was thrown into the air.

Bear shoved Blanche onto the other side of the altar rail before she realized what had happened. "Run!" he ordered her. "Get the police!"

She bolted down the aisle, and heard Bear's voice as she went, "Cut it out, Freet. You're only digging yourself further into the pit."

Another shot came, and a voice emanated from the grim hole. "Tell the girl to come back, Arthur. I've got you in range, now. And you know you can't go anywhere with those handcuffs on."

Blanche froze in the center of the aisle.

"You don't have many bullets left, do you?" Bear said coolly. "I've been counting."

"I have one more," Freet's voice said. "And I'd like to use it."

"Look, Freet," Bear said patiently. "Even if you shot me, you still wouldn't be able to get out of the cellar before Blanche got the police. And why should you add on another murder? On the other hand, if you let me live, there's a chance you'll get off with fewer charges. You'd be better off taking whatever chance you can get."

Faintly, Blanche heard the sound of sirens in the background. Police. But they wouldn't be coming here, would they?

"It's over, Freet. You'd be better off quitting while you're ahead," Bear went on. He looked up at Blanche, and he seemed suddenly very far away from her. The gap of eternity had opened up between them. Her throat contracted.

"You don't understand, Arthur. It would be very satisfying to shoot you."

"A costly satisfaction," Bear said.

"Or I could shoot myself," Freet added.

"I wouldn't advise it," Bear said.

"Of course not. You're such a moralist. But it would solve a lot of problems for me. I've broken some bones, and I can't possibly get away before the police come. Wouldn't you rather I shot myself than you?"

"Honestly, I wouldn't. I'm not fond of you, Freet, but I won't wish hell upon you."

"You would if you knew everything I've done," Freet's voice giggled.

"I know enough," Bear said evenly, although Blanche saw he was struggling to hold his composure. "I can guess the rest."

"And none of that makes you want to send me to hell?" Freet said derisively.

"What I want doesn't matter. Hell is far worse than anything," Bear said with the same calm voice.

"So you'd prefer I shot you?" Freet asked.

Bear shrugged.

"No!" Blanche cried. She couldn't be so intellectual about this.

Freet's laughter echoed weirdly on the walls, a disembodied voice coming from the cellar. "She's more sensible than you are, Bear."

"She doesn't want to see me die," Bear said, almost unconcerned. He was not looking at Blanche. She couldn't tear her eyes away from him.

"Do you know why I strangled Father Raymond after I shot him?" Freet's voice asked.

Bear was quiet, and Blanche could see his body turn rigid.

"Because he wanted to save your lives. He wouldn't tell me where he had hidden the priceless set I was after. I offered him the choice of living or dying, but he chose to die. For you."

"I guessed that." Bear's voice shook slightly.

"And now you've made his death pointless. Because I am going to kill you. I just wanted you to know that—that you've wasted his death."

"It wasn't wasted," Bear said recklessly. "Go ahead, then." He knelt down, shaking but erect, pushing his twisted bleeding arm against the altar rail.

Suddenly a door banged in the back of the church and a voice shouted, "Police!"

Blanche saw Bear go flying atop the altar rail as Freet fired again. Then suddenly several men ran down the aisles, pushing her aside. She stumbled and tried to run forward, but someone held her back. There were policemen pointing their guns at Bear, and at the hole in the floor. But her eyes were fixed on Bear's body, slumped on the altar rail.

She heard, as though far off, a policeman order Freet to

drop the gun. Radios crackled behind her. She saw Bear's head moving as he slid back onto the ground.

He raised his head, and their eyes met. Slowly, painfully, he smiled at her.

After what seemed like an hour of sitting in the cellar, waiting in anxious trepidation, Rose heard a car pull up in front of Freet's house. Doors slammed, and two policemen ran down the alleyway. She tried to peer past Fish's shoulders to see the men, but all she could see was their boots.

"We've been trapped in this cellar," Fish explained. "Kidnapped."

"Is there anyone else in the house?" she heard one officer ask.

"No. The kidnapper's gone to St. Lawrence."

"We're coming in the back," the policeman said.

"The door code's six-six-six!" Rose shouted as the police ran down the alley.

"I never thought I'd be glad to see a policeman," Fish muttered. He offered her his arm to lean on as they walked up the cellar stairs.

"By the way, Fish—thanks," Rose said when they reached the top and waited by the door.

"Oh, don't mention it," Fish said offhandedly. "Thanks for coming after me in the first place. You're a good kid."

"I'm almost seventeen," she said, slightly offended. She wasn't a *kid.*

"So old," he said, and she thought she could make out his smile.

At long last, there were footsteps in the kitchen and the bolts on the cellar door were slid back.

Fish and Rose stood blinking in the twilight at the two cops standing there with guns drawn.

"It's just us," Fish said, raising his hands. "We're the ones you came to rescue."

"And thank God you came," Rose added, stepping forward shakily, suddenly realizing that the adventure was over. She felt inclined to kiss the linoleum floor.

One of the cops raised his thick black eyebrows in astonishment, recognizing her. "If it isn't Miss Brier," he said in a disgusted but unmistakable tone, putting away his gun. "I suppose you forgot your keys again?"

Officer Cirotti's voice was intimidating as before, but his eyes were amused. She managed a smile.

"Can I call my mother?" she asked.

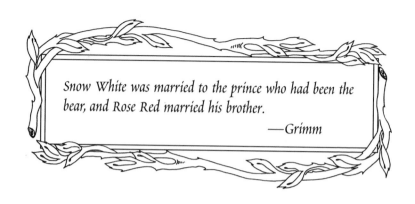

Snow White was married to the prince who had been the
bear, and Rose Red married his brother.

—Grimm

Chapter 20

THE TWO GIRLS stood in the shadows of the hallway, gazing at each other. Blanche was wearing a white
linen dress with a lace collar. Rose wore a linen flowered
print frock, scattered with red roses and leaves. She held a
straw hat with trailing ribbons in her hands.

"It's hard to believe, isn't it?" Blanche murmured, running her hands over the material of the dress. It felt even
richer than it had looked that one night in the store window.

"I can't imagine how he found the very dress we were
admiring that night after the opera. It must be the first
time in the history of shopping that a man ever remembered the name of a woman's clothing store," Rose laughed.
She turned her sister around and began to adjust the white
roses that she had woven into Blanche's braids.

"Not just that. I mean, everything that's happened,"
Blanche said, wincing as her sister pulled a stray hair.
"Mr. Freet being captured, you and Fish turning up alive
—and yes, these dresses. Are you sure you don't want to

wear the white one?" Blanche asked, turning back to her sister.

"Oh, no. The delicate shade suits you better. You'd be overwhelmed in a big print like mine. Besides, I think Bear bought the rose dress for me. After all, that's my name." Rose set the hat on her red hair and adjusted it. "I *am* glad that he remembered to buy me a hat, though."

"I don't even like to think about what these presents cost him," Blanche confessed.

"Well, I suppose he would say it was worth it. Besides, now that he's been exonerated from the drug charges and gotten his inheritance back from his father, he could buy us dresses like these every day if he wanted to." Rose put a hand on her hat and spun around so that her skirt flared satisfactorily.

"Ugh! That would ruin it!" Blanche shivered and smoothed down the sleeves of her dress. "It would be sort of like having chocolate mousse for breakfast every day—too much!"

Rose was inclined to agree. "Still, I'll never forget how I felt when that man from the store knocked at the door and brought in these two huge boxes. I had no idea what they were! Oh, and the wrapping paper—floral outside and silver inside! It was a treat just to open the box, let alone to see what was inside." She arched her back and gave a luxurious sigh. "I must say, Bear has good taste. It would have taken me years to pick out a dress that I liked on my own—and I like this one very much."

"I think his mother was a clothes designer," Blanche murmured. "He says I look a lot like she did when she was young."

Mother, talking on the phone in the kitchen, smiled at both of them. She was dressed in her Sunday best and was

talking to their aunt in California. Ever since the girls'
escapade a few weeks ago, Mother had been calling one
relative after another to tell them the story.

"Oh, I wish the boys would get here soon!" Rose fretted,
going to the living room window to peer out again. She
turned away with a sigh, took off her hat, and fluffed up
her bangs with her hand.

"You look really nice, Rose," Blanche said to her sister.
Rose was wearing her hair braided in front and long in the
back. The bruises on her face were barely visible now, and
she had regained her rose-petal complexion. Her small chin
was raised in a look of confident assurance, spunk, and
good humor, and her eyes were radiant. Blanche looked
down. Was it really fair that her sister was so gorgeous? She
fought with the usual jealousy. C. S. Lewis had said something about true humility being the ability to rejoice in
somebody else's good fortune as if it were your own. So she
took in the picture of her sister, with her smooth, shining
hair, sparkling eyes, and slim figure, and sighing, counted it
all joy. She even managed to begin to feel less nervous.

"Stand up straight," Rose prompted her sister, and straightened her own shoulders. "You look absolutely beautiful, sister."

Rose thought her older sister had never looked so lovely.
Let people say what they would—Blanche was the prettier
one in the family. That smooth, pure white skin without a
single zit! Maids of other eras would have killed for it, Rose
was sure. The problem was, she decided, that Blanche lived
in the wrong century. And her hair! Rose had dreamed so
often of what it would be like to have soft inky black hair
like Blanche's. But no, her hair was a plain red. And when

Blanche wore pale colors, she looked like a flower, delicate and airy.

"You should always dress like that," she told her sister.

"I thought you said before that I should wear stronger colors," Blanche accused.

"Well, I've changed my mind. Strong colors are *my* favorite, but it's okay if you want to wear pastels. I used to think it made you look weak, if you know what I mean. But I guess that's okay, sometimes, to be weak."

Blanche laughed and put a timid hand to her head to feel the petals of the creamy roses in her hair. "I feel silly," Blanche confessed.

Somehow, that was the wrong thing to say, Rose felt. One should keep a quiet composure, or say "thank you" graciously—not say you felt silly.

"You look like a princess," Rose said firmly. "I don't care what you say."

"Rose, do you ever get envious of other people?" Blanche said at last.

Rose thought for a moment, head on one side. "Yeah. But when I do, I try to think about something else. Then I forget."

"Oh," Blanche paused. "I guess I'm not distracted so easily. Oh, I wish they would come so I could stop thinking stupid things!"

"Yes, exactly—where are they?" Rose wrinkled her nose in consternation.

"Mother said they had something to do. I think maybe another meeting with the district attorney about Mr. Freet."

"I wish he would confess to Father Raymond's murder as well as to attempting to kill me. It would make it so

much easier for them. Did Bear tell you that their father—their real father—completely washed his hands of
them when they were arrested for drugs? When they got
out of detention, they had no place to go. They had to stay
at a homeless shelter." Rose reluctantly turned from the
window again, resigning herself to wait. "But I must say
that their father turned out to be very reasonable once he
heard about Mr. Freet's arrest and everything that's happened. He probably feels guilty that he's neglected his sons
for so long. Even if they haven't gotten their juvenile re-
cord revoked yet, at least they've proved their innocence."

"That must mean a lot to them. I think Bear has had a
hard time forgiving their dad for abandoning them," Blanche
reflected. She had suddenly realized how blessed they were
to have had such a good father. Dad was dead, but at least
he'd always loved and stood by them.

"Poor Dr. Freet," Rose said softly. "It must have been very
hard for him to find all this out about his brother. Especially
his connection with the school drug ring, when Dr. Freet
had spent so much time on anti-drug campaigns."

They sat down on the couch, and Blanche stared at her
white-linen covered lap and her folded hands. "You know,
when you've had someone point a gun at you, it's almost
like having died, somehow. You're never the same."

"I know what you mean." Rose rubbed her eyes and
shook her head. "Brrr! You feel as though you're living on
borrowed time."

"Yes. That's it. You might have died, but instead, you're
alive. You know," Blanche pressed her hands together to
feel their warmth and the life in her muscles, "things like
this make you realize that God is in charge of everything.
Everything. I mean, even if things had gone the other way,

and Freet had killed Bear—or you—or Fish—somehow I would still know that God's in charge."

Rose had leaned back against the couch and gently felt the pimple on her nose to make sure it wasn't too noticeable. "It's as though the curtain that covered the machinery of the universe was pulled aside for a moment, and you saw how things work, isn't it?"

"Yes, that's it." Blanche was surprised. "How'd you know?"

Rose shrugged. "I always sort of knew, but now I know that I know. Boy, we're profound, aren't we? Let's go outside to wait for these slow-pokes."

The summer sun was shining across a blue sky as they stood on the porch steps. Blanche tried to cover up her embarrassment at being on the street in such a fancy dress by examining the roses in the flower boxes. "I almost wish we hadn't cut them. They just started blooming."

"Nonsense. Mother said we should, and your hair looks simply elegant with white roses in it. I would have put red roses in my hair, but they symbolize passionate love, and I don't want that Fish person to get any ideas."

"I doubt that he would think you were sending him a secret message. Besides, you're wearing red roses all over your dress."

Rose gave a start and her face turned the color under discussion. She squeaked faintly in dismay. "Oh, bother."

Blanche had picked a red blossom from Rose's window box. "Never mind about flower language. You should pin it on your dress."

Rose rallied. "Good, maybe the thorns will send another kind of message."

Blanche hid a smile. "You are hardly the picture of disinterest, Rose."

Rose heaved a sigh. "Unfortunately, disinterest has never been one of my stronger qualities."

Just then, a sleek white car pulled over in front of their house, and two men got out of the front seats. Both of them wore suits, and were strangely familiar.

"Is that—them?" Blanche whispered uncertainly to Rose.

Rose was staring. "I don't think so. They look too—nice."

The two young men in question halted before the stoop and looked up at them, expectantly. The tall one with short dark hair had his arm in a sling. The other one's lighter hair was cut a bit longer, and he held a flat cap in one hand.

The two girls stared at them in perfect incomprehension for several moments.

"Oh, come on," said the one with lighter hair. "We don't look all that different, do we?"

"Bear?" Blanche said, and "Fish!" exclaimed Rose at the same time.

The tall, dark-haired guy with the arresting good looks laughed and held out his hand to Blanche. "Snow White?" he said, imitating her voice.

She knew him then, for certain, and went to him happily. He put his one arm around her and kissed her. "You look lovely in that dress," he said. "Or is it the idea of the dress that makes you beautiful?"

"You cut your hair!" she said at last. She couldn't believe what a difference it made in the way he looked, with his head free from the heavy mat of dreadlocks. He was standing taller, too, and smiling.

"I did. Call it the fulfillment of a vow. My head feels ten pounds lighter," he said, grinning.

"Where are you princes going to take us?" Rose asked,

still looking at Fish suspiciously as though she weren't completely certain it was him. He crossed his eyes at her.

"I thought we could start out by taking you to see how far they've gotten with the renovation of St. Lawrence," Bear said offhandedly.

"The renovation? But I thought it was all closed down!" Rose exclaimed.

"Oh, it was. Until—uh—the diocese received a substantially large grant to repair the roof and floor." Bear suddenly seemed interested in the state of his cuffs.

"Two substantial grants, actually. I think my money's going to repair the roof since Bear destroyed most of the floor himself." Fish raised one eyebrow at his brother.

"It was supposed to have happened a long time ago— my mother had planned it, and Father Raymond was going to oversee the project, but that all fell apart when he died. And then our dad decided to take everything away from us and—you know the rest." Bear squinted at Blanche in the sunlight. "I understand a new religious order is going to be taking over the church and the old rectory fairly soon. St. Lawrence is being repaired just in time."

"Sister Geraldine will be so glad to hear that," Blanche said.

"Oh, she knows. I think we've given her a new lease on life. Father Raymond always used to tell her she should go back and stir up her Dominican congregation—I wouldn't be surprised if she went off and did it now," Bear said.

"Should I tell Mom we're leaving?" Rose asked.

"Is she ready?"

"I think so. She was just talking on the phone when we came outside. I'll go and fetch her." Rose danced up the steps, swirling her dress in pleasure as she went in.

Fish watched her go, shaking his head. "What drama," he said. "Is she always like this?"

"Yes, I'm afraid so," Blanche said to him with a smile. "Life is always an adventure for her."

"It would be. Well, I suppose I'll have to get used to it." He dropped his hat on his head with a sigh. "You two get in the car. I'll wait for them."

Bear opened the car door for Blanche, and got in the back seat beside her. With a sigh of contentment, he put his good arm around her shoulders.

"How's your other arm?"

"Looking very good. It's mostly healed."

She noticed he looked utterly at peace. "Where are we going?"

"Oh, someplace in the country. I think it's time for us to leave the City for a while," he said. "I hope to get out for good, eventually. What would you think about that, Blanche?"

"I'd hate to see you go," she said shyly, looking up into his brown eyes.

He laughed and squeezed her hand. "Then you can come with me, my lady."

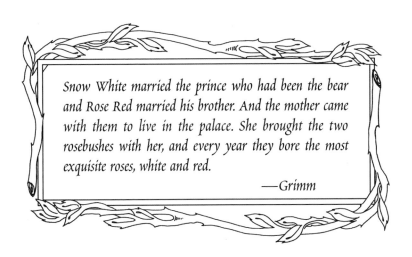

Snow White married the prince who had been the bear and Rose Red married his brother. And the mother came with them to live in the palace. She brought the two rosebushes with her, and every year they bore the most exquisite roses, white and red.

—Grimm

THE END

About the Author

Regina Doman writes: "I had loved the Brothers Grimm tale of *Snow White and Rose Red* ever since childhood, when I read a stage version of it in a school reader. In the version I knew, the brother of the prince was turned into a fish by the wicked dwarf, and it was Snow White who dispatched the dwarf in the end by cutting off his magic beard . . . two elements missing from the original Grimms' tale. Sadly, I have not been able to find this version anywhere, but as the reader can see, the one I knew in my childhood has shaped the story significantly."

When Miss Doman was eighteen, she and friends did a video version of *Snow White and Rose Red,* and though the shooting went well, the video camera shorted out and the film was lost. Soon after this minor disaster, the author decided that if she were to do any more with this particular story she would change the setting to an urban, modern-day one. Five years later, she found herself living and working in New York City—and writing her first novel.

Now married and the mother of two young children, the author makes her home in Front Royal, Virginia. She says, "This book may be the end of my experimentation with the fairy tale, *Snow White and Rose Red.* But it is not the end of the story of Blanche, Bear, Rose and Fish."